The Betrothed

ALSO BY KIERA CASS

The Betrothed

KIERA CASS

HARPER TEEN
An Imprint of HarperCollins*Publishers*

HarperTeen is an imprint of HarperCollins Publishers.

The Betrothed
Copyright © 2020 by Kiera Cass
Map by Virginia Allyn

For information address HarperCollins Children's Books, a division of
HarperCollins Publishers, 195 Broadway, New York, NY 10007.
www.epicreads.com
Library of Congress Control Number: 2019956232
ISBN 978-0-06-229164-6
Typography by Sarah Hoy and Erin Fitzsimmons
22 23 24 25 26 LBC 6 5 4 3 2
❖
First paperback edition, 2021

For my punk brother, Gerad.
Who would carry me across the Serengeti.
Allegedly.

From the

CHRONICLES OF COROAN HISTORY,

BOOK I

And so, Coroans, preserve the law,

For if we undo one, we undo them all.

ONE

It was the time of year when the sunrise still had frost on it. But winter was fading, and the flowers were starting to bloom, and the promise of a new season filled me with anticipation.

"I've been dreaming of spring," I sighed, staring out the window at the birds sailing boldly across a backdrop of blue sky. Delia Grace tied the last of the laces of my gown into place and moved me over to the vanity.

"Me, too," she replied. "Tournaments. Bonfires. Crowning Day is on the horizon."

Her tone implied I should be more excited than the average girl, but I still had my reservations. "I suppose."

I could feel her exasperation in the movement of her hands. "Hollis, you will undoubtedly be His Majesty's partner and escort for the festivities! I don't know how you can be so calm."

"Thank the stars we have the king's attention this year," I said, keeping my tone light as she braided back the front pieces of my hair, "or it would be as dull as a tomb here."

"You say that as if your courtship were a game," she commented, sounding surprised.

"It is a game," I insisted. "He'll move along soon enough, so we need to enjoy this while we can."

I watched Delia Grace chewing her lips in the mirror, not looking up from her task.

"Is something wrong?" I asked.

She quickly perked up, lifting her lips into a smile. "Not a thing. Just perplexed by your cavalier attitude toward the king. I think there's more to his attentions than you're seeing."

I looked down, thrumming my fingers across the table of the vanity. I liked Jameson. I'd be mad not to. He was handsome and wealthy and, for goodness' sake, the king. He was also a fair dancer and most entertaining to be around, as long as he was in good spirits. But I was no fool. I'd watched him flit from girl to girl over the last several months. There had been at least seven, including me—and that was just counting the ones everyone at court *knew* about. I'd enjoy this for as long as I could and then accept whatever lump of a person my parents chose for me. At least I'd have these days to look back upon when I was a bored old lady.

"He's still young," I finally replied. "I don't see him settling down with *anyone* until he gets through a few more years on the throne. Besides, I'm sure he's expected to marry for political advantage. I can't offer much there."

There was a knock at the door, and Delia Grace went to answer it, disappointment on her face. I could tell she really thought I stood a chance, and I instantly felt guilty for being so difficult. In our decade of friendship, we'd always supported one another, but it was different these days.

As we were ladies at court, our families had maids. But the highest-ranking noblewomen and royalty? They had ladies-in-waiting. More than servants, your ladies were your confidantes, your attendants, your escorts . . . they were everything. Delia Grace was stepping into a role that didn't exist for me yet, convinced that, at any moment, it would.

It meant more than I knew how to say, more than I knew how to handle. What is a friend but someone who thinks you're capable of more than you do?

She returned with a letter in her hand and a glint in her eye. "There's a royal seal on this," she teased, flipping the paper over in her hand. "But, since we don't care how the king feels about you, I suppose there's no urgency to open it."

"Let me see." I stood and held a hand out, but she quickly retracted the letter, a smirk on her face. "Delia Grace, you wicked girl, give it to me!" She took a step back, and in a split second I was in pursuit, chasing her around my apartments, squealing with laughter. I managed to corner her twice, but she was always faster than I was, and wriggled out of the spaces before I could get ahold of her. I was nearly breathless from running and laughing when I finally caught her around the waist. She held the letter out as far as she could. I might have managed to wrestle it back from her, but as I was stretching upward, my mother burst in through the doors that attached my rooms to hers.

"Hollis Brite, have you lost your senses?!" she scolded.

Delia Grace and I pulled apart, placing our hands behind our backs and curtsying quickly.

"I could hear you girls shouting like animals through the walls. How can we hope to have a suitor matched with you if you insist on behaving like this?"

"Sorry, Mother," I murmured contritely.

I dared to peek up at her. She was standing there with the same exasperated expression plastered to her face she usually wore when speaking with me.

"The Copeland girl got engaged only last week, and the Devauxes are in talks now as well. Yet you're still acting like a child."

I swallowed, but Delia Grace had never been one to stay silent. "Don't you think it's a little premature to pair Hollis with someone else? She has as good a chance as anyone at winning the king's heart."

My mother did her best to suppress her condescending smile. "We all know that the king's eye is prone to wander. And Hollis isn't quite queen material, wouldn't you agree?" she asked with a sharply raised eyebrow, daring us to think otherwise. "Besides," she added, "are *you* really in a position to talk about anyone's potential?"

Delia Grace swallowed hard, her expression stone-like. I'd

seen her don that mask a million times.

"And there you have it," Mother concluded. Having made her disappointment with us clear, she turned on her heel and left.

I sighed, turning to Delia Grace. "Sorry about her."

"It's nothing I haven't heard before," she admitted, finally handing over the letter. "And I'm sorry, too. I didn't mean to get you into trouble."

I took it from her and cracked the seal. "No matter. If it wasn't this, it'd be something else." She made a face that said I was right, and I went to reading the note. "Oh dear," I said, patting at my loose hair. "I might need your help pulling this back again."

"Why?"

I smiled over at her, waving the letter like a flag in the breeze. "Because His Majesty requires our presence on the river today."

"How many people do you think will be there?" I asked.

"Who knows? He does enjoy having a crowd around him."

I pursed my lips. "True. I'd like to have him to myself just once."

"Says the girl who insists this is all just a game."

I looked over at her, sharing a smile. That Delia Grace, she always seemed to know more than I ever wanted to admit to.

We rounded the hallway and saw that the doors were already open, welcoming the new spring sun. My heartbeat picked up when I saw the red robe trimmed in ermine draped across the back of a slim but sturdy figure at the end of the walkway. Though he wasn't facing me, his mere presence was enough to fill the air with a warm tickling feeling.

I fell into a deep curtsy. "Your Majesty."

And I watched as a pair of glossy black shoes turned to face me.

TWO

"MY LADY HOLLIS," THE KING said, holding out his ring-bedecked hand. I took it and rose, looking into a beautiful set of honey-brown eyes. Something about the deep and purposeful attention he bestowed upon me whenever we were together made me feel a little like I did when Delia Grace and I were dancing and I'd spun around too quickly: slightly warm and dizzy.

"Your Majesty. I was so pleased to receive your invitation. I love the Colvard River."

"So you've mentioned. I remember, you see," he said, wrapping his hand around mine. He then dropped his voice. "I also remember you mentioning that your parents have been a little . . . *overbearing* recently. But I had to invite them for the sake of propriety."

I peered behind him and saw a larger party than I'd been

expecting for our excursion. My parents were present, as were some of the lords on the privy council, and plenty of the ladies who I knew were waiting impatiently for Jameson to finish with me so they could have their turn. In fact, I spotted Nora looking down her nose at me with Anna Sophia and Cecily right behind her, smug in their certainty that my time was soon to end.

"Don't worry. Your parents won't be on our barge," he assured me. I smiled, thankful for a small reprieve, but unfortunately my luck didn't extend to the winding ride in the coach down to the river.

Kereseken Castle was set atop the Plateau of Borady, a marvelous and unmistakable sight. To get down to the river, our carriages had to weave slowly through the streets of the capital city of Tobbar . . . and that took some time.

I saw the gleam in my father's eye as he realized this carriage ride was his chance to have an extended audience with the king. "So, Your Majesty, how go things along the border?" he began. "I hear our men were forced into a retreat last month."

I had to avoid rolling my eyes. Why would my father think that reminding the king of our recent failures was the way to strike up a conversation? Jameson, though, took the question in stride.

"It's true. We only have soldiers along the border to keep the peace, but what are they expected to do when attacked? Reports are that King Quinten insists Isolten land goes all the way to the Tiberan Plains."

My father scoffed, though I could see he wasn't truly as calm as he appeared. He always twisted the silver ring on his pointer finger when he was nervous, and he was doing just so now. "That has been Coroan land for generations."

"Precisely. But I have no fear. We are safe from attacks here, and Coroans make for excellent soldiers."

I stared out the windows, bored by the talk of inconsequential squabbles along the border. Jameson was usually the best company, but my parents killed any joy in the coach.

I couldn't help sighing in relief when we pulled up to the dock and I could exit the stifling carriage. "You weren't joking about your parents," Jameson said when we were finally alone.

"The last two people I'd invite to a party, that's for sure."

"And yet they made the most charming girl in the world," he said, kissing my hand.

I blushed and looked away, my eyes finding Delia Grace as she climbed out of her carriage, followed by Nora, Cecily, and Anna Sophia. If I thought my ride had been unbearable, her clenched fists as she walked over to me told me hers had been much worse.

"What happened?" I whispered.

"Nothing that hasn't happened a thousand times before." She rolled her shoulders back, pulling herself up taller.

"At least we'll be together on the boat," I assured her. "Come. Won't it be fun to watch their faces as you climb onto the king's ship?"

We walked down to the landing, and I felt a thrill of heat

run up my arm when King Jameson took my hand to help me onto our boat. As promised, Delia Grace joined us, along with two of the king's advisers, while my parents and the remaining guests were escorted to various other boats at His Majesty's disposal. The royal standard was sitting proudly atop its pole, the bold Coroan red flicking back and forth so quickly in the breeze off the river that it looked like fire. I happily took my seat to Jameson's right, his fingers still laced through mine as he helped me settle in.

There was food to enjoy, and furs to cover us if the winds were too chilly. It seemed anything I could desire was right there before me, which was something I was still surprised by: the lack of want when I sat beside a king.

As we made our way down the river, people standing on the banks stopped and bowed when they saw the standard, or called out blessings for the king. He was so poised as he nodded his head in acknowledgment, sitting as upright as a tree.

I knew not every sovereign was handsome, but Jameson was. He took great pains with his appearance, keeping his dark hair short and his bronze skin soft. He was fashionable without being frivolous, but he liked to show off the best of his possessions. Taking the boats out this early in the spring could prove that point quickly enough.

And I liked that about him, if only because I got to sit here beside him, feeling unmistakably regal.

Along the side of the river, near where a new bridge had been built, a weatherworn statue stood, casting her shadow down the slope toward the blue-green waters. As tradition dictated, the gentlemen on the boats rose to stand while the ladies dropped our heads in respect. There were books filled with the tales of Queen Albrade riding along the countryside and fending off the Isoltens while her husband, King Shane, was off in Mooreland for matters of state. Upon his return, the king had seven statues of his wife placed across Coroa, and every August, all the ladies at court did dances holding wooden swords to remember her victory.

Indeed, the queens throughout Coroan history were often remembered more vividly than the kings, and Queen Albrade wasn't even the most revered. There was Queen Honovi, who walked the far line of the country, setting the boundaries and blessing with a kiss the trees and rocks she used as markers. To this day, people would look for the stones in particular—as they were placed by the queen herself—and kiss them, too, for luck. Queen Lahja was famous for taking care of Coroan children at the height of the Isolten Plague, so named because when people contracted it and died, their skin turned as blue as the Isolten flag. She walked bravely into the city herself to find the little ones who survived and placed them with new families.

Even Queen Ramira, Jameson's mother, was known across the country for her kindness. She was, perhaps, the opposite of her husband, King Marcellus. Where he tended to strike first without question, she was known to seek peace. I'd heard at least three potential wars were stopped by her gentle reasoning. The young men of Coroa owed a debt of gratitude to her. As did their mothers.

The legacies of Coroan queens left a mark on the entire continent, which was probably part of Jameson's draw. Not only was he handsome and rich, not only would he make you a queen . . . he would make you a legend.

"I love being on the water," Jameson commented, drawing me back to the beauty of the moment. "Probably one of my favorite things as a boy was sailing to Sabino with my father."

"I remember your father was an excellent sailor," Delia Grace remarked, inserting herself in the conversation.

Jameson nodded enthusiastically. "One of his many talents. I sometimes think I inherited more of my mother's traits than his, but sailing stayed with me. His love of traveling, too. What of you, Lady Hollis? Do you like to travel?"

I shrugged. "I've never really had the chance. I've lived the entirety of my life between Keresken Castle and Varinger Hall. But I've always wanted to go to Eradore," I breathed. "I do love the sea, and I've been told the beaches there are a thing of beauty."

"They are." He smiled and looked away. "I've heard it's the fashion now for couples to take a trip together when they get married." He met my eyes once more. "You should make sure your husband takes you to Eradore. You'd look radiant on the white beaches."

He looked away again, popping berries into his mouth as if it was nothing to speak of husbands and trips and being alone. I looked at Delia Grace, who stared back at me with astonished eyes. I knew once we were in private, we would pull apart every piece of that moment to figure out just what it meant.

Was he trying to say he thought I should marry? Or was he hinting that I should marry . . . him?

These were the questions on my mind as I sat up, looking across the water. Nora was there with her sour expression, watching with the other wretched girls from court. As I peeked around, I noted several pairs of eyes settled, not upon the beauty of the day, but on me. The only set that seemed angry, though, was Nora's.

I picked up a berry and hurled it over at her, hitting her square in the chest. Cecily and Anna Sophia laughed, and Nora's jaw dropped in shock. But she quickly picked up some fruit of her own and threw it back at me, her expression shifting to something resembling happiness. Giggling, I picked up more, and began a war of sorts.

"Hollis, what in the world are you doing?" Mother called from her boat, just loud enough to be heard above the slaps of paddles on the water.

I looked at her and replied in all seriousness, "Defending my honor, of course." I caught Jameson's chuckle as I turned back to Nora.

There was a stream of laughter and berries going in both directions. It was the best fun I'd had in a while until I leaned a little too far over for a rather determined throw and ended up toppling into the water.

I heard the gasps and cries of those around me, but I managed to get in a good breath and came up without choking.

"Hollis!" Jameson exclaimed, reaching an arm out for me. I grabbed on and he pulled me safely back into the boat in a matter of seconds. "Sweet Hollis, are you all right? Are you hurt?"

"No," I sputtered out, already shivering from the chill of the water, "but I seem to have lost my shoes."

Jameson looked down at my stockinged feet and burst out laughing. "We shall have to fix that, won't we?"

There was laughter all around now that I was fine, and Jameson took off his coat to wrap it around me, keeping me warm.

"Back to shore, then," he ordered, still smiling. He held me close, looking deep into my eyes. I sensed that in this moment—shoes gone, hair a mess, soaking wet—he found me irresistible. And yet, with my parents just behind him, with a dozen demanding lords hovering nearby, he was forced to settle for placing a warm kiss on my cool forehead.

It was enough to send new waves through my stomach, and I wondered if every moment with him would feel like this. I'd been dying for him to kiss me, hoping every time we got a brief second to ourselves he'd pull me close. So far, though, it hadn't happened. I knew he'd kissed Hannah and Myra, but if he'd kissed any of the others, they weren't telling. I wondered if his not kissing me yet was a good sign or a bad one.

"Can you stand?" Delia Grace asked, bringing me back to the moment as she helped me onto the dock.

"The dress is much heavier when drenched," I admitted.

"Oh, Hollis. I'm so sorry! I didn't mean to make you fall!" Nora exclaimed once she climbed off her own boat.

"Nonsense! It was my fault, and I learned a very valuable lesson. I shall only enjoy the river from my window from now on," I replied with a wink.

She laughed, almost looking as if she did so in spite of her better judgment. "Are you sure you're all right?"

"Yes. I may have a runny nose tomorrow, but I'm right as rain, and twice as wet. No hard feelings. I promise."

She smiled and it felt genuine.

"Here, let me help you," she offered.

"I've got her," Delia Grace snapped.

Nora's smile instantly faded, and she went from looking quite pleased to unimaginably irritated. "Yes, I'm sure you do. Seeing as you never had a chance of getting Jameson's attention on your own, holding on to Hollis's skirts is the best a *girl like you* could do." She raised an eyebrow and turned. "I'd keep my grip tight if I were you."

I opened my mouth to tell Nora that Delia Grace's situation had never been her fault. But I found a hand on my chest, stopping me.

"Jameson will hear," Delia Grace said through gritted teeth. "Let's just go." The heartbreak in her voice was unmistakable, but she was right. Men battled on open fields; women battled behind fans. I held on to her with a firm grip as we made our way back to the castle. After so much abuse in one afternoon, I wondered if she might retreat into solitude the next day. She'd done that often when we were young and her heart couldn't bear to hear another word.

But the following morning, she was in my room,

wordlessly pulling my hair into another intricate design. It was in the middle of this that a knock came at the door, and she opened it to an army of maids bringing in bouquet after bouquet of the first blooms of spring.

"What exactly is this all about?" Delia Grace asked, directing them to set the flowers on any open surface they could find.

A maid curtsied before me and handed me a folded note. I smiled to myself as I went to read it aloud. "'In the event you have caught cold and were unable to venture out into nature today, I thought that nature ought to come to its queen.'"

Delia Grace's eyes widened. *"Its queen?"*

I nodded, my heart racing.

"Find my golden dress, please. I think the king deserves a thank-you."

THREE

I WALKED DOWN THE HALLWAY with my head high, Delia
Grace just behind my right shoulder. I met the eyes of older
attendees at court, smiling and nodding at them in acknowledgment. Most paid me no mind, which wasn't surprising.
I knew they felt there wasn't much point in them getting
attached to the king's latest fling.

It wasn't until we approached the main hallway to the
Great Room that I heard something that set me on edge.

"That's the one I was telling you about," a woman whispered loudly to her friend, in a tone that made it impossible
to mistake the words for praise.

I froze, looking at Delia Grace. The squint of her eyes
told me she'd heard it, too, and didn't know what to make
of it. There was a chance they were talking about her. About
her parents, about her father. But gossip surrounding Delia

Grace was old news, and the teasing surrounding it was usually reserved for young ladies looking for someone to take a dig at; everyone else looked for new stories, exciting ones.

The kind that might surround King Jameson's latest love interest.

"Take a breath," Delia Grace commanded. "The king will want to see you're well."

I touched the flower I'd tucked behind my ear, making sure it was still in place. I straightened my gown and kept moving. She was right, of course. It was the same strategy that she'd used for years now.

But by the time we walked into the Great Room, the stares were unmistakably disapproving. I tried to keep my expression unreadable, but underneath it all, I was a trembling mess.

Against the wall, a man was standing, arms crossed, shaking his head.

"It would shame the whole country," someone muttered as they passed me.

Out of the corner of my eye, I saw Nora. Going against every instinct I'd had up until yesterday, I walked over to her, Delia Grace trailing like a shadow.

"Good morning, Lady Nora. I'm not sure if you've noticed, but some of those at court today are . . ." I couldn't find a word for it.

"Yes," she answered quietly. "It seems someone on our outing yesterday shared the story of our little battle. No one appears to be upset with *me*, but of course, I am not the king's favorite."

I swallowed. "But His Majesty has been moving from lady to lady this last year as if it were nothing. He can't be planning to keep my company much longer, so what's the problem?"

She made a face. "He took you out of the palace. He let you sit under the flag. As casual as you might think yesterday was, it was unique to all of his interactions with women to date."

Oh.

"It's the lords, isn't it?" Delia Grace asked Nora. "The ones on the council?"

In their first civil interaction in all the years I'd known them both, Nora gave a quick and sympathetic nod.

"What does that mean?" I asked. "Why would the king even care what anyone thought?"

Delia Grace, who'd always been a quicker study at government and protocol, only half rolled her eyes at me. "The lords run their counties for the king. He is dependent upon them."

"If the king wants peace in the outreaches of the land and expects taxes to be collected properly, he needs the lords on the council to handle it," Nora added. "If the lords are unhappy with the way things are done, well, let's just say they can become lazy at their jobs."

Ah. So the king could lose both income and security if he

made the foolish mistake of aligning himself with someone the lords didn't like. Someone like a girl who fell into a river while flinging fruit at another girl, all while still in sight of the statue honoring one of the greatest queens the country had ever known.

For a split second, I was completely overcome by humiliation. I'd read far too much into Jameson's words, into his attentions. I'd really thought that becoming queen might be a possibility.

But then I remembered: I'd always known I wouldn't be queen.

Yes, it would be fun to be the wealthiest lady in all of Coroa, to have statues erected in my honor . . . but that wasn't realistic, and surely Jameson was only moments away from being swept off his feet by another pretty smile. The best I could do was enjoy Jameson's elaborate flirtations while they lasted.

Taking Nora's hand, I faced her. "Thank you. Both for the bit of fun yesterday and your honesty today. I owe you."

She smiled. "Crowning Day is in a few weeks. If you and the king are still attached, I assume you'll choreograph a dance for him. If you do, let me be a part of it."

Plenty of girls performed new dances for Crowning Day, hoping to gain favor by honoring the king. I supposed, if Jameson was still entertaining the idea of me then, I would be expected to have one ready. From what I remembered, Nora was pretty graceful. "I'll want all the help I can get.

You absolutely have a place."

I motioned for Delia Grace to follow me once more. "Come. I need to thank the king."

"Are you mad?" she whispered, aghast. "You're not really going to let her dance with us, are you?"

I looked back at her, incredulous. "She just showed me great kindness. And she was more than polite to you. It's just a dance, and she's very light on her feet. It will make us all look better."

"Her actions today can hardly make up for past wrongs," Delia Grace insisted.

"We're growing up," I told her. "Things change."

Her face said she wasn't at all pacified by that answer, but she stayed silent as we made our way through the sea of people.

King Jameson was on the raised stone dais at the head of the Great Room. It was wide, built with room for a large royal family to occupy it, but it currently held only a single throne with two small seats on either side for whoever his most important guests were at the moment.

The Great Room was used for everything: receiving guests, balls, and even dinner each night. Along the eastern wall, the steps up to the gallery for the musicians were lined with tall windows that let in ample amounts of sunlight. But it was the western wall that drew my gaze each time I entered the room. Six stained-glass windows spanned the length, stretching from the height of my waist all the way to the ceiling. The windows depicted scenes from Coroan history in glorious illustration, cascading color and light throughout the room.

There was one window depicting Estus being crowned, and another of women dancing in a field. One of the original panes had been destroyed in a war, and it was replaced seamlessly with a scene of King Telau bending his knee to Queen Thenelope. It might have been my favorite of the six. I wasn't entirely sure of her role in our history, but she was deserving enough to be immortalized in the room where all the important day-to-day living of the palace was done, and that alone was impressive.

While large tables were brought in and out for dinners, and people would come and go with seasons, the windows and the dais were always the same. I moved my eyes from the depictions of kings past to the one upon the throne now. I watched as he engaged in a deep discussion with one of his lords, but when the gold of my dress caught his eye, he turned for a second. Then, realizing it was me, he summarily dismissed the lord. I curtsied and approached the throne, welcomed by a set of warm and gracious hands.

"My Lady Hollis." He shook his head. "You are the rising sun. Gorgeous."

At those words all my resolve was undone. How could I be sure I meant nothing when he looked at me like that? I hadn't watched him closely with the others; I didn't think it was important at the time. But it felt completely unique, the way he moved his thumb back and forth on my hand, as if a single patch of skin wasn't enough for him.

"Your Majesty is too generous," I finally answered, ducking my head. "Not just with your words, but with your gifts. I wanted to thank you for the entire garden you sent to my room," I said pointedly, to which he chuckled. "And I wanted you to know I was well."

"Excellent. Then you must sit with me at dinner tonight."

My stomach flipped. "Majesty?"

"As well as your parents, of course. I could use a change of company."

I curtsied again. "As you wish." I could see there were others waiting for his attention, so I quickly backed away, positively giddy. I reached out for Delia Grace's hand, clutching her for support.

"You're going to be set beside the king, Hollis," she murmured.

"Yes." The thought left me as breathless as if I'd run across the garden.

"And your parents as well. He hasn't done that before."

I gripped her hand even tighter. "I know. Shall . . . shall we go tell them?" I looked into Delia Grace's all-seeing eyes, the ones that could read my simultaneous excitement and fear, the ones that saw I didn't understand what was happening.

Those very eyes brightened as she smirked. "I think a lady of your importance should simply have a letter sent."

We laughed as we left the room, not caring if anyone looked or made comments. I still wasn't completely convinced of

Jameson's intentions, and I knew that the people at court weren't thrilled by my presence, but none of that mattered right now. Tonight, I would dine beside a king. And that was something to celebrate.

Delia Grace and I sat in my room, completing the reading time she insisted we have daily. She had a variety of interests: history, mythology, and the great philosophers of the day. I preferred novels. Usually, I'd be transported to places dreamed up in the pages of a book, but today, my ears were on edge. I was listening, glancing over at the door every few minutes, waiting for them to storm in.

At the one moment I finally stumbled upon an interesting section, the doors flew open.

"Is this a joke?" my father asked, his tone not angered but shockingly hopeful.

I shook my head. "No, sir. The king extended the invitation just this morning. You seemed so busy, I thought a letter would be more appropriate."

I shot a conspiratorial look at Delia Grace, who pretended to still be immersed in her book.

My mother swallowed, her body never fully settling in one spot as she spoke. "We are all to sit with the king tonight?"

I nodded. "Indeed, madam. You, Father, and myself. I'll need Delia Grace with me, so I thought her mother might join us as well."

At that, Mother's excited fidgeting stopped. My father

closed his eyes, and I recognized the action from many a time when he wanted to think over his words before he spoke them.

"Certainly you would prefer to be solely in the company of your family for such a momentous occasion."

I smiled. "There is room for all of us and more at the king's table. I hardly think it will matter."

My mother looked down her nose at me. "Delia Grace, would you please leave us to speak with our daughter?"

We shared a tired look, and Delia Grace closed her book, setting it on the table before she left.

"Mother, honestly!"

She moved quickly, coming to tower over me where I sat. "This is not a game, Hollis. That girl is tainted, and she shouldn't be in your company. At first it seemed sweet, like charity. But now . . . you have to sever ties."

My mouth fell open. "I most certainly will not! She has been my closest friend at court."

"She's a bastard!" my mother hissed.

I swallowed. "That is a rumor. Her mother has sworn she was faithful. Lord Domnall only threw that accusation at Delia Grace's mother—eight years after the fact, mind you—so he could arrange a divorce."

"Either way, a divorce is enough of a reason to stay away from her!" Mother argued.

"It's not her fault!"

"Too right you are, dear," Father added, ignoring me.

"If her mother's blood isn't bad enough, her father's is. Divorced." He shook his head. "And to have eloped at all, let alone so quickly after."

I sighed. Coroa was a land of laws. Many of them centered around family and marriage. Being unfaithful to your spouse meant you were, at best, an outcast. At worst, there would be a trip to the tower. Divorce was something so rare, I'd never actually seen it happen with my own eyes. But Delia Grace had.

Her father claimed that his wife, the former Lady Clara Domnall, had an affair that resulted in the birth of their only child, Delia Grace. On those grounds, he demanded and was granted a divorce. But within three months he'd run off with another lady, handing off the titles Delia Grace was set to inherit to this woman and any offspring they might produce. Of course, what were titles with such a reputation? Eloping meant an awareness of widespread disapproval and was seen as a last resort, with some couples choosing to separate rather than take such desperate action.

Still a lady in her own right, Lady Clara reclaimed her maiden name, and brought her daughter to court so that she might be able to grow up with the influence of the gentry. What she got instead was endless torment.

I'd always found the whole story questionable. If Lord Domnall had suspected his wife had been unfaithful and that Delia Grace wasn't his, why did he wait eight years to bring it up? There had never been any proof to back up the claims, but he was granted his divorce all the same. Delia Grace said he must have fallen hard for the woman he eloped with. I tried to tell her it was nonsense, but she shook her head at me.

"No. He must have loved her more than my mother and me combined. Why would you leave for something you cared for less?" The look in her eyes was so resolute that I couldn't argue with her, and I never brought up the topic again.

I didn't need to. Half the palace did on our behalf. And if they weren't judging her to her face, they were at least thinking it. My parents were proof enough of that.

"You are being too hasty," I insisted. "It was very generous of the king to invite us to dinner, but it doesn't mean anything more will come of it. And even if it does, after all this time, doesn't Delia Grace—who has always been a model of perfection at court—deserve to stay at my side?"

My father huffed. "People have already passed judgment about your escapades on the river. Do you want to give them more ammunition?"

I thrust my hands into my lap, thinking it was pointless to argue with my parents. When had I ever won? The closest I ever came was when Delia Grace was beside me.

That was it!

I sighed, looking up at my parents, their faces still determined.

"I understand your concerns, but perhaps our wishes aren't the only ones to be considered here," I offered.

"I owe nothing to that scandal of a girl," Mother spat.

"No. I mean the king."

At that they silenced themselves. Finally, my father ventured to speak.

"Explain."

"I only mean that His Majesty has become quite enamored of me, and part of what makes my days so easy is Delia Grace's companionship. Furthermore, Jameson is much more compassionate than his father and might understand taking her under my wing. With your permission, I'd like to pose the question to him."

I'd chosen my words carefully, measured my tone. There was no way they could call me sulky or whiny, and there was no way they could pretend to have a higher authority than a king.

"Very well," Father said. "Why not ask him tonight? But she is not invited to sit with us. Not this time."

I nodded. "I'll write her now so she understands. Do excuse me." I kept my serene air about me as I fetched some parchment from my desk, and they left, looking puzzled.

When the door closed, I giggled to myself.

> Delia Grace,
> I'm very sorry, but my parents have made a stand about the dinner tonight. Don't fret! I have a plan to keep you by my side always. Come and find me later tonight, and I will explain everything. Have courage, dear friend!
> Hollis

There were still judgmental glances being cast at me as I made my way to dinner, and I realized I didn't much care for it. How had Delia Grace survived this kind of scrutiny? And from such a young age?

As it was, my parents didn't care about the glares, but instead walked in as if they were showing off a purebred mare they'd just inherited, and that only garnered more attention.

Mother turned around to look at me, assessing even as we approached the head table. I'd kept my golden gown on, and she'd let me borrow one of her headpieces, so I had a string of jewels across my golden hair.

"It's not really showing up," she said, looking at the head-piece. "I don't know how your hair came out so blond, but it just ruins the look of jewels across your head."

"Nothing I can do to help it," I replied. As if I didn't know already. My hair was a shade or two lighter than that of most of the crowd, and more than one person had noted it across my lifetime.

"I blame your father."

"I wouldn't," he snapped.

I swallowed, seeing the tension of the moment was truly getting to them. It was a well-observed rule of the family that all bickering was reserved for the privacy of our apartments. Suddenly remembering this, they bit back their bitterness as we approached the head table.

"Your Majesty," Father greeted him, a false wide smile on his face. But Jameson hardly noticed they were there. His eyes rested solely on me.

I curtsied low, unable to look away. "Your Majesty."

"Lady Hollis. Lord and Lady Brite. You look in good spirits. Please, come and sit." He held his hand out, gesturing for us to come behind the table. My breath sped up as I settled beside the king, ready to weep with joy when he kissed my hand. Turning around, I saw the Great Room as I'd never seen it before.

Elevated on the dais, it was easy to see everyone's faces, to watch as rank dictated who took which seat. Surprisingly, where all the attention as I walked in left me uneasy, taking in those same stares when I was beside Jameson gave me a thrill. From his side, I could see the same thought lingering in every gaze: *I wish it were me.*

After a few quiet moments of staring into my eyes, Jameson took a deep breath and turned to my father.

"Lord Brite, I hear your estates are some of the prettiest in all of Coroa."

My father's chest lifted. "I would say so. We have a magnificent garden and good, comfortable lands. There is even a tree with a wooden swing that I used as a child. Hollis climbed up the ropes once herself," he said, then made a face like he wished he hadn't. "But it's hard to make time to travel back when Keresken is so beautiful. Especially for the holidays. Crowning Day in the country just doesn't compare."

"I imagine not. All the same, I'd like to see it sometime."

"Your Majesty is always welcome." My mother reached

over and touched Father's arm. A visit from a royal meant lots of preparation and money spent, but it was quite a win for any family to earn a visit to their estates.

Jameson turned back to me. "So you climbed up the ropes of your swing, did you?"

I smiled, thinking back to the moment fondly. "I saw a nest and very much wished to be a bird myself. Wouldn't it be lovely to fly? So I decided I would go live there, with the mother bird, and see if she took me into her family."

"And?"

"I was scolded for ripping my dress instead."

The king roared with laughter, drawing the attention of most of the room. I could feel the heat of a thousand eyes on me, but all I could think about were his. Delicate crinkles lined the corners of his eyes as they lit with joy; it was beautiful.

I could make Jameson laugh, and very few people possessed such a talent. It amazed me that such a silly little story entertained him so.

I'd actually climbed up the ropes of the swing many times, never getting too far, partly because I feared the height and partly because I feared my parents' reproach. But I remembered that day in particular, the mother bird with her little ones, flying off to get food for them. She seemed so worried for her babies, so ready to meet their needs. I had to ask myself later how desperate I must have been to want a bird for a mother.

"Do you know what I want, Hollis? I want to hire someone

to walk behind us and ink down every single word you say. Every compliment, every story. You are endlessly entertaining, and I don't want to forget a second of it. I'm already looking forward to what tales I'll hear at dinner tomorrow."

My smile came back to me. Tomorrow. It seemed Jameson intended to keep me at his side for a while. "Then you must tell me all of your stories, too. I want to know everything," I said, resting my chin on my palm, waiting.

Jameson's lips lifted into a devilish smirk. "Don't worry, Hollis. You will know everything soon enough."

FOUR

"Why didn't you come to dinner? You could have attended still," I said, wrapping my arms around Delia Grace. The palace halls were empty, and that made our voices echo even more than they usually did.

"I thought it would be easier to just not be there rather than go with my mother and explain why I wasn't sitting beside you for the first time in ten years."

I made a face. "My parents . . . sometimes I think they're too stuck-up to even be seen with *me*."

She giggled a little. "Have they ordered that I stay away, then?"

I crossed my arms. "If they did, it wouldn't matter. Seeing as Jameson said you should be with me always."

Her face lit up. "Really?"

I nodded. "After you left, my parents made their case for

setting you aside—as if I could ever find a better friend! But I calmly reminded them that you help get me through my days now, and if that pleases the king, then it ought to be good enough for them. So, of course, my mother brought the issue up at dinner, citing your reputation, as if you had anything to do with it."

Delia Grace rolled her eyes. "Of course she did."

"But listen, listen! Jameson asked, 'Is she truly such a good friend?' And I said, 'Second only to you, Your Majesty.' And then I batted my lashes at him."

"That man *loves* to be flattered." She crossed her arms, waiting for more.

"I know. So he asked, 'Do you really consider me your friend, dear Hollis?' And—I still can't believe I dared to do this in front of so many people—I lifted his hand in mine and kissed it."

"No!" she whispered excitedly.

"Yes! And I said, 'There is no one in this world who shows me such respect and care as you . . . but Delia Grace is close.' He stared at me for a second, and, oh, Delia Grace, I think he would have kissed me had we been alone. Then he said, 'If it makes Lady Hollis happy, then Delia Grace must stay on.' And that was the end of it."

"Oh, Hollis!" She threw her arms around me.

"So there. I'd like to see my parents try to wriggle their way around that."

"I'm sure they'll try." She shook her head. "It sounds like he's willing to give you anything you want."

I looked down. "I wish I could just be sure of what *he* wanted." I sighed. "But even if I was, I don't know how to win people over, and I'd have to do just that to make the lords happy with his choice."

Her eyebrows knit together in thought. "Go get some sleep. I'll be in your room in the morning. We will figure this out."

She'd have a plan. When had Delia Grace ever not had a plan? I hugged her and kissed her cheek. "Good night."

The next morning, I awoke feeling anything but refreshed. My mind had been racing through the night, and all I wanted to do was talk through each of my thoughts and pull at the threads until I found the answers tied up at the end of one.

I still couldn't believe that Jameson might truly want to make me his queen. But the more I considered whether it was a real possibility, the more exciting the thought became. If I could just do something to make the people comfortable with me as a choice, I, too, could be adored. People could kiss the places I'd visited, like Queen Honovi, or have festivals for me, like Queen Albrade. Save for Queen Thenelope, who'd been royal in her own right, every other queen had been a Coroan girl, like me. They'd all come from good families, all been embraced, all left a mark on history. . . . Maybe that could be me, too.

Delia Grace walked in carrying a handful of books while I was still hugging my knees to my chest in bed.

"Do you think becoming queen means you get to sleep in

all the time now?" she joked. I could hear the hint of a bite to her words but decided not to address it.

"I didn't sleep well."

"Well, I hope you're ready to work regardless. We have a lot to cover." She went to the vanity and nodded at it, her way of instructing me to come and sit.

"Like what?" I walked over, letting her pull my hair off my face.

"When it comes to dancing and entertaining, I believe you can top any lady at court. But your understanding of international relations is weak, and if you want to convince the lords of the council that you are a serious choice, you need to be able to speak to them about politics of the court."

I gulped. "Agreed. So, what do we do? I feel like if I have to sit through a lesson with a stuffy old tutor, I might just die."

Delia Grace placed her pins quickly, pulling the top section of my hair into a simple bun while leaving the rest of it down. "I can help you. I have some books, and anything I don't have, the king would certainly provide."

I nodded. If Jameson really intended to take me as a bride, he'd want me as educated as possible.

"And languages," Delia Grace added. "You need to learn at least one more."

"I'm rotten with languages! How am I . . ." I sighed. "You're probably right. If we ever visit Catal, I don't want to be completely lost."

"How solid is your geography?" she asked.

"Solid enough. Let me get dressed." I hopped up to go to my armoire.

"Might I suggest Coroan red?"

I wiggled a finger at her. "Good thinking."

I tried to consider other small, strategic things we could do to curry favor, but, as Delia Grace had so astutely pointed out, I was much more gifted at entertaining than planning. As she cinched up the last string of my kirtle, a knock came at the door.

She tied off the knot and went to answer it as I looked at myself in the mirror, making sure everything was straight before my company came in.

Lord Seema was standing there, his expression looking as if he'd recently been eating a lemon.

I sank into a curtsy, hoping my shock didn't show on my face. "My lord. To what do I owe this honor?"

He wrung his fingers back and forth over the paper in his hands. "My Lady Hollis. It has not escaped my notice that you have gained the king's special attention in recent weeks."

"I'm not sure about that," I hedged. "His Majesty has been very kind to me, but that's all I can really say."

He glanced around the room, looking like he wished he had another gentleman to share the moment with. Finding no one worthy, he sighed and went on. "I can't tell if you are playing ignorant or if you truly can't tell. Either way, you *do* have his attention, and I was hoping you might do me a favor."

My eyes darted to Delia Grace, who raised her eyebrows as if to say, "Go on!" I clasped my hands in front of me, hoping to look modest and attentive. If I needed to learn about the politics of court, I supposed this was as firsthand a lesson as I was going to get.

"I can't make any promises, sir, but please, tell me why you've come."

Lord Seema unfolded his papers and handed them over to me. "As you know, Upchurch County is at the farthest edge of Coroa. To get there or to Royston or Bern, you have to take some of the oldest roads in the country, the ones made as our ancestors slowly worked their way toward the forests and fields at the end of our territory."

"Yes," I said, and, for what it was worth, I did remember that little bit of Coroan history.

"As such, these roads are in the greatest need of repair. I have fine carriages, and even they struggle. You can imagine the strain this puts on the poorest of my community who might need to travel to the capital for any reason."

"I can." He made a good point. Back home at Varinger Hall, we, too, owned and kept lands, and we had many families who lived on them and paid rent to us in money and goods. I'd seen their old horses and weathered carts. It would have been a challenge to come even from our closer county to the castle with those things. I couldn't picture trying to do it from the farthest reaches of the country. "What is your aim here, sir?"

"I'd like a royal survey of all the roads in Coroa. I've

tried to mention this to His Majesty twice this year, and he's brushed it off. I was wondering if you could . . . encourage him to make it a priority."

I took a deep breath. How in the world would I go about that?

I looked down at the papers I had no hope of understanding before handing them back to Lord Seema. "If I can get the king to focus on this, I would ask a favor of my own in return."

"I assumed nothing less," he replied, crossing his arms.

"If this project moves forward," I began slowly, "I expect you to speak kindly of me to anyone you pass who mentions my name. And if you discuss this interaction with the other lords, would you please tell them I received you graciously?"

He smiled. "My lady, you make it sound as if I would have to lie. You have my word."

"Then I will do all I can to help you with this worthy project."

Satisfied, he gave me a deep bow and left the room. As the door shut, Delia Grace burst into a fit of laughter. "Hollis, do you realize what this means?"

"That I need to learn how to make the king care about old roads?" I offered.

"No! A lord of the *privy council* just came asking for your help. Do you see how much power you have already?"

I paused for a moment, letting that thought sink in.

"Hollis," she said with a grin, "we are on our way up!"

This time, when I walked into the Great Room for dinner and Jameson waved me to approach the head table, Delia Grace came with me. My parents were already to the king's left, chatting up a storm, so I went up thinking I had some time to figure out how to casually work road repair into the conversation.

"How in the world am I going to do this?" I asked Delia Grace quietly.

"No one said it had to happen today. Think on it more."

I didn't know how to explain why this felt bigger than earning Lord Seema's allegiance. I wanted Jameson to see me as someone serious. I wanted him to know I could be his partner, that I had a mind capable of handling important decisions. If he could . . . then a proposal surely wouldn't be far off.

As Delia Grace and I listened to my parents go on and on about how Mother's favorite tiara had gone missing last Crowning Day, and she was hoping the culprit would show up with it this year so she could finally get it back, I thought back on how easy our conversation had been the night before. How would I have said something then? A crumb of an idea hit me, and I waited until my mother finally let the king have a break from her incessant talking.

"I had a thought," I began sweetly. "Remember that old swing back at Varinger Hall?"

Jameson smirked. "What of it?"

"I think I would like to go back to it, and have the strongest hands in all Coroa push me on it. Maybe then I would finally feel like I got to be a bird," I teased.

"That sounds positively charming."

"There are many places in Coroa I'd like to see with you," I continued.

He nodded seriously. "As you should! More and more, I'm thinking you need to be well versed in all of Coroa's history."

I added that little tick mark to the list of things the king had said that made me think he wanted me as queen.

"I hear the mountains in the north are so beautiful, they'll bring you to tears."

Jameson agreed. "The way the mist settles on them . . . it's as if they're from another world entirely."

I smiled dreamily. "I would very much like to see that. Maybe it would be a good time to go on a tour of the country, let your people see you. Show off your great possessions."

He reached over, wrapping a strand of my hair around his finger. "I do have some beautiful things, though there is one gem in all of Coroa I am aching to call my own."

Tick.

I lowered my voice to a whisper. "I would go anywhere with you, Your Majesty. Although . . ." I peeked around him at Father. "Father, didn't you have trouble on the road the last time you went up to Bern?"

After swallowing his oversized spoonful of food, he answered. "Broke a wheel. Those roads are rough out there."

"Are they?" Jameson asked.

Father nodded gravely, as if everything he spoke of with

the king was of utmost importance. "Unfortunately, yes, Majesty. Not enough people out there to keep them up. I'm sure there are plenty more in the same state of disrepair."

"Well, that won't do," I said. "I wouldn't want Your Majesty injured. Perhaps another time."

Jameson wiggled his finger at me. "Who was it . . . Ah! Lord Seema!" he called. Out of the crowd, Lord Seema lifted his head and rushed forward to bow before the king.

I sat up straighter as Jameson began.

"Was it you who was saying something about the roads in Upchurch?"

Lord Seema flicked his eyes between Jameson and me. "Yes, Your Majesty. They're in considerable disrepair."

Jameson shook his head. "I am thinking of taking the Brites on progress, but I cannot do so if this pearl of a lady might be stranded on the road."

"No, Your Majesty. With your permission, I could assemble a committee and survey the roads. Afterward, I could organize a proper budget, if you like. I'm very passionate about all the citizens of Coroa being able to travel easily, wherever they like, and would happily oversee it myself."

"Granted," Jameson replied quickly. "I'll expect reports."

Lord Seema stood there, stunned. "Yes. Yes, of course," he stuttered as he backed away, mouth still hanging slightly open.

"What fun!" I sang. "I shall finally see all of our great country."

Jameson kissed my hand. "All of Coroa. All of the continent, if you wish."

Tick.

I settled back into my seat, looking over at Delia Grace.

She lifted her cup as her smile tightened. "Impressive."

"Thank you." I looked out at the mass of people, finding Lord Seema. He tilted his head toward me, and I did the same in reply. Maybe I could do this after all.

FIVE

WITHIN DAYS, MY WORLD CHANGED. Jameson was still sending flowers and trinkets to my room anytime he seemed to
see something he thought I'd like, but now nobles left gifts
for me as well. With all the new jewelry at my disposal, I
truly was as Jameson said: as radiant as the sun. I had two
chambermaids assigned to me, and when I walked through
the palace, people would smile at me in passing, if sometimes
a little tightly. I didn't know if I had Lord Seema to thank for
this or if my new attempts to be as regal and lovely as possible when I was with Jameson were finally being seen, but
I certainly didn't mind the attention. I had thought nothing
could be as much fun as winning over the heart of a king,
but I was wrong. It was much more thrilling to win over the
hearts of countless people at once.

This thought filled my head as I walked with Delia Grace

to the Great Room, graciously acknowledging courtiers and wishing them a good morning. Jameson seemed to have a special sense for when I was entering a room, and he would turn the full force of his attention on me when I came near. I was now greeted with a kiss on the cheek in the full view of the court anytime I joined him. And while I noted some disapproving glances when it happened, I took that as more of a challenge than a disappointment.

"You got my letter?" he asked.

"You mean the page of absolute poetry that ended with a request that I meet you this morning? Why, yes, I did."

He chuckled. "You bring words out of me that I didn't know existed," he confessed, not looking the slightest bit shy about making such a statement with so many people in earshot. "Tell me, is everything well? Your new maids? Do you like your new clothes?"

I stepped back so he could see the full glory of one of my recent gifts. "They are the most beautiful I've ever had. And, yes, my maids are quite helpful, thank you. As always, you are too generous."

At that he wiggled his eyebrows. "Those tokens will look like pebbles when—"

He broke off at the sound of hurried footsteps, and I turned, following his gaze. An older gentleman, one of Jameson's many advisers, rushed in and bowed his head.

"Your Majesty, forgive me. There is a family here from Isolte seeking sanctuary. They come to present their case."

It was customary among all the kingdoms of the continent

to ask a king's permission before settling in his land. If a family was found without a royal grant, well, on a good day they'd be removed. I'd seen what had happened on bad days, when Jameson's father, Marcellus, sat on the throne.

His Majesty sighed, seeming put out to be drawn away from our conversation. "Very well, show them in." As if the idea had struck him just then, his gaze came back to me. "Lady Hollis, perhaps you'd like to sit for the proceedings?" He waved his hand to the seat beside him. The gentleman in it, Lord Mendel, looked quickly between the two of us.

"Your Majesty, I—"

Beside him, Lord Seema gave a discreet nudge to his arm. Lord Mendel sighed but stood, bowing to both the king and me. I gave Lord Seema a grateful nod as I took my place.

I shot a look at Delia Grace, who was quietly smug on my behalf; she'd always known, hadn't she? I heard disgruntled murmurs swarming around us—yes, I still had hearts to win over—but I focused my attention on Jameson. This was an opportunity to prove exactly what I was capable of. I could be demure and intelligent if the moment required it.

I sat up as straight as I could, keeping my chin down and my breathing slow. I wanted everyone to see me as poised, capable. Maybe then Jameson would be ready to make me his queen.

An older gentleman and his wife entered the room, her hand gracefully perched upon his. Behind them followed their four children, three boys and a girl.

The children all had pale skin and hair in varying shades of yellow, while their parents were starting to gray. The youngest boy was on edge, clutching his sister's hand tightly, while she was canvassing the room in a much different way, her eyes suggesting she was looking for something.

The father knelt, bringing his knee to the floor, before rising and presenting himself to the king. Even if we hadn't been told they were from Isolte, it would have been obvious. The land was dreadfully windy in the summer, and the winter went on far longer than it did here. I wouldn't have been surprised to hear they were still seeing light snow, even now. As such, Isoltens spent more time indoors, and the sun-kissed cheeks seen everywhere in Coroa were missing on them.

"Good morning, sir," Jameson said, inviting the man to speak.

"Your Majesty, I pray you will forgive our poor state, but we came straight here," the father began humbly.

I would not have called their appearance poor. Velvet draped across every member of the family, with plenty to spare . . . which forced me to press my lips together so I didn't giggle. Honestly, who in the world designed those sleeves? I could make an extra gown from the yardage draping off their arms. And the hats! For my life, I never understood the fashion from Isolte.

In truth, I never even understood people from Isolte. The word that came to mind most of the time was *unoriginal*.

Yes, I'd heard of their great findings in astronomy and herbology, and that the medicines discovered by their doctors were yielding great benefits for their people. But the music they made was bland at best, the dances they performed were copied from ours, and most other efforts at art were modified forms of something seen elsewhere. Their fashion seemed to be their best attempt at something no one else laid claim to. And why would they?

"We come asking for your mercy, to allow us to settle in your land, offering us sanctuary from our king," the father continued, his tone carrying an edge of nerves.

"And where is it that you come from, sir?" Jameson asked, even though he knew the answer.

"Isolte, Your Majesty."

"What is your name, sir?"

"Lord Dashiell Eastoffe, Your Majesty."

Jameson paused. "I know that name," he murmured, brow creased in thought. Once his memory came back to him, he eyed the visitors with something that looked like a mix of suspicion and pity. "Yes, I can see why you would want to leave Isolte indeed. Oh, Hollis," he said, turning to me with a playful glint in his eye, "do you ever thank the gods that you have me for a king and not that grouch, King Quinten?"

"I thank the gods that we have you above *any* other king, Your Majesty." I batted my lashes flirtatiously, but I truly had thanked the heavens for him. He was younger and stronger than any king on the continent, much kinder than his father, and far less temperamental than the other leaders I'd heard about.

He chuckled. "If I were in your position, I, too, might have fled, sir. Many families have chosen to immigrate to Coroa recently." There was one such family living in the castle, but I never saw them. "It makes me wonder just what dear old King Quinten is up to these days to strike such fear into his subjects."

"We also have a gift for Your Majesty," Lord Eastoffe offered instead of answering the question. He nodded to his oldest son, and the young man moved forward, bowing before the king and holding up a long velvet parcel.

Jameson walked down the dais steps to the young man and flipped the fabric back. Beneath it was a golden sword with an array of jewels resting in the hilt. As Jameson lifted it, the new spring sun bounced off the blade, temporarily blinding me.

After inspecting the sword, Jameson pulled out a lock of the young man's long hair and sliced through it with his gift. Chuckling as it cut away with ease, he held the sword up again. "This is impressive, sir. I've never seen its equal."

"Thank you, Your Majesty," Lord Eastoffe said gratefully. "Alas, I cannot take credit for it. I was raised a gentleman, but my son has settled upon this craft, choosing to be capable of supporting himself, with or without land."

Jameson looked down at the boy whose hair he'd just so

graciously trimmed. "You made this?"

The boy nodded, his eyes downcast.

"As I said, impressive."

"Your Majesty," Lord Eastoffe began, "we are simple people, without ambition, who have been forced to abandon our estates due to serious threats on our lands and our lives. We ask only to settle here peacefully, and vow to never stir a foot against any natural Coroan, and join in their faithful service of you."

Jameson turned away from them, his eyes going from thoughtful to focused as they settled on my face. He grinned, suddenly looking exceptionally pleased with himself. "Lady Hollis, these people have come seeking refuge. What would you say to their plea?"

Smiling, I looked down at the family. My gaze passed cursorily over the youngest children and their mother, and settled on the eldest son. He was still on his knees, hands clutching the velvet wrap. His eyes locked with mine.

For a moment, the world stilled. I found myself completely lost in his gaze, unable to look away. His eyes were a shocking blue—a color rare enough in Coroa and completely unique to anything I'd seen before. It wasn't the shade of the sky or of water. I didn't have a word for it. And the blue pulled me in, refusing to let me go.

"Hollis?" Jameson prodded.

"Yes?" I couldn't look away.

"What would you say?"

"Oh!" My eyelids fluttered as I came back to the present.

"Well, they have come in all humility, and they have shown they will contribute to our society through their artisanship. Most important, they have chosen the finest kingdom to settle in, offering their devotion to the goodliest king alive. If it were for me to decide?" I looked at Jameson. "I would let them stay."

King Jameson smiled. It seemed I'd passed the test. "Well, there you have it," he said to the Isoltens. "You may stay."

The Eastoffe family looked at one another, embracing joyfully. The young man bowed his head to me, and I did the same in return.

"A family of your . . . *caliber* must stay at the castle," Jameson instructed, his words sounding more like a warning than an invitation, though I didn't understand why. "At least, for now."

"Of course, Your Majesty. And we will be most happy with wherever you choose to keep us," Lord Eastoffe replied.

"Take them to the South Wing," Jameson ordered a guard, giving a flick of his head. The Isoltens bent their heads in acknowledgment before turning and filing out.

"Hollis," Jameson whispered beside me, "that was beautifully done. But you must become accustomed to thinking quickly. If I ask you to speak, you need to be ready."

"Yes, Your Majesty," I replied, fighting a blush.

He turned to speak with one of his advisers, while I focused my eyes on the back of the hall, watching the Eastoffe family. I still didn't know the eldest son's name, but he looked over his shoulder at me, smiling again.

A quick flutter of whatever had made him hold my gaze before rushed through me, and it felt like a tiny pull in my chest was telling me to follow those eyes. But I dismissed it. If there was anything I knew as a Coroan, it was that Isolten blue was not to be trusted.

SIX

"Now that that's done, I have something to show you," Jameson whispered in my ear. I turned to look at his devilishly excited eyes, remembering that I'd come in this morning at his invitation. I was thankful to have something—anything—to pull me away from the strange sensation humming through my chest.

I took his hand gratefully, but as soon as he wove his fingers through mine, he looked troubled. "You're trembling. Are you unwell?"

"I don't know how you handle all those eyes looking at you all the time," I replied, trying to explain it away. "You have to make so many decisions, and so quickly."

His eyes were alight with wisdom as he led me to the edge of the dais. "I was fortunate enough to have an excellent teacher in my father. My bride, whoever she may be, will have to do her best to learn the trade of ruling from me."

"That's no small task, Your Majesty."

He smirked. "No. But it does come with some rewards."

I waited for him to say more, but he simply stared straight ahead. "Majesty?"

He kept smiling with his chin up, ignoring me.

We walked down the steps, and I drew in a breath as he led me to one of the doors at the front of the Great Room. I shared a look with him as the guards let us through; I'd never been here before. The king's rooms—his private chambers, rooms used for prayer, and the spaces he gave to those working on the privy council—were separated from everyone else by the Great Room. It allowed him to make a rather impressive entrance, and it was easier to keep him secure.

"Majesty, where are we going?"

"Nowhere," he sang coyly.

"It is decidedly not nowhere," I insisted, the excitement bubbling up in my stomach.

"Fine. It's someplace I've been thinking about taking you since the night we truly met."

I rolled my eyes. "You mean the moment I made the world's biggest fool of myself?"

He laughed. "The moment you became the most charming girl in all of Coroa."

"I have to tell you, it's made me so happy to know I've brought any measure of joy to your life," I admitted. "Not every lady can say she's made a king himself laugh."

"In my case, not a single girl at court can say it. You're

the only one, Hollis. Everyone else? They want something. But you give and give." He raised my hand to kiss it. "So it delights me to give to you in return."

We walked past two more sets of guards before we reached the room Jameson wanted to show me. Once we were there, one of the guards had to take out a special key and hand us a lantern.

"There are some lanterns in the room already," Jameson assured me, "but there are no windows, so any bit of light helps."

"Am I being escorted to a dungeon?" I joked, feigning fear.

He laughed. "Not today. Come. I think this may end up being your favorite room in the castle someday."

Tick.

I hesitantly followed him through the doors, taking a moment to let my eyes adjust and then forgetting completely how to breathe.

"Some of these are mine," he began. "I'm sure you recognize the seal I wore on my coronation day. These rings here, I've worn many times. And this . . ."

"The Crown of Estus," I breathed, completely awestruck. "It's even more beautiful up close."

I stared at the piece for a long time, feeling tears gather at the corners of my eyes. Just over seven generations ago, Coroa was under constant civil wars for leadership. Rulers were made and undone in a handful of years, and it left us at war with ourselves and defenseless against other countries that might take our land. Finally, the Barclay tribe—the very same Barclays who Jameson was descended from—conquered what was left of their enemies, and, though the fighting was brutal, the people were grateful to have one clear leader. The people collected scraps of gold and jewelry, melted them down, and forged them into a crown. A holy man blessed it, and everyone came to watch King Estus Barclay be crowned, the people giving over their rights to his leadership.

The Crown of Estus was only taken out once a year, on Crowning Day, and only those fortunate enough to be born into a noble family would ever catch a glimpse.

"Your Majesty, thank you. Your trust in me must be very great to let me so close to something so special, and I am humbled by it." I could hardly express the awe I was feeling, but I knew how privileged I was in that moment. I turned to face him, tears still blurring my vision.

He took my hand, kissing it again. "I do trust you, Hollis. It's like I said: you constantly give. Your time and affection, your laughter and care. You have already given me a thousand gifts in them. Which is why I must tell you that seeing the Crown of Estus is not your gift . . . this is."

He gestured to the wall to my left, which was covered in shelves of yet more jewels. Ropes of sapphires and laces of diamonds were laid out before me. We didn't need windows in this room—the little light we had was enough to make them sparkle blindingly.

"These are the queen's jewels. Every year, the kings of

Coroa and Isolte meet to renew our peace. King Quinten will be coming for his annual visit at the end of the week, and I want you to look like royalty."

Part of me wanted to faint. Part of me wished my parents were here to see this. But every last piece of me wanted to wear that necklace set with rose-tinted jewels and diamonds.

I walked closer to it, afraid to so much as even point at any of these gorgeous pieces. "Are you quite sure? I know how precious they are."

"There's no one I'd trust with them more. And, genuinely, since that night in the ballroom, I've been imagining you with something as pretty as these along your neck." He gestured across the wall of jewels, as if offering them all to me.

Satisfied, I pressed my lips together and lifted my fingers to touch the smooth, cold stones, hovering somewhere between pink and red. "This one."

"Perfect."

The thrill of knowing I was going to wear something distinctly made with a queen in mind ran over me, and I turned around, throwing my arms around Jameson. "You are too good to me."

"Are you happy?"

"Almost too happy," I answered, holding on to him tightly and realizing something. "Your Majesty. We've never been all alone before."

He smiled. "Well, you are a rather virtuous lady. I'm surprised I managed to get you to slip away with me now."

"You're very clever."

And because we were so close, and alone, and swept up in our own world, when he bent down to kiss me, I leaned into it. To finally be kissed was a wondrous thing, and to be kissed by a king was even more thrilling. Jameson drew me close, holding my chin and pulling away when he deemed the kiss long enough.

Something in his eyes shifted, as if he'd settled upon a decision. His tone became very serious.

"You must brace yourself, Hollis. Many changes are coming for us."

I swallowed. "For us both, Majesty?"

He nodded. "Over the next few weeks, I intend to make all of Coroa aware of just how much I adore you. That will mean many things. Some will beg for your favor; others will curse your name. But none of that matters, Hollis. I want you for my bride."

It took all the strength I had to even whisper a reply. "And I would be honored . . . but I worry I'm not worthy."

He shook his head, carefully tucking a loose curl behind my ear. "I think many who marry into royalty feel that way, but you needn't worry. Just think of my great-grandmother Albrade. They say that she was as pale as an Isolten when she took her vows," he joked, "but look at the legend she became."

I tried to smile, but it was hard to imagine myself doing anything so brave as winning a war.

"I am no soldier," I replied meekly.

"And I don't want you to be. All I ask is for you to be everything you already are. That, my sweet Hollis, is what I love you for."

Love you for, love you for, love you for . . .

The words echoed in my heart, and I wished I had a way to save them in a bottle. He was kind enough to give me another moment to steady myself before going on.

"I've grown up without any siblings. My parents both died far too soon. Above anything, you have given me the company in this life that I have longed for. That is all I ask for from you. Anything else anyone wants is superfluous. If you think you can be happy being my partner in this world, then all will be well."

He spoke so sincerely, with such feeling, that my eyes welled once more. His affection was overwhelming, and as I looked into his eyes, only inches away from mine, I trusted that I could do any task that might be demanded of me so long as I was beside him.

It was such a strange sensation, so very new. In that instant, I knew this must be love. It was more than the weak knees, but the unflinching resolve he inspired in me . . . all of this was unique to Jameson.

I nodded. It was all I could do. But, for him, it was enough.

"I ask that you keep this a secret for now. The lords are still trying to convince me to marry the princess from Bannir for the sake of the border, but I cannot stomach the thought. I need some time to convince them that you and I can make Coroa secure on our own."

I nodded again. "I shall do the same."

He looked as if he might kiss me again, but then thought better of it. "I must take you back before anyone has room to question your honor. Come, sweet Hollis, into the madness we go."

As the doors opened to the Great Room, I blushed as everyone's focus turned to us. My heart fluttered mercilessly, and I wondered if they could see it.

They were looking upon their queen.

SEVEN

OVER THE NEXT FEW DAYS, Delia Grace hounded me relentlessly. I sometimes hummed as if I hadn't heard a single thing she was saying, or occupied myself with another task entirely, smiling the entire time. Today I was bent over some embroidery on a new dress, but, as focused as I tried to be, Delia Grace could only be ignored for so long.

"Why won't you at least tell me what you saw?"

I giggled. "It's nothing more than a collection of rooms. It just so happens that Jameson lives in these ones."

"What in the world took you so long?"

I pulled carefully at my gold thread, trying to keep the design clean. "We were gone for all of five minutes."

"Fifteen!"

I looked over my shoulder at her in shock. "Surely not."

"I was out there, waiting with the rest of court. I assure

you, we were all keeping time."

I shook my head, smiling. "You'll know about everything soon enough."

"Did he marry you?"

I nearly pricked my finger. "Do you think so little of me? King or no king, getting married without a witness is as bad as eloping. Do you honestly think Jameson would tarnish my reputation in such a way?"

She at least had the decency to look apologetic. "No. Sorry, Hollis. But then why won't you tell me the truth?"

"Can I not enjoy a little surprise every once in a while? Or a secret? Goodness knows they're impossible to keep at court."

She rolled her eyes. "Well, if that's not true, then nothing is." Sighing, she walked over, placing her hands on my shoulders. "If something important happens, you will tell me, yes?"

"Trust me, I wish I could tell you everything." I pulled at my stitches again. The dress looked rather nice, and it was a welcome change to have something else to occupy my thoughts.

"Just tell me this: Are things going as I suspected they would?"

I pressed my lips together, looking up at her from under my lashes. Her responding smile was enough.

"Very well, then," she said. "You're going to need ladies."

I set the dress down. "No. I don't want to build a circle of false friends. Most of the girls at court have been staring daggers at me since the night of the ball; I don't want them near me all the time."

"You need people to attend you."

"No," I replied. "A *queen* needs people to attend her. I have no such title . . . at the present."

"Hollis."

"And if I attempt to amass a household, the lords will talk. It seems they're still hesitant, and I don't wish to do anything that might bring hardship upon Jameson."

She sighed. "Fine, then. If you were going to ask *one* more person at court to see to your needs, who would it be? And, in the name of Estus, don't you dare say that pig-nosed Anna Sophia."

I sighed. "Can I think about it?"

"Yes, but not for long. This is no game, Hollis."

I remembered when, not even a few weeks ago, I had thought of it all as just that. But Delia Grace was right; these were the paths of our lives being forged right before us. It was nothing to play with.

"Where do you think I'd find more thread?"

Delia Grace stood up. "The royal seamstress ought to have loads. I can go find her."

"No, no," I said. "Let me. I'm sure you have lots and lots of plotting to do for my life," I added with a wink.

I left through the side door from my room in my family's apartments, which let out into the middle of the castle, a bustling intersection of activity. I took a second to gaze around. Even though I had spent a significant amount of time at Keresken Castle, I still always found myself in awe of my surroundings.

The wide hallways were grand and ornately decorated; the stonework was even and beautiful; and throughout there were spectacular arches that formed canopies above every space wide enough for them. They often reminded me of upside-down bridges, their spindles coming down as if they wished to touch the tips of our expectant fingers. Magnificent spiral staircases looped through the three upper floors of the castle, and we'd been told the collections of sculptures and paintings housed here surpassed any of those that foreign ambassadors had seen anywhere else on the continent.

My family's apartments were located on the inner edge of the East Wing, which was a respectable location. Those of great importance lived in the very small North Wing, which was closest to the Great Room, and therefore closest to the king. There were also empty apartments in the North Wing that were reserved for nobles and dignitaries. It was where King Quinten would stay when he came to visit.

Families with long Coroan bloodlines were next, living on the near sides of the East and West Wings, and then those with shorter lines but valuable ties and land on the outer edges. Then less important families, and if you got beyond a certain juncture in the hallways, well, it was clear most people didn't care if you were present or not. High floors meant you could stay but weren't necessarily expected to be seen, and the servants made their homes in the floors below the main level.

Beyond the back of the palace, along the high crest of the hill the castle claimed as its own, there were outbuildings, larders, and other spaces where the masses of people who kept the palace operating did the majority of their work. I hoped that was where I might find the seamstress.

"Oh!" I gasped as I rounded a corner a little too quickly.

The two young men I'd almost crashed into looked at me and then dropped into a deep bow. Their hair alone made them unmistakable; these were the boys from Isolte. They wore very loose shirts, the kind men in Coroa wore *under* their doublet, and they both carried leather bags with tools sticking out of them.

"Oh, please, there's no need for that," I insisted, urging them to stand.

The boy with the blinding blue eyes lifted his head. "Perhaps there is, Lady Brite."

I smiled. "I see you've learned my name. But it is my mother who goes by Lady Brite. I am simply Hollis."

He rose, eyes never breaking contact. "Hollis," he said. We stood there for a moment, my name hanging between us, and, once again, I found myself having a difficult time looking away. "I'm Silas," he finally added. "And this is my brother Sullivan."

The brother merely tipped his head. Silas placed a hand on his shoulder. "Why don't you go ahead and take those supplies to the outbuilding? I'll follow along in just a moment."

Wordlessly, Sullivan stumbled down into another bow before exiting quickly.

"Sorry about that," Silas said, turning back to me. "Sullivan is very shy if he doesn't know you. Actually, he's shy even if he does."

I giggled. "Well, you'll have to apologize for me. I didn't mean to startle you."

"Since when do you have to apologize for anything, my lady? They say you are to be queen."

My eyes widened.

"Is it not true? I didn't mean to presume. It's just, everyone says so when you pass."

I looked down. "These people . . . do they sound happy when they say it?"

He nodded. "Plenty of them. If they happen to be around about our age, let's just say the tone is a bit more envious than awed."

I sighed. "Understood. Well, there is no ring on my finger, so no one can really say one way or the other."

"Then *if* this all comes about, I hope that you two will be very happy. Isolte has a queen, but it is universally acknowledged that she lacks a level of strength and generosity one should expect from a leader. Your people will be fortunate to have you."

I looked at my feet, feeling a blush coming on, and noticed the tools in his hands again.

"Forgive me, but why is it you're still working now that you're here? You've left Isolte—which, by the way, may be one of the smartest things a person could do—so why not start over and be a gentleman like your father? It would certainly be cleaner."

He laughed. "I'm proud of what I can do. I'm best with swords and armor, but if Sullivan doesn't mind working with me, I can make jewelry, too." He shrugged, still looking quite pleased with himself. "After presenting that sword to your king, I—"

"Ah, but he is your king now, too," I commented.

The boy—Silas—nodded. "Forgive me. We're all still adjusting, and I'm a bit suspicious of kings at the present."

He took a pause before returning to our conversation. "Since presenting our sword to the king, we've received several requests for more, and I think my mother even managed to talk someone into commissioning a necklace."

I put my hands on my hips, staring at him, impressed. "And here I didn't take Isoltens to be artists." He smiled and shrugged. "That's a rather handy skill. How did you learn it if you were a courtier yourself?"

"Our manor was close enough to the castle that we could come and go with ease, so most of our time was spent at home." A whimsical smile crept across his face. "My father's greatest regret is not developing a practical skill in his youth, so when I expressed an interest in metalwork, he made it possible for me to learn. The first sword I made was for my cousin Etan?" He said it like I might have some idea who he was talking about. "He needed a good battle sword for a tournament. The handle shook too much for him to trust it, and a huge chip came out on his very first swing, but he used it for that whole tournament just the same." He said all this with an expression that told me he was picturing the whole scene. "It's been three years, and I'm proud of what I can do, but I'm always trying to improve. We all are. Even my sister does metalwork, though she does mostly finer things, the finishing touches on the jewelry Sullivan and I make." He held up his hands. "Our fingers are too big."

I studied his hands, noting they were dry and there was soot along the beds of his nails. He might have been raised a noble, but his hands were anything but gentlemanly. Something about that made them strikingly beautiful to me. I tucked mine behind my back, sighing in admiration when I answered. "That's amazing."

He shrugged. "Not so impressive in Isolte. The arts aren't quite as important there."

I raised my eyebrows, allowing that. "Is it as cold as everyone says?"

"If you're speaking of the winds, yes, they can be brutal sometimes. And if you're speaking of the general public . . ." He raised his eyebrows. "I find that being around some people in Isolte can make the temperature drop even further." He chuckled at his own joke. "Don't you know what it's like? Haven't you ever been yourself?"

The surprise in his voice was fair. If a Coroan was going to visit anywhere, Isolte was the easiest place to go . . . though perhaps not the most welcoming.

"No. My father is always working, and if he travels, he

prefers to go alone or with Mother. I've asked to go to Eradore—I heard the beaches there are breathtaking—but it's never happened." I didn't want to say that I'd stopped asking ages ago, when it became clear they wouldn't have minded my company so much if I'd had the common sense to be born a boy, or at least have come after I had a brother. But that didn't happen, and I didn't know where the blame for that belonged, but they decided it was mine.

I had Delia Grace anyway; she was better than a long ride in a stuffy carriage, regardless of the destination. That's what I told myself.

He hoisted the bag back up onto his shoulder. "Well, I'm sure His Majesty will take you anywhere your heart desires. It sounds as if he'd do anything for a lady he rescued from a freezing river." He made a teasing face.

"That happened before you even got here! And it wasn't frozen! *And* I was defending myself from an onslaught of berries. If anything, I didn't do enough."

"I'd have liked to have seen that," he commented playfully. "The ladies back in Isolte don't even bend to touch their hands to the water, much less risk slipping in."

"Probably for the best. That river claimed a very dear pair of shoes."

He laughed, kicking at the stone floor idly. "Well, I suppose I should find Sullivan. The staff was kind enough to find a space for us to work, and it'll be nice to feel . . . useful."

"I know what you mean. Which reminds me, have you

seen a seamstress's or dresser's room back this way? I'm looking for thread."

"Yes," he answered enthusiastically. "Take the next stairway to the second floor. There isn't a door on the room, so you should be able to see it."

"Ah. Well, thank you very much, Silas."

He nodded his head. "Anytime, Lady Hollis."

He hurried on his way, and I walked back to the stairwell, thinking that it was much darker back here than I was used to. As I climbed the stairs, I thought upon the countless visits of kings and dignitaries, of emissaries and representatives that had happened since my family made Keresken Castle our primary residence. I'd *seen* people from all over the continent. And yet, speaking in the hallway with Silas Eastoffe marked the first time I'd ever spoken to a foreigner.

I was surprised to find he was not so different from me, not so difficult to see at home within these castle walls.

EIGHT

THE FOLLOWING MORNING, THE KNOCK came right on time.

"Which do you think it is?" Delia Grace wondered aloud. "Either gifts from His Majesty or another lord coming to seek your favor?"

I avoided her eyes, unsure how this would unfold. "Neither."

"Lady Nora Littrell," the maid announced as my guest rounded the corner.

"What's she doing here?" Delia Grace asked under her breath.

"I invited her," I clarified, standing to greet my guest. "Thank you for coming, Lady Nora."

"Happy to be here. What can I do for you?"

I swallowed, knowing the following statement would

shock Delia Grace. "I've asked you here to offer you a position in my household."

Sure enough, Delia Grace looked positively aghast as she sputtered, "What? Why her?"

"Because she was lady enough to apologize when she did something foolish, and gracious enough not to hold my own foolishness against me." I looked back at my dearest friend. "Our reach at court is limited. Lady Nora knows people we don't, and she's bright. As you've pointed out, I need all the help I can get."

At that Delia Grace dropped her head, blushing, looking as if she were crushing her teeth together behind her lips.

"Granted, my place isn't official yet," I began again, looking back to Nora, "but if you want it, I'd like you both to be in my entourage. Delia Grace, of course you will be primary lady-in-waiting, and Nora, if you want to join us, you can be a lady-in-waiting as well. If things continue like they have been, and Jameson proposes, I will ask for your help in assembling the rest of my household, so that we can assure that it is the happiest it could possibly be. And, naturally, any favor that comes upon me, I will gladly share with you."

Nora walked over, taking my hands. "I'd love to be your lady! Hollis, thank you!" Her smile was genuine, and any resentment she'd harbored toward me for winning Jameson's heart was clearly gone. Maybe it had never even been there to begin with.

Delia Grace, however, was still fuming.

I stared evenly at her. "This will only work if the two of

you can cooperate. You are very different ladies with different personalities and gifts, and I don't know how I'm to get through this without you both. Please."

Delia Grace's arms were crossed, her expression unmistakably telling me I'd just betrayed her in the deepest way possible.

"I was always going to have to get other ladies. You suggested it yourself," I reminded her.

"I know. I just didn't think . . . . She'll answer to me, right?" Delia Grace asked.

"You're the primary lady-in-waiting," Nora said before I could reply. "*Everyone* would answer to you."

"I expect you to be fair," I cautioned her, "but, yes, you outrank everyone who comes after."

She sighed. "Fine." She looked at me, her eyes clearly disappointed. "If you'll excuse me, my lady, I have a headache. And it seems you have someone else to tend you now."

With that she stormed off, the slamming door echoing in her wake.

"I guess I couldn't have expected that to go any better," Nora admitted.

"It will take a lot to undo everything that's passed between you two," I replied.

"Yes. I have to say, with how . . . distant we've all been with her, I'm surprised you're willing to give me a chance at all."

I turned to her. "Well, I'm a big supporter of second chances. I'm hoping that Delia Grace will give you one as well. And that you'll try to make a new start with her."

Her discomfort was written across her face as she worked up the nerve to answer. "That might be nice. Sometimes . . . it's easier being at court when all the negative attention is on someone else, if that make sense."

I sighed. "Yes. Yes, it does."

She gave a sad shrug. "My family has scandals of its own—almost all noble families do—but it made life here easier knowing there was someone to direct all the gossip at."

"I understand. But that is all in the past. Sooner or later, you will have to offer her an apology. I need your help, but I cannot be without her."

She nodded. "I won't let you down, my lady. I'm pleased beyond words just to be a part of this. You're going to be in the history books. Do you realize that?"

I took in a shaky breath through my smile. "I do. . . . I think that's why I'm so nervous."

Nora kissed my cheek. "Don't worry. You have Delia Grace, and now you have me."

Before I could thank her, my mother burst through the door, looking as if she was ready to wage war.

She looked between Nora and me, Nora's hands still in mine, and pointed an accusing finger. "Did you really let that girl into your household?"

After a moment of shock, I understood. "I assume you ran into Delia Grace."

"I did."

"I wonder why you finally saw fit to take anything she says seriously. Could it be because she brought up a piece of my life you forgot to wrap your hands around?"

She didn't deny it. She didn't say she was looking out for me, or that there was a better way to go about it that I hadn't considered. It was just one more thing that was meant to be mine but, in her eyes, wasn't.

"What makes you think you have the capacity to arrange your own household?" she spat. "I expected you to keep Delia Grace; there was no way around that." She rolled her eyes, bitter that the only friend I'd had at the castle chose to stay by my side. "And I'll allow this because Nora is of a more reputable family than most, but from here on in, your father and I will be choosing your ladies. Is that understood?"

It was exhausting, bearing the weight of her constant demands. Was it not enough that I was all but betrothed to a king? No one else could have given her that; a *son* couldn't have given her that.

She huffed and stormed out as quickly as she'd come.

"Don't worry," Nora whispered. "I've got an idea."

Delia Grace was in the garden, stripping petals from the flowers and tossing them at the ground. It was a place we both loved and often retreated to. In a world where everything was fast and people were always chasing after something, the garden was a breath of quiet.

But not for long.

"How could you go complain to *my mother*?" I called, marching across the grass. "She's now demanding to build my entire household. Don't you think her choices would be far worse than anyone I could choose?"

Delia Grace rolled her eyes. "Your mother has some sense about her. That's more than I can say for you."

"We can't stay alone in my room forever! Eventually, we're going to have to find out who we can trust and who we can't."

She laughed shrilly. "And you think the best place to start is with the person who teased me the most for the last ten years?"

"Nora was wrong, and she told me so. I think she's too ashamed to admit it to you yet, but she knows she has a lot to make up for."

"Oh, yes, I'm sure you inviting her into your household has *nothing* to do with her sudden change of heart."

I sighed. "Even if it does, shouldn't we take it? This is why I didn't tell you what I was thinking. Nora's the only lady at court beyond you I thought I could ask for help. But I knew you would prevent it if you could."

She just sat there, shaking her head.

"Didn't you say I should make a household?" I reminded her. "Weren't you the one who wanted me to learn more, be better?"

At that, she finally stood. "Would you please stop throwing my own ideas in my face?" She took a few deep breaths, wiping at her forehead as if she could erase the worry in her creased brow. "Next time, would you please tell me? Before you add someone, would you let me know? Then I can brace myself."

I went over and took her hands, pleased she was willing to even let me hold them. "You say that as if I did this to intentionally hurt you. I promise, I didn't. I thought bringing Nora in would help us. And I think she's genuinely sorry for how she's hurt you."

Delia Grace stood in front of me, shaking her head again. "She's a consummate actress. You're too simple to see through it all."

I swallowed the ache of the insult. "Well, I may be simple, but I am also on the right hand of the king. So I need you to trust me. And I need you to help; you know I can't do this alone."

She propped her hands on her hips, considering. For a moment, I wondered if she'd actually leave me.

"Just don't let her forget her place, all right?"

I shook my head. "You don't have to like her."

"Good. Because right now I hardly like you." With that she barreled off, leaving me in my favorite place feeling decidedly unpeaceful.

NINE

"Lady Hollis," the maid whispered, her voice shaky. I was still in bed as she was getting fresh water and stoking the fire. "His Majesty demands you come immediately to the Great Room for an urgent matter."

I turned and saw a guard standing behind her shoulder. No wonder the poor thing was so on edge. What did it mean that someone had to chaperone me? My gut told me nothing good. Still, I kept my voice steady as I spoke.

"If His Majesty demands it, then I am ready. My robe, please."

The maid helped me into my dressing gown and quickly pinned the front pieces of my hair back. I would have felt so much better if Delia Grace had been the one doing it. She would have talked because, within seconds, she would have had a plan. I wiped water across my face so I looked a little more awake and took a deep breath.

"Please lead the way," I instructed the guard, as if I somehow couldn't find my own way to the Great Room. The hallways echoed so when they were empty. Usually, it sounded like a special kind of music to me. But being escorted in my nightclothes for an unknown reason completely knocked the notion from my head.

When I arrived, I saw Jameson was sitting on his throne, holding a letter in his hand and looking cross. My parents were there as well, escorted by their own guard, and glaring at me as if I'd summoned them at this early hour. Their presence was not unexpected, but that of the entire Eastoffe family was. Everyone in the room was in various stages of getting dressed, even Jameson himself. Though I had to admit he looked rather dashing with his hair rumpled and his shirt untied.

I curtsied before him, judging by his expression that this might not be the best time to mention that. "Your Majesty. How might I serve you?"

"In due time, Hollis. First, I have some questions." Both his expression and tone were calm, calculating. He looked across the faces in the room, as if deciding who to start with first. "You," he finally said, pointing to the Eastoffes.

"Your Majesty," Lord Eastoffe began, falling on one knee.

"Have you been in contact with your former king?"

He shook his head fervently. "No, Your Majesty, not at all."

Jameson pursed his lips a little, tilting his head. "I find that hard to believe after receiving this," he said, holding up the letter. "The kings of Coroa and Isolte meet annually, as you know. I suspect you've been in dear old King Quinten's entourage these many years past."

Lord Eastoffe nodded.

"This is my second time meeting with him as a sovereign in my own right, but isn't it interesting that he suddenly has decided to bring his queen with him?" Jameson raised his eyebrows. "Can you think of any reason he might do that?"

"Who could guess at his motives, Your Majesty? As you know, he's very impulsive, and recently, he's become less and less predictable." Lord Eastoffe was clearly sweating. "I find it as surprising as you do, as he rarely lets the queen accompany him abroad."

"I think he has heard my heart has finally settled," Jameson announced. "I think he knows I intend to give Coroa a queen, and he is bringing that wench to compare her to the fairest lady in our kingdom."

He wasn't shouting the words, but he was very close, so it was hard to know if it was intended to be a compliment or not. After all that fretting in my room, I couldn't see why I'd gotten so bothered for something that seemed so common. Didn't kings often travel with their wives? What did it matter if we were seated side by side?

Then I pushed down the only reason that crossed my mind as to why this could be a bad thing: that when placed next to a proper queen, I would look foolish, and all the lords we'd been swaying to support me would be lost.

I ducked my head as he went on.

"I'm just very curious how he only learned of her importance the week after you arrived." He leaned back on his throne. "I've known that man my whole life. He will come and disparage the Lady Hollis in any way he can, and I ought to know, as he's attempted to do the same to me."

"Your Majesty, regardless of what he thinks—"

"Silence!"

Lord Eastoffe lowered his head even deeper into a bow, wiping at the sweat across his brow. Behind him, his wife reached for her daughter's hand, clutching it tight.

Jameson stood and stalked across the raised platform like an animal in a cage, looking for the weak link in the bars to break through.

"You will be front and center for all events, and, as new *Coroan* citizens . . . on your absolute best behavior. Should Quinten come across anything about you to draw complaint, you'll find yourselves a head length shorter."

"Yes, Your Majesty," the Eastoffes chorused back at him breathlessly. Even I was having a hard time finding my lungs.

"I believe there are three or four other high-ranking Isolten families in the castle. You will pass on this instruction to them. If you want to stay here, I expect perfect allegiance."

"Yes, Your Majesty."

"Lady Eastoffe, you must train Lady Hollis in Isolten manners. I want her to make that girl Quinten put on the throne look like a joke."

"Yes, Your Majesty." This woman, who I'd only seen that one time in passing, offered me a small but reassuring smile. Something about her expression said that she wouldn't let me fail.

"Lord and Lady Brite," Jameson said to my parents. "I am charging you with making sure Hollis knows enough of what's happening with Mooreland and Great Perine to be able to speak should she be approached."

My father heaved out a ragged sigh, twisting that silver ring again. It was a very special ring, one of hundreds passed down from men who'd served directly under King Estus in battle. One would think it'd be handled with care. All he ever used it for was worrying. "That is a lot to cover, Your Majesty."

"And any shortcomings on that will be accounted to you, sir. I am well aware of how capable Lady Hollis is, and I will *not* be made a fool of," Jameson thundered.

"Yes, Your Majesty." Father bowed deeply.

"Anyone else have something to say?" Jameson asked, his dark eyes searching us. I hesitantly raised my hand, and he nodded toward me.

"As the Eastoffes are artisans, mightn't it be nice to have something made to mark the occasion? Twin items of some kind for you and King Quinten, something to mark you as peers, especially if he is intimidated by your youth and strength, which very well may be the cause for him parading his wife. Perhaps it would pacify him to offer up a gesture of . . . peace." I quickly peeked over at Silas, his long hair still a mess from sleep. Like his mother's, his eyes were reassuring, and I sighed, hoping this idea would be good for both of us.

Jameson smiled, though it was colder than usual. "See, Lord Brite? Your daughter's mind is faster than yours, even on your best day." He turned to the Eastoffes. "Do as she says. And make it quick. They will be here on Friday."

My stomach plummeted to the floor. Friday? That was . . . that was *tomorrow*. Jameson *had* told me they'd be coming at the end of the week. . . . How had I completely lost track of the time? And worse, how was I supposed to prepare everything in a day?

He stood, ending the meeting, and everyone dispersed.

I pressed my hand against my stomach, watching Jameson's angry back as he stormed away. I didn't know what I was going to do. Besides the fact that they had been longtime enemies of Coroa, I didn't know much about Isoltens. Lessons in their manners? Understanding continental politics? I doubted even Delia Grace could manage all that in such a short time.

"When shall I come to you, my lady?" Lady Eastoffe asked quietly, dropping into a deep curtsy, a gesture I was still adjusting to.

"I'm sure you haven't had a chance to eat yet. Do that first, and then come as soon as you are able."

She nodded and left with her family, the littlest one sniffling. Lord Eastoffe got on his knee again to speak to him. "You have nothing to fear, Saul," he promised. "This is a different king, a kinder king. See how he asks us to help? All will be well."

Behind this little one, Silas and Sullivan were there to ruffle his hair and offer comfort. Silas looked up from his brother and offered me another smile similar to his mother's, though, admittedly, her eyes didn't sparkle like his. In truth, I'd never seen anyone's eyes sparkle like his.

"You'd better be up to this," Father warned me in passing, making me aware that I'd been staring. "You will not humiliate us in front of the lords again."

I sighed. I'd gone from being the lady Jameson was going to dance with at dinners to his official companion for a visit from a foreign king. From what I remembered of Jameson's mother, dozens of tasks fell on her for state visits. Was I expected to do everything a queen would? I shook my head. I couldn't handle this alone; I needed my ladies.

TEN

"No," I said as Nora pulled out another dress. "Too dark."

"She's right," Delia Grace agreed reluctantly. "Maybe we should have something altered. The Isoltens do wear different sleeves."

"I would knock over every single goblet on the table," I commented with a laugh, which she joined in with rather quickly.

"And look like a jester," she added.

I shook my head. "I just want to seem regal. I want to look like I *belong* beside Jameson."

"I think you need to stick with your signature gold," Delia Grace insisted. "And then, for the tournament, the rose dress will look nice in the sun."

Nora agreed. "Rose looks lovely against your skin. And Delia Grace and I can see what we own that will look best behind you. I promise we won't distract."

Delia Grace was visibly inhaling slowly through her nose, not looking pleased to have someone speak for her. "I think anything in a cream color will look nice. Or the obvious Coroan red. Whatever you'd like, my lady."

Some of the anger had passed. But not all of it.

Delia Grace went to answer the knock at the door, and I trailed behind her, knowing it would be Lady Eastoffe. She entered quickly, followed by her daughter, and they both sank into curtsies.

"My Lady Hollis, please allow me to introduce my daughter, Scarlet."

"Very nice to formally meet you both. Please come in."

She clasped her hands together as she walked. "Where would you like to start?"

I sighed. "I'm not entirely sure. I . . . I'm not the best pupil, but I just need to learn enough about Isolte to not look like an absolute fool."

Lady Eastoffe's face was equal parts sweet and serious as she weighed her words. "Every woman in your position has had a moment like this, when their era, so to speak, began. We will do everything we can to help you shine."

My shoulders slumped as she broke the tension I'd been carrying ever since I'd woken up this morning. "Thank you." I held my hand out, gesturing that they should settle in at my table.

Lady Eastoffe took the seat closest to me. "We have very little time, so we need to get to the important things first.

I need to tell you about King Quinten," she said, looking grave as I took my place. "He is a dangerous man. You may already know that the line of the Pardus family is almost as old as the Barclay family."

I nodded, though I was only sort of aware of that fact. Jameson was the seventh descendant from King Estus, and no one on the continent could boast a direct line as long as the Coroans'. That I knew.

"Like all countries, we have had good kings and bad ones, but there is something . . . dark about King Quinten. He has always been hungry for power, wielding it as carelessly as a child. But fear has made him worse with age, and now he's old and paranoid. His first wife, Queen Vera, miscarried several times and has been in the grave for six years now. Prince Hadrian is his only living child, and he is of a sickly disposition. King Quinten recently married a very young woman in hopes of producing more heirs—"

"Valentina?"

"Valentina," she confirmed. "But so far, it's been fruitless. All of his hopes now rest on Prince Hadrian—who I've heard some princess is reluctantly marrying next year. The poor boy looks as if he could die at any moment."

"Is he really so ill?" I asked. Lady Eastoffe made a face at her daughter, who answered for them.

"He's managed to live this long, so who can tell?" Scarlet hedged. "Perhaps he was just meant to be a pale shade of green."

I allowed that comment a little smile before flopping back

in my chair. "So your king is worried because his line may end with either himself or his son?"

"Yes," Lady Eastoffe replied.

"And there is no one to pick it up and maintain peace?"

She hesitated. "He tends to eliminate those who could usurp him."

"Oh . . . So . . . I don't think I understand. What good does that do him?"

"None as far as anyone with any sort of reason can see," Scarlet answered quickly. "But, as we said, fear has made him mad, and the best anyone can do is steer clear at this point."

Lady Eastoffe continued. "Of course you should obey your king. Shine, be the best you can be. But also stay away from King Quinten if you can."

I nodded. "What of Valentina?"

"I'm sorry to say that we don't know her well," Scarlet began, sharing a concerned glance with her mother. "Few people do. But she's young, like us, so if you can keep her entertained, that might get you on her good side."

I turned to Nora and Delia Grace. "Entertaining is generally my strong suit. But I'm not sure how to do that without knowing her interests."

Nora sighed. "Perhaps we can take her to the town, show her some of the shops?"

"Good. Yes. And we will think of more," I promised Lady Eastoffe.

"And I will continue to think," Scarlet added. "If I

remember anything, I'll make sure to tell you. And since plenty of courtiers will come with the king, we can ask some of them when they arrive if they have any ideas."

I sighed in relief. "Thank you. I've been told my whole life that Isoltens were more like stones than people. It seems I was misinformed."

Lady Eastoffe smiled conspiratorially. "Maybe wait until you meet the king before you change your mind completely."

I laughed easily, and she and Scarlet joined in. I was grateful that if I had questions over the visit, I had someone I could go to.

"I admire you," Lady Eastoffe admitted. "So young and so brave."

I made a face. "Brave?"

"It's no small thing to become queen. Even Valentina I admire for it, regardless of how I might feel about her otherwise."

I swallowed. "I'd be lying if I said I wasn't nervous."

"Which is natural. But you are already doing the best thing any of us could: you're encouraging your king to favor peace." She shook her head. "No one could do more."

I nodded, looking down at my hands. Her words were generous, but that didn't stop me from worrying that I would be the weak link in the chain, causing chaos to break out at any moment.

"King Jameson seems quite taken by you," Scarlet offered. "How *did* you manage to catch his eye?"

I saw Delia Grace place a hand on her hip, her smirk saying everything.

"It was mostly chance," I replied. "The king had been flirting with a few girls at court, though it was clear to most everyone that they weren't serious. His father had been in the grave about a year and a half at that point. His mother passed maybe three months after King Marcellus."

"Yes," Lady Eastoffe said. "My husband and I came to both funerals."

I noted that curiously. They must have been a very high-ranking family to accompany King Quinten on so many international trips.

"Delia Grace and I, we were dancing together one night in the Great Room. We were holding one another by the wrists, spinning and spinning like tops, when we lost our grip and fell backward. Delia Grace fell into the arms of some other ladies, and I fell into Jameson's."

I had to laugh for a moment. It was a bit ridiculous that this was how I'd won Jameson's heart.

Lady Eastoffe sighed, and Scarlet rested her head on her chin, taken in by the tale.

"I was so overcome with the hilarity of the moment, I was laughing, blissfully unaware of who was holding me. By the time I stood up to thank him, he was laughing, too. Everyone said it was the first time they'd heard him laugh since his parents died, and I've been living to make him smile ever since. I think everyone thought he'd move on eventually—"

"Not everyone," Delia Grace reminded me.

"Almost everyone," Nora chimed in with a wink.

I smirked at that before turning to Delia Grace. "Well, you've always had more confidence in me than I ever have. But it really was all chance. Had it been another quarter turn, we'd have both landed on our bottoms. Another half turn, and I'd have been on the floor, and Delia Grace would be hosting you today while I faithfully served her."

Nora nodded, then spoke again. "Well, if she'd have us."

She had a fair point, and it made me laugh yet again. Even Delia Grace had an amused little grin on her face. "I *suppose* I'd be lucky to have you both," she teased.

"It's good you have a close group of friends," Lady Eastoffe said. "It's wise to know exactly who you can trust. Why, even Queen Valentina only keeps one lady."

"Really? I might have to ask her about that. I'd prefer to keep my household small. I mean, when the time comes."

Lady Eastoffe grimaced. "You might have to wait awhile to speak to her at all."

"Why?"

"Protocol. Only the head of house speaks first. As you are not married, your parents should introduce you, but the king may bypass them and do it himself. Either is fine. But typically the higher-ranked person speaks first, and if that doesn't happen . . ." There was a long pause. Was I not going to speak to this woman at all? "If you have any doubts, treat Quinten and Valentina like they're superior in every situation. Even if they're not, they'll appreciate the flattery and be more likely to respond kindly."

"Right. What about meals? I've been sitting on the king's right, but I'm assuming that will go to King Quinten now. Should I try to—"

Without knocking, my parents barged in, my father holding several books and scrolls in his hands.

"You can go," my mother said briskly to Lady Eastoffe.

"Mother, Father. Lady Eastoffe is my guest. Please show her—"

"The king gave me a job," my father interrupted. "Are you suggesting I ignore it?"

Lady Eastoffe smiled and rose from her seat. "Call on me anytime, Lady Hollis. If we think of anything else concerning the queen, we'll send word. A pleasure, Lord Brite. Lady Brite."

My father shoved my flowers aside, rolling out a map. "Sit. We have a lot to discuss. Great Perine is on the edge of civil war, and I don't even know where to begin with Mooreland."

I sighed, looking at the mud-colored maps. It wouldn't have mattered who was teaching me; about twenty minutes in, and my mind was already full to the brim. Between protocol and current affairs, there wasn't space for anything else. And what was worse was that I was nowhere close to knowing everything I needed to for tomorrow.

ELEVEN

AFTER MY PARENTS LEFT, NORA and Delia Grace spent the rest of the day testing me on what I'd learned thus far. For every answer I got right, I got to take a bite of pie, so, naturally, I was starving by dinnertime.

As we walked to the Great Room, Nora whispered over my shoulder. "Try not to look so glum. This is a great honor."

"I can't help it. I'm never going to be able to get all this right, not this fast."

Delia Grace leaned in. "She's right. Smile. None of this matters as much as you keeping Jameson happy."

I sighed, pulling myself up taller as we entered to bows and polite smiles. Jameson was, as always, delighted to see me. I thought of his words when he'd taken me back to the jewel room. He'd said himself that all he wanted me to be was exactly who I was. How was I supposed to balance that with the things everyone else expected me to be? Surely if I failed him in front of a not-quite-enemy, his affections would fade.

Part of me wondered if that wasn't such a bad thing.

I shook my head, trying to get myself together. Only an idiot would pass up a king.

"My own heart," Jameson greeted me, kissing my cheek in front of the entire court. "How has your day gone?"

"I'm just going to hope that King Quinten's hearing is starting to fade so he won't know how little I've remembered from my lessons."

Jameson laughed at that, and I wished I could laugh myself.

"Oh, I suppose you're right to have a healthy fear of Quinten. Growing up, I did myself. Had to get over it when I took the crown," he said casually, reaching for his cup.

"What did you, of all people, have to fear? You're the king."

He made a face. "Well, I wasn't when we met. He's looked like a villain from an old tale since the first time I laid eyes on him. As I got to see him in action, I've realized that *villain* might be too kind a word."

"Gracious." I had quite suddenly lost my appetite. "What has he done that made you think that?"

Jameson didn't say anything straightaway, looking as if he had a hard time choosing his words. "It's not any one thing. It's everything. He acts as if the world has caused him some great offense, and he spends his waking hours trying to get his revenge."

"On what? On who?"

Jameson lifted his cup to me as if I'd made a great point. "No one can ever be sure, my darling Hollis. My father spent his days prepared to make war with Quinten, and if it hadn't been for my mother, they'd have battled more often than they already did. But if I must go to war, I want there to be clear gain behind it; none of these silly squabbles. I'm sure a time will come when I go after Quinten for a very good reason, but until then, I will strive for peace."

I smiled at him in complete adoration. "You are a wonderful king. From the bottom of my heart, I mean that."

He reached for my hand, taking it in both of his and kissing it with fervor. "I know you do," he whispered. "And I have no doubt that you will make for a remarkable queen."

The word still sent my heart racing. It was going to be an unimaginable thing, the day I was given a crown.

"That reminds me," he said, "I have a surprise for you."

I looked at Jameson pointedly. "I swear, if you've invited some king or another to join tomorrow's festivities and I have to learn a whole other set of protocol tonight, I will go back and jump in the river. I'll stay there this time, I mean it!"

He laughed and laughed, and I couldn't tell if he enjoyed seeing me under pressure or if I was just very good at fooling him. "No, it's nothing like that. Just something to help you. But," he said, looking back to Nora and Delia Grace, "I think I will need some assistance."

Then he held up his napkin.

TWELVE

"Don't you dare peek," Jameson insisted, holding the cloth tightly around my eyes.

I giggled. "So long as you promise not to let me fall!"

"Don't worry," Delia Grace whispered, holding my hand. "I'll keep a lookout for you. As always."

I gripped her hand a little tighter as we made our way up a curving set of stairs, thankful that, despite our recent ups and downs, I could still count on her.

"Your Majesty, where in the world are you taking me?"

"Just a few more steps," he sang into my ear, his breath tickling my neck. "Nora, could you please get the door?"

I heard her sigh—a hushed sound of awe—and felt Delia Grace pause, gripping my hand. I reached my hand higher up Jameson's coat, taking in a handful of velvet as I held on tightly, hoping not to fall.

"All right, Hollis. Step this way." Delia Grace reached around, positioning me, taking a while before she was content.

With a swift flick of his hand, Jameson sent the fabric flying. The first thing I saw was him. I had turned to see his expression, hoping to find him glowing with contentment. And he absolutely was.

Oh, those sparkling honey-brown eyes that made the stars jealous. Even at the end of a horrible day, just being able to look up at that smile and know I put it there was enough to make it all better.

The second thing I saw was exactly where I was standing. I took in the Queen's Chambers and my heart very nearly stopped beating. "The last four queens of Coroa have slept in these rooms. Seeing as you will be receiving Queen Valentina and her company tomorrow, it's only proper they belong to you."

"Your Majesty," I whispered. "No."

"Maybe if you can look at the river you won't feel the need to go jump in it again," he commented casually, ushering me over to the window. The moon was low in the sky, fat and full. It was shimmering off the river in the distance and casting light upon the city. I remembered the view Delia Grace and I'd had of the Colvard River one night in empty apartments a floor or two higher than this. We snuck up with a bottle of mead and very thick shawls, talking and waiting for the sun to rise. When it did, the river reflected it back, and it was as if the entire city was covered in gold.

I remembered thinking there was no possible way another room in the castle could match it. I was wrong.

"I've had new linens put in, of course," Jameson said, walking me in. "And these rugs on the walls are new, too. I thought they might help with the draft."

My heart was skipping beats left and right, trying desperately to keep up. I leaned into him. "Your Majesty . . . I am not queen."

He smiled again, so pleased with himself. "But you will be." He kissed my hand. "I am simply bestowing upon you what is rightfully yours . . . a few months ahead of schedule."

I could hardly catch my breath. "You are far too good to me, Your Majesty."

"This is nothing," he whispered. "When you are queen, you shall be drowning in jewels and gifts and praise until death. And I suspect for many years after," he added with a wink. "Look around the room. Settle in. My men will be moving all your things in the morning before Quinten arrives."

I was still quite stunned. I was to live in the queen's apartments. They were mine.

"It seems silly to tell the sun good night, but I do it anyway. Good night, Lady Hollis. I'll see you in the morning."

The second the doors closed, Nora and Delia Grace shared their first moment of true camaraderie. They clasped each other's hands, jumping and squealing as if the apartments had been gifted to them.

"Can you believe this?" Delia Grace exclaimed. She

grabbed my hands and pulled me back from the entry space, where the queen received her guests, to the bedroom proper. To the right of the large four-poster bed was the sweeping window that looked down upon the city and the river, and to the left along the wall was a passage to an antechamber. I knew from my few visits to the queen's rooms that her ladies slept in that space. But along the wall behind the bed, there was another door, one I'd never been through.

Nora and Delia Grace followed in hushed awe as I pushed the heavy door open. The apartment went on and on. There were desks for writing and rooms for private meetings and, in another antechamber, a collection of armoires for my clothes.

I felt faint, like the floors were set upon the river itself, lilting with the tides.

"Delia Grace, will you walk me back to the bed?" I asked, holding out an arm. She came and grabbed it quickly, concern painting her face.

"Hollis?"

"Here." Nora pulled back the drapes on the bed and I settled down, slowing my breathing.

"Aren't you happy?" Delia Grace asked. "You're getting what every girl in the kingdom wants!"

"Of course. It's just . . ." I had to stop to slow my breathing. "It's so much at once. I'm to entertain a queen, take all of these lessons, and move to new rooms? In a day?" I lamented. "They'll be here *tomorrow*!"

"We're here to help you," Nora offered.

I shook my head, starting to cry. "I don't think I want this."

"You need sleep," Delia Grace said before turning to Nora. "Get her shoes."

"I don't even have a nightgown," I sniveled.

"I'll go and fetch one. Just stay calm." Nora was gone in a flash, and I was left with Delia Grace, who had moved on to the task of taking off my shoes.

There was no water in the pitcher, no fire in the hearth. Linens had been brought and candles had been lit so the room would be suitable for presentation, but the apartments weren't quite ready to be lived in.

"Let's go back to my room tonight," I murmured. "We can do this in the morning."

"No!" she insisted, pushing me back onto the bed. "The king will see it as a slight. You've been given the second-best lodgings in the entire palace, and you want to leave them for a handful of personal items? Have you lost your senses completely?"

I knew she was right, but it felt like I'd gone from spinning out of Delia Grace's hands to the right hand of the throne overnight, and I did not know how to handle it.

I lay on my side as Delia Grace made short work of loosening my dress. Within a few minutes, Nora was back with a nightgown, robe, and slippers. She also had my brush and a small vase.

"I thought you'd appreciate seeing something of yours in here," she said. "Shall I put it on the vanity?"

I gave a small nod, managing to get out a smile as she set it in place. Delia Grace sat me up as Nora pulled back the curtain to see into the antechamber. "Space for four or five, I think, should you want to go ahead and choose your ladies."

"*If* it goes beyond the two of you, you can choose. But not today."

"Nora, see if you can find some maids," Delia Grace commanded. "I'm going to get her in bed and get the trimmings—firewood, flowers."

"Should we go back to her room and move some more of her belongings?"

"The king said he'd do it in the morning. It can keep until then."

They planned around me, like I wasn't even there, like this wasn't all happening for and because of me. And because I couldn't bear to think of anything more for the day, I let them. The drapes were closed around my bed, making for a cozy and quiet space, but it didn't entirely block out the sound of them moving around the apartments or the maids building a fire.

I didn't go to sleep. But I heard when Delia Grace and Nora finally did. And that was when I found my shoes and quietly slipped out of the room.

THIRTEEN

By this point in the night, I knew the moon would be shining through the stained-glass windows of the Great Room. I passed corners where couples whispered and giggled, and I was bowed to by guards and servants working at even this late hour.

In the Great Room, the fire from the wide hearth was down to glowing embers, and a lone servant was stoking it, getting the last bits of heat where he could. I stood in the middle of the archway, looking at the explosion of color on the floor. Nothing, of course, could match the way the colors danced in the roaring light of day, but there was something other, something almost sacred about the way they fell by moonlight. Still the same designs, the same patterns, and yet quieter, more deliberate.

"Is that you, Lady Hollis?"

I turned. The person I'd thought was a servant at the fire was actually Silas Eastoffe.

Of course he was here. In the moment when I was wondering if it would be worth abandoning my king, I ran into someone who'd done something similar to his. And who could say which of us was a better criminal?

He might be the worst person I could have come upon. Not just because he too had been tempted to the life of a traitor—tempted and succumbed—but because there was something about those blue eyes that made me think . . . I couldn't even say what they made me think.

I tried to look dignified, as if my night robe was the same as a gown in my eyes. It was difficult under the weight of his stare. "Yes. What are you doing up at such an hour?"

He smiled. "I could ask the same of you."

I stood taller. "I asked first."

"You really are going to be queen, aren't you?" he said in a teasing tone. "If you must know, *someone* thought it would be a good idea to make two matching pieces of metalwork for two great kings in a single day . . . Sullivan and I only stopped working about twenty minutes ago."

I bit my lip, my attempts at being aloof vanishing before my guilt. "I'm so sorry. When I said that, the date of the visit had completely slipped my mind. It's taken me by surprise as well."

"Has it? My mother said you were quite a willing student

today." He crossed his arms and leaned sideways against the wall, as if this were an everyday meeting, as if he knew me so well.

"Willing, yes, but good? That remains to be seen." I pulled my robe a little tighter. "I've never been the brightest of the girls at court. If I ever forget that fact, Delia Grace reminds me. Or my parents. But your mother and Scarlet were quite patient with me today. I may need them to come by again tomorrow. I mean, today, I suppose."

"I can tell them if you like."

"You'll also have to tell them I've moved."

"Moved? In a day?"

"In an hour." I brushed my hair back and swallowed, trying not to sound as irritated as I felt. "King Jameson moved me into the queen's apartments tonight. I don't think my parents even know about it yet. I have no idea how the privy council is going to take it once the news becomes public." I rubbed at my forehead, trying to smooth the wrinkles of worry away. "He wanted me to look the part before King Quinten arrives. I have jewels coming. He mentioned some new dresses. And suddenly, I have new rooms. . . . It's all a bit much," I confessed.

"Isn't this what you want, though? You will be the best kept woman in the kingdom."

I sighed. "I know. So I'm not sure what . . ." I paused. I was telling this boy far too much. He was a stranger and a foreigner. Who was he to ask about my life? But in that same moment, I realized I'd rather talk to him about my troubles than anyone else, even the people who were truly meant to know everything about me. "I suppose it's not the gifts I'm receiving, but the pace at which they're coming. You're quite right, I have everything I could ask for and more."

His smile didn't seem as genuine as it had before. "Good."

I could sense an ending coming that I wasn't prepared for, so I quickly changed the subject. "How are you settling in? Are you enjoying Coroa so far?"

He smiled. "I knew the food would be different, and the air would smell different, and that the laws are different. It's just, in the past, when I've visited, I've always known I was going home. I don't mean to seem ungrateful. I'm thankful His Majesty let us stay for more reasons than I can even list. But there are times I'm sad, knowing I won't ever see Isolte again."

I bent my head down and softened my tone, coaxing him to be more positive. "Surely you'll go back to visit. You have family there still, yes?"

He gave me a very thin smile. "I do. And I'll miss them. But when we see King Quinten tomorrow, I hope, with all of my heart, it will be the last time I ever lay eyes on that man."

Something about his words sent a chill through me, and I realized they were strangely similar to what Jameson had said.

"If he's so awful, then I shall wish for that myself. And for your family's happiness for as long as you live in Coroa."

"Thank you, my lady. You are the gem everyone says you are."

I wanted to tell him that, to my knowledge, no one but Jameson thought I was a gem. But it was such a kind thing to say, I didn't want to spoil it.

He tucked a loose strand of hair behind his ear. The rest of it was tied back with a cord, and I realized that must have been the piece that Jameson cut, and now Silas was left with a section of hair that would not obey. I also realized now that when the sword was brought near Silas's face, he did not flinch.

"I guess I'll be on my way, then," he said. "Don't want to keep you."

"What were you doing here, by the way?" I threw out quickly. I wasn't ready for him to leave, not just yet. "It's quite a distance from your corner of the castle."

He pointed up. "Like I said, we're great thinkers in Isolte, but not great creators. The art here, the architecture . . . there's something about it. I'd describe it if I could, but I don't have the words." He looked back to the windows. "I like watching the light in the glass. It's . . . calming."

"It is, isn't it? All the light cast down looks broken, but if you look up, you can see there was a plan all along."

He nodded. "And you say you're no student. I admire how you think, Lady Hollis." He bowed. "I'll tell my mother to come see you after breakfast. We'll probably need Scarlet to stay and help us finish the pieces."

"I really am sorry."

He shrugged, his expression easy again. "It was a good idea. Especially given the kings' tumultuous past. But could you give me some more notice next time you have a stroke of brilliance? A boy can only do so much."

I giggled. Without thinking, I reached out to reassure him, taking his hand. "I promise."

Caught off guard, he looked down, staring at our hands. But he didn't rush to pull his away. And neither did I.

"Thank you, my lady," he whispered, nodding quickly before vanishing into the corridors of the castle. I watched until he became another shadow of Keresken, blending into the night. And then I looked down at my hand, stretching out my fingers as if I could remove the warm feeling in them.

Shaking my head, I brushed the sensation away. Whatever had just happened, it was the least of my concerns right now. I turned back, looking at the explosion of color on the floor.

If I wanted to, I could walk across the room and knock on the door to Jameson's apartments. I could tell a guard I needed to speak with the king, urgently. I could tell him how I needed more time, how, as someone not born to the position, I was struggling to keep up.

But.

I looked across the Great Room, considering. I cared for Jameson. I really did. That alone made me want to try harder, to look like I could handle it all, even if I wasn't quite there yet.

The love of a king could drive one to attempt anything. And there was nothing as intoxicating as being adored by him, and by the people who adored me for his sake. Tomorrow,

I would have the privilege of telling my parents about my new rooms. I would get to see the lords as they conceded to Jameson's desires, knowing that I had been raised not only above every girl in the kingdom, but also above every available princess on the continent. I would, very soon, be queen.

I gazed up at the window one last time, then walked back to my new rooms. It was a bit of a thrill, walking up the stairs to a room that wasn't just made for royalty, but was also a space independent from my parents. That alone was something to be grateful for. And all those things combined made me ready for anything.

FOURTEEN

THE FOLLOWING MORNING WAS A bustle of activity as all of my worldly goods were brought up to my new rooms. Amid the chaos, a page arrived carrying a box. He was flanked by two guards who watched as he carefully placed the box on a table. Nora and Delia Grace exchanged a confused look as I gave the page a nod saying he could open it. I thoroughly enjoyed the collective gasp from the girls as they took in the blinding sparkle of the rose-colored necklace.

"My goodness, Hollis!" Delia Grace said, coming to peer over the edge of the box but not daring to touch it.

"This was what was happening that day in the king's chambers. He was letting me choose something for today."

"You did a spectacular job," Nora commented.

"I know that necklace," Delia Grace said, awestruck.

"That was made for Queen Albrade herself, Hollis. That was made for a warrior."

I smiled, thinking I could use something made for going into war. I was reaching over to pick up the necklace when another page carrying a box walked in. "Forgive me, Lady Hollis," he said. "His Majesty thought this would go well with your necklace."

He didn't wait for instructions to open his package, presumably acting on the king's orders to shock me. I reached over, clutching Delia Grace's hand when I took in the headpiece that Jameson had picked out. It was breathtaking, tipped with the same gemstones as the necklace, fanning out like the sun bursting over the horizon.

Like the sun. He'd chosen this with care.

"Help me, ladies. It won't do if we're late." I sat down at my vanity as Delia Grace took the headpiece and Nora carried the necklace.

"You will be exhausted by noon! It's so heavy." Nora set the clasp, and once the weight of it was fully on me, I thought she might be right. But, tired or not, I wouldn't take this thing off my neck until sunset.

"Here," Delia Grace said, setting the headpiece in my hair and securing it with a few extra pins.

I sat at the vanity, looking at myself. I'd never felt so beautiful. I wasn't sure if I looked like myself, but I couldn't deny that I looked like royalty.

I swallowed. "I'm counting on you to rescue me if you catch me about to do anything foolish. I have to be poised and beautiful so King Quinten doesn't have anything to critique."

Nora brought her face next to mine, meeting my gaze in the mirror. "I promise."

"Obviously," Delia Grace added.

I nodded. "Then let's go."

I kept my hands gracefully clasped in front of me as we took the short walk from the queen's apartments to the Great Room. I could feel myself growing more and more confident with every gasp and bowed head we passed. I could see in their eyes that my goal had been met: with my best gold dress, and the headpiece Jameson had chosen, I looked like a radiant queen.

Toward the head of the room, the Eastoffes waited, front and center as Jameson had requested. Lady Eastoffe gave me a warm smile, mouthing the word *beautiful* and touching her hand to her heart. Beside her, Silas stumbled as he went to bow, trying to keep his eyes on both the floor and me. I suppressed a smile, then worked to give myself a steadier expression as I continued up to Jameson.

His mouth hung slightly open and it took him a moment to remember to extend his hand to receive me.

"Goodness, Hollis. I forgot how to breathe." He shook his head, staring at me as I blushed. "For all of my life, I shall never forget you in this moment: a rising queen and a rising sun."

"Thank you, Your Majesty. But you must take some of the credit. This is beautiful," I said, touching the headpiece. "I love it."

He shook his head. "I'm glad you enjoy the jewels, but I assure you, there isn't another woman in this room who could have done them justice."

We were still staring into one another's eyes when the fanfares sounded in the distance, announcing King Quinten was near. Jameson signaled for the musicians to be ready, and I moved my gaze to Delia Grace, who motioned for me to straighten my necklace, centering the largest jewel.

By the time King Quinten and his party arrived, we were prepared, looking like a painting as he walked down the red woven carpet laid up the center of the great hall. I'd last seen him when he came for Queen Ramira's funeral, and I desperately wished I'd taken note of him then. All I remembered was that my black dress was scratching my arm, and I spent the majority of the service trying to fix the sleeve. But that didn't matter, as I felt I knew him now; he was everything Lady Eastoffe had told me.

His hair was thinning and though there were hints of yellow to it, most of it was gray. He walked with the assistance of a cane, his shoulders slightly hunched, and I wondered if part of the difficulty was the weight of so much fabric. But it was his expression that chilled me: as I looked into his eyes, I felt my heart go cold. There was something about him, as if he had both everything and nothing to lose, and the power accompanying those notions made him fearsome to behold.

I looked away as quickly as I could, training my eyes on Queen Valentina. She truly wasn't much older than me, and that made the gap between her and King Quinten very great indeed. She smiled without showing teeth and kept her right hand settled protectively on her stomach.

On the king's other side, Prince Hadrian was unmistakable. Yes, most Isoltens looked like they needed to see the sun, but he was closer to a ghost. I, too, wondered if he might be one soon. He kept his lips pressed tight as if to hide the effort all this movement was taking, but the line of sweat across his brow was obvious. That man ought to be in bed.

With these three before me, I realized I should have no fear. Coroa may have been a much smaller country than Isolte, but our king was far greater.

"King Quinten," Jameson said loudly, opening his arms. "I am so pleased you and your family have made your way to Coroa in safety. The Lady Hollis and I welcome you as my father did, as a fellow sovereign, placed by the gods, and as a dear friend."

Several quiet things happened at once. King Quinten rolled his eyes at the mention of the gods, Prince Hadrian lifted a shaky hand to wipe sweat from his upper lip, and I sighed in relief because we'd all been introduced.

Jameson descended from the dais, which had been outfitted with enough seats for our guests, and went to greet King Quinten. He shook his fellow sovereign's hand with both of his own, causing the room to burst into rapturous applause. My eyes kept flickering back to Valentina. She stood so tall, but I couldn't tell what was keeping her upright. Not happiness, it seemed, nor pride. . . . She was unreadable.

Jameson invited King Quinten, Valentina, and Hadrian to come and sit with us, and those in Quinten's party began to mingle with those of Jameson's court. The visit had officially begun.

I turned to Valentina, who'd been placed next to me, hoping to make her feel comfortable.

"Your Majesty, Isolte is such a large country. Whereabout were you born?" I asked.

Her returning look was smug. "You don't speak first. I speak first."

I was taken aback. "My apologies. I assumed that the king's introduction was sufficient."

"It was not."

"Oh." I paused. I was quite certain I had this right. "Well, what about now? As you've already spoken to me?"

She rolled her eyes. "I suppose. What is it you asked? Where I was from?"

"Yes," I replied, resurrecting the smile on my face.

She inspected the many rings on her hands. "If I told you, would you even recognize the name?"

"Well . . ."

"I doubt it. From what I hear, you've lived your whole life between your family's manor and Keresken Castle," she said, raising an eyebrow.

"Between the two, I've had all I could want in the world," I admitted. "Perhaps I could show you some of the architecture later? Some of the stonework on the—"

"No," she answered quickly, cutting me off and placing

her hand again on her stomach. "It is very important that I have my rest."

She lay back in her seat, looking bored, and I felt sure that I was failing Jameson. I sighed, looking away. I'd spent the better part of the last twenty-four hours worrying that I wouldn't be able to speak to Valentina at all, and now I'd be fine if I never heard her speak again.

I looked out among the guests, searching for my parents; they would know how to restart the conversation. Delia Grace might have an idea, too. . . . But I saw no one I recognized save for the Eastoffes.

I left my place to go ask for their help, catching them as they were warmly greeting another family.

"I didn't know you were coming," Lord Eastoffe was saying, gripping an older gentleman tightly. "I'm glad we get to tell you about how we're settling in face-to-face; a letter never quite catches everything."

The gentleman and his wife stood with a young man who was clearly their son, based on his nose and cheekbones. Though the couple was all smiles at being reunited with their friends, their son looked as if he'd rather be mucking out a stall.

"Scarlet," I whispered.

She turned. "Lady Hollis, you look radiant!" She smiled brightly, an almost sisterly warmth on her face.

"Thank you," I replied, feeling a little more at ease with her. "Listen, I need your help. Please tell me you've thought of something for me to say to the queen. She clearly has no interest in speaking with me."

Scarlet sighed. "She's like that with everyone—it's probably why she only has one lady. But I did remember this morning that I've heard she's interested in food. If there's a chance to show her a new dish, she'll probably enjoy that. Here." She grabbed my arm, pulling me forward. "Uncle Reid, Aunt Jovana? This is the Lady Hollis. She is to be queen." Scarlet beamed with pride, and I placed a hand on hers.

"It is a pleasure to meet you, my lady," Scarlet's aunt said. "News of your upcoming betrothal has reached Isolte. People have spoken frequently of your beauty, but they have not done you justice."

I felt my heart beat a little faster as I tried to take it all in. It was surreal to know that people in other countries had heard about me, knew my name.

"You are too kind," I answered, hoping to come across steadier than I felt.

"These are the Northcotts," Silas explained. "Our aunt and uncle, and this is our cousin Etan."

I looked at the young man, who was content to glower at me.

"Very nice to meet you," I said.

"Yes," he replied curtly.

Well, he was about as abrasive as Valentina. He only let a tiny smile come to his face when Saul came and wrapped his arms around him. Saul's head barely came up to his chest, and Etan scratched his hands playfully through his cousin's hair. After that moment, he was back to being as impassive as a suit of armor.

"We hear there is to be a joust," Lord Northcott said. "I hope I will see one of you out there." He pointed between Sullivan and Silas.

Sullivan merely ducked his head, and Silas spoke for them both. "We might be on the sidelines this time, but I'm very excited to watch. This is the first time we've been here for something this festive; I don't know if things are done differently in Coroa. I've never seen."

He looked to me for confirmation. "I doubt it," I said, my tone teasing. "Seeing as so much in Isolte is, well, let's say *imported* from Coroa, I'm sure it will all be quite familiar."

Most of them allowed that, chuckling at the observation. But not Etan.

"Isolte is just as sovereign as Coroa. Our traditions just as valuable, our people just as sacred."

"Absolutely. The privilege of knowing your cousins has taught me so much already about the world beyond Coroa," I said, smiling at Scarlet. "I hope to visit Isolte myself one day."

"I hope so, too," Etan spat, his tone sarcastic. "I'm sure you'll be greeted with fanfare at the border."

"Etan," his father snapped. There was a shuffling of feet and many ducked heads, but the comment went above me.

"I don't understand, sir."

Etan looked at me as if I were a child. "No. Of course you don't. Why would you?"

"Etan," his mother whispered urgently.

"How have I offended you?" I asked, genuinely confused how both he and Valentina were so quick to find fault with me.

He smirked. "You? *You* cannot offend anyone." He motioned to my headpiece, which was still making light dance every time I took a step. "You are an ornament."

I inhaled sharply, hating that I could feel my skin turning red.

"Excuse me?"

He motioned up to the dais where Queen Valentina was sitting beside my empty seat. "What do you see up there?"

"A queen," I replied firmly.

Etan shook his head. "That is an empty vessel, chosen to be something nice to look at."

"Etan, that's enough," Silas growled. But his cousin would not be deterred.

"If you don't know what's happening along your own border, what's happening to your own people, I can only conclude that you, my lady, are exactly the same: decoration for your king."

I swallowed, wishing I were as cold and clever as Delia Grace. She would have torn this boy to shreds. But part of me sensed that, on some level, he was right. If I was soon to be queen, I had to look at the line of women I was going to be added to.

I was no soldier. I was no cartographer. I wasn't book smart or exceedingly kind or remarkable in any way that anyone had ever taken note of.

I was pretty. And there was nothing wrong with that, but on its own, that had very little value. Even I knew that.

Still, I refused to be shamed for being the one thing I was capable of.

"Better an ornament from Coroa than a knave from Isolte," I hissed, pulling my head up high. "Welcome to Coroa, Lord and Lady Northcott. So glad you could come." With that, I turned on my heel and returned to my seat, which I hoped Etan noted was basically a throne. I drew the image of the sun rising over the river to mind, thinking of things that made me happy and calm.

I was not going to cry. Not here, not now. I wasn't going to give anyone in this room—particularly someone from Isolte—reason to think that I was not poised and patient and good enough to be at the right hand of a king.

FIFTEEN

"Please," I begged. "She's terrible."

Jameson chuckled as he walked around his private rooms, removing some of the heavier accessories he was wearing now that the opening of our visit had officially passed. "They're all terrible," he agreed.

"She thinks she's so *superior*. I cannot spend an evening with her." I crossed my arms, remembering her pinched face. "I'd rather eat in the stables."

He laughed outright at that, the sound matching the roars of the crowds still gathered on the other side of the door. "As would I! But don't you worry, my Hollis. This visit is a short one, and they'll be gone soon enough." He came close, wrapping his hands around my waist. "And we can get back to more important things."

I smiled. "You are the most important thing in my world.

So, if you insist I eat a meal with that wretched lady, I will."

He put a hand under my chin, tilting my face up to his. "I will spare you. This time," he added in a tone that was close to serious. "But unfortunately, I have to be at dinner tonight with Quinten to talk through a few deals and trades . . . things that would bore you. So go ahead. Spend the night with your ladies."

I took the hand that was beneath my chin and held it up so I could kiss it. "Thank you, Your Majesty."

There was a glittering look of satisfaction in his eyes, and it was difficult to concentrate under the weight of his stare.

"You'd best get back," he said. "Don't worry, I'll make an excuse for you tonight."

"Tell her I suffocated under a pile of Isolten dresses," I joked, and left with the sound of his laughter ringing in my ears.

Outside, Delia Grace and Nora waited anxiously. "Come, ladies, I'm not feeling well," I said in mock solemnity. "I think it's best I retire for now."

Delia Grace caught on right away, and she fell into step behind me as I walked cautiously through the crowd. In a corner, I finally caught sight of my parents. My mother was looking down her nose as people came up to her, presumably to congratulate her and Father on their great success. Wouldn't it be something to tell everyone I'd been chosen by the king by being the opposite of everything they'd tried to turn me into?

Even with all that had happened, they hardly spoke to

me, save to correct me or attempt to make a decision on my behalf. Their distance only made it that much easier to defy them.

I looked over my shoulder at Nora. "Why don't you gather a few other ladies to come by my room? It will be nice to have some more people in that space."

"Of course, my lady," she replied gleefully.

"I'll see if we can get ahold of a musician or two. Make an afternoon of it," I thought aloud. This plan was sounding better by the minute. I caught Nora before she moved too far. "And get ahold of Scarlet Eastoffe if you can. In fact, if the entirety of the Eastoffe family would like to escape the presence of their former king, tell them they are welcome in my apartments."

She nodded and broke off to build us a small party. At least this day could take a slight turn for the better; I'd been saved from an evening in the company of Valentina, and now I got to dance instead.

Nora opened the door for Yoana and Cecily as I helped Delia Grace put the last of the chairs against the wall.

The main space in the greeting area was now cleared for dancing and talking, and I'd called up one of the court musicians so we could have music. After the madness of moving and the tension of meeting Valentina, this was going to be a treat.

"Thank you for inviting us." Cecily came and greeted us with a little curtsy.

"Oh, you're quite welcome. You remember Delia Grace, of course," I said, gesturing over to her. Delia Grace stood with her head high, knowing that finally she was in a position no one could deny was exalted.

"Yes." Beside her, Yoana swallowed. "Very nice to see you."

"Delia Grace, dear, won't you show them to the refreshments?"

She nodded, not needing to speak to anyone she didn't want to at the moment, and I felt sure she was enjoying the knowledge that if anyone so much as breathed at her wrong, I'd eject them from the room.

Another knock came, and Nora opened it again.

"Scarlet!" I called. "So glad you could make it."

I was pleased to see her parents and Saul walk in behind her, but I was surprised to note that the Northcotts had joined her as well. And then, as if he was determined to be seen as an afterthought, Silas Eastoffe walked in the door. And there went my heart, skipping as if being trapped in my chest was just too far away for comfort.

I cleared my throat, turning to greet my guests.

Lord Eastoffe came over, bowing before me. "Thank you for letting us come along. It was more . . . unnerving than any of us thought it would be to see King Quinten again."

I tilted my head in sympathy. "You may all hide here as long as you like. The apartment extends for days, and we have plenty of food—we'll make a camp," I joked. "Please make yourselves comfortable."

Delia Grace was already moving to the music, and I joined her, doing a dance that we'd choreographed ourselves last year.

"That's very pretty," Nora commented as Delia Grace and I touched wrists and walked around one another.

"Thank you," Delia Grace answered. "We spent weeks on it."

"You should try your hand at choreographing the one for Crowning Day," Nora added.

Delia Grace seemed almost stunned by the kind suggestion. "If Lady Hollis wishes it. Thank you."

When the dance ended and a new song played, I watched as Nora started up a dance of her own. Honestly, if she and Delia Grace choreographed our dance, it would probably be one of the best I'd ever done.

More than once, I got distracted by a pair of blue eyes watching contentedly from a chair against the wall. I looked over at Silas, speaking as I swayed to the music.

"Do you dance, sir?"

He sat up a little straighter. "On occasion. But of everyone in the family, Etan is the best," he said, nodding to his cousin across the room. I searched and found him frowning as he studied the tapestries, hands behind his back, looking as if he were very much here against his will.

"You must be joking."

Silas chuckled. "Not at all."

"Well, please don't be offended if I don't extend him an invitation."

He made a face. "In his current mood, I don't think he'd accept if you did."

I sighed, believing that. "Would you?"

He swallowed and looked at the floor. "I would . . . though perhaps not today." When his face came back up to me, I noted the hint of a blush on his cheeks, and I couldn't blame him for not wanting to dance in front of such an intimate gathering.

"Lady Hollis, come and see," Cecily called, and I went quietly across the room, which thankfully gave me time to clamp down the growing smile on my face. What was it about Silas Eastoffe that turned the air in the room into something sweeter? He made everything feel . . . easy. Words came out clearer, thoughts became less foggy. I hadn't realized people could do that, could make everything sharper.

The room separated into relaxed conversations and fits of giggling, leaving me in a blissfully happy mood. And when I somehow ended up having little Saul as a dance partner, it seemed perfectly natural. I spun him around to much applause, and it was nice to see his tears from yesterday replaced with laughter. When the song ended, I bent down and kissed Saul on the cheek. "Thank you, sir. You're a fine dancer."

The violinist played on in the background as everyone spoke, and as we all sat and conversed, the new apartments felt like they could eventually be a comfortable place. There was a promise of it.

"The king must care for you very much," Silas said,

coming to stand next to me. "These rooms are amazing. They remind me of our rooms back at Chetwin Palace. But the Coroan architecture is so different. I think the stones alone change everything."

"How so?" I asked. It was the same stone I'd known all my life.

"In Isolte, the buildings are tinted slightly green or blue. It's a mineral in the stones by the northern coast, and they're very pretty, but in the winter especially, it makes thing seem dark. These stones of yours have such warm colors in them. So everything looks brighter, welcoming. And when you combine that with the impressive scope of the apartments, it's quite striking."

I nodded, many feelings playing through my heart. "It's easily the most beautiful place I've ever rested my head, but I'd be lying if I said I didn't I miss the simplicity of my old room, not to mention knowing what was going to happen most days."

I swallowed, once again wondering if I'd said too much but still feeling there was no one I'd rather share too much with.

He smiled softly. "There's a beauty in simplicity, isn't there?" He looked around the room again. "At one point in my life, I might have chosen the new clothes, the finer food, all the trappings of court. But I can say that, in losing them, I've learned that nothing in this world can replace loyalty, patience, and genuine affection."

I sighed. "I think I might be forced to agree with you.

The most valuable thing you can own is the assurance of your place in someone's heart. It is far better than any necklace, far better than any apartment."

We shared a quiet look.

"Would you exchange your crown of gold for one of flowers, then?" he asked with a smile.

"I think I just might."

"I think it would suit you," he commented, and I found myself holding eye contact with him for just a moment too long.

"I told your father you were welcome to hide here as long as you like. If you need anything at all, you know where my rooms are. Don't be afraid to ask."

He shook his head. "You've given us so much already. Look at how happy Scarlet is, and Saul. I couldn't ask for more."

He was right. Everyone was smiling . . . with one exception.

"Thank you, by the way. For attempting to defend me earlier."

Silas glanced up, finding his cousin as I had: alone and looking miserable. "If he knew you, he wouldn't say such things. I told him how good you'd been to us, how kind. I told him how highly my sister speaks of you, how even Sullivan smiles when he hears your name."

"Does he?" I gushed.

Silas nodded proudly. The compliment of Sullivan's quiet approval was not lost on me.

"My mother praises your bravery, my father says you're wise for your age, and I—"

He stopped quickly, and I looked up at him, dying to know the end of that sentence.

"And you?"

He stared down at me intently, and I could see the words trapped in his mouth. He looked at the ground, took a deep breath, and came back to me.

"And I am so pleased to have found a friend in Coroa. I genuinely thought it might be impossible."

"Oh." I glanced around the room, hoping no one could read the disappointment on my face. "Well, with how thoughtful your family is, it hardly seems impossible to me. And you shall always have my friendship."

"Thank you," he whispered.

"Silas?"

We both turned to his mother's voice.

"Please excuse me," he said, and I had the distinct sensation of being rescued.

"Absolutely. I need to make rounds anyway," I said as he moved away.

For reasons I couldn't say, I picked up a glass of ale and walked over to the scowling figure at the sweeping window.

"Is something wrong, Sir Etan?" I asked, offering him the cup. He took it without a word of thanks.

"I mean no offense. Your rooms are very pretty. I'm sure you were dying to show them off."

I shook my head. "That's not why I invited you."

"I expect your king wants us to go home with reports of how well he treats his future queen. But I don't have time for gossip. I'd just rather be home."

"Ah, look at that. Something we have in common." I turned and walked over to Delia Grace, refusing to let him ruin my mood.

"That man is awful. If he wasn't related to people who have been helping me so much, I'd kick him out right now."

"What's this?" Nora asked, hearing the end of my sentence.

"Nothing. Just the Eastoffes' cousin Etan being a bit of a snob."

"As if any Isolten has the room to be snobbish here," Delia Grace grumbled.

I looked over my shoulder, hoping no one was close enough to hear that.

"By the way," she continued, "I think I'm going to take Nora's advice and start choreographing our dance for Crowning Day. Just so we're prepared."

"Good idea. Everything feels so rushed lately."

"I want to keep it small, only four girls. So you need to pick one more, and we're all set."

"Good idea. Hmm." I mentally ran through the other girls at court. I didn't know many very well, and I wasn't too fond of the ones I did. Goodness, if I couldn't think of one I wanted to dance with, how was I supposed to fill out a household? I glanced around the room, trying to see if anyone would make a good addition, when my eyes alighted on the one person I knew would be perfect.

"Scarlet?" I asked, walking over to her as she chatted with her aunt.

"Yes, Lady Hollis?"

"Do you know about Crowning Day?" I squinted. "I dare say I don't know any of the holidays in Isolte."

"I've heard of it. Isn't it meant to celebrate the forming of the royal line?"

"Yes! We symbolically recrown the king and pledge our loyalty. It's probably my favorite holiday. Most people sleep all day, and the feast begins in the evening, and everyone celebrates through the night."

Lady Northcott's eyes widened. "This sounds like my kind of holiday. Perhaps we will move here, too."

I giggled at her enthusiasm. "Well, part of the celebration is dancing. Nearly every girl at court is in one dance or another, so of course we'll have one. Would you be willing to join Delia Grace, Nora, and myself? It will be a great opportunity to impress the king."

Her face lit up. "Oh, I'd love to! When do we start?"

"After King Quinten leaves, at least. I won't have any time to think about dancing until then."

"Of course. Let me know when you're practicing, and I'll be there."

Her aunt looked so pleased on her behalf, and in the corner, I saw Silas trying not to smile.

Sure, Valentina had been cold, and Etan had been rude. Twice. But when I saw Silas's glittering eyes looking back at me in appreciation, all I could think of was that it had been such a good day.

SIXTEEN

THE NEXT MORNING, I SAT up in bed, hopefully inhaling the morning air. If anything could cheer an anxious mood, it was the jugglers and musicians and games on the tournament field.

"I'm so excited for the tournament." Nora came and nudged me to move over on the bed. I obliged, and she pulled my hair over my back and started brushing.

"Me, too." I curled my legs up to my chest and wrapped my arms around them, almost feeling like I needed to hold the feeling in.

"Is Jameson riding today?"

I shook my head. "He's going to accompany King Quinten for the whole thing, and, seeing as the armor alone would knock Quinten to the ground," I said with a pointed look,

"I think he'll stay in the stands today. I'm not even sure if I'll bother wearing a token."

"Why not? You don't have to give it away."

"We'll see. Either way, I want to wear the red underskirt, but with my signature gold on top."

She nodded. "That will look nice. We should probably tuck your hair up so it doesn't get dirty. Come on." We moved over to the vanity so she could secure my hair back in a golden net, using a wide band of red satin to keep the front of my hair in place.

"No question who I'm pulling for today, is there?"

"Not with that much red." She smiled.

I squinted up at her. "Where's Delia Grace?"

"Something was wrong with her dress, and she had to go find thread."

I raised my eyebrows. "No wonder it's so calm in here."

Nora chuckled as I looked through my drawer, fishing out ribbons and handkerchiefs. "Remember to cheer loudly and be careful that your heart doesn't get stolen by a handsome knight," I warned her. Though I knew Jameson would be sitting beside me, I flipped a handkerchief over and over in my hand. I supposed Nora was right; I could have one and not give it away. I slid it up the sleeve of my dress as Delia Grace entered the room, already tense.

"Why is the blasted seamstress so far back in the castle? Doesn't anyone on this side of the palace ever need a needle and thread?" She huffed as she made sure our dresses were sitting properly and our hair was in place.

"I'll make it my first order of business to allot some rooms in these halls for the dressers," I promised. "I'm sure more people need that than we could guess."

She tucked a stray hair at my neck back into the net, nodding intently. "Sometimes, Hollis, I think we're the only ones who actually know what's going on here. There, you're good."

"Off we go, ladies," I said, handing a ribbon to Delia Grace before we moved outside. I kept my head high as I walked across the crowded grounds to where Jameson was settling into the king's box. King Quinten was sitting to his left with his precious queen beside him. I sighed. At least with her sitting on the other side of the box, the chances of us needing to interact were slim.

As I got closer, I saw a young man in armor approaching me.

"Why, Silas Eastoffe, is that you?" I asked, though the answer was plain enough by the sight of his parents and dreadful cousin flanking him.

He pulled off his helmet and gave me a quick bow. "Indeed, it is, my Lady Hollis. I'm trying my hand at the sword fight after all. And look," Silas continued, turning a full circle. It didn't take long for me to understand.

I met the eyes of his parents, who wore expressions somewhere between satisfied and wary. "You wear no red, you wear no blue."

In the distance, his aunt and uncle called out. Lord and

Lady Eastoffe waved and started over as I turned to my ladies. "Delia Grace, Nora. You may go to our seats. I'll be along shortly." They quickly obeyed and I was left with Silas and Etan, though I wished Etan would take his sour expression and follow his aunt and uncle.

"Are you not worried about offending someone?" I asked Silas quietly.

"On the contrary. I'm proud of my past and my present, so I hope to honor both kings today."

Every time I learned something new about Silas, I found I admired him even more. "That's very noble, sir."

Next to him, Etan rolled his eyes.

"And what of you, Sir Etan?" I asked. "Will you not participate today? Do you not have the stomach for tournaments?"

He looked down upon me as if I were a bug.

"I do not play at wars, my lady. I fight real ones. A lance and a blunted sword don't frighten me."

I looked back at Silas. "My cousin has volunteered for the Isolten army many times," he said proudly. "He fights to keep peace along the border."

I didn't like that I was spending time with someone who was fighting against my countrymen, but I couldn't deny it took bravery to do that.

"Well, then, you have my admiration for your courage, and my compassion for the sacrifices I'm sure you've made."

He sneered at me. "I don't need either. Not from you."

I shook my head and gathered my gown. "I'm glad you've sheathed your sword today, Sir Etan. If you could do the same with your tongue, you might find your company much more appreciated."

With another fussy expression, he stormed off, leaving me alone with Silas. Finally.

"I tried."

He smiled with a shrug. "I know. I like that about you. You're always trying."

I considered that. Etan had called me an ornament, Delia Grace took every opportunity to remind me I was a poor student, and my parents . . . well, they found endless fault with me. But Silas kept catching things that I didn't know about myself. He said he liked the way I thought. And he was right, I had plenty of good ideas. And he said that I tried, and he was right about that, too. I had a hard time giving up.

I found myself wishing I had a reason to stay near him just a little bit longer. Instead, I bowed my head to him to take my leave and walked away, looking back as I went. There was some unnameable thing that I felt when I was near Silas, like there was a string connecting us, pulling on me if I wandered too far. I was starting to think that fate had made our paths cross, but, considering how differently our paths had begun, I couldn't guess at why. Impulsively, I pulled my handkerchief from my sleeve and let it fall to the ground before rushing away.

As soon as I reached the royal box, I dropped into a curtsy before King Jameson. "Majesty."

"My Lady Hollis, you look radiant today. How am I to focus on the games?"

I smiled, then nodded at King Quinten and Queen Valentina. "Your Majesties. I hope you slept well."

Queen Valentina blinked at me, seemingly confused by the kindness. "Thank you."

I took my seat and tried to pay attention as the games began. As usual, Jameson's least favorite event, spear on foot, was up first. I couldn't blame him; it was too slow paced even for me, and I was never sure of the scoring. Some of the other events were much more straightforward.

"Ha ha!" King Quinten shouted. "That's another victory won by my men!"

"You have superb soldiers," Jameson agreed amicably. "My father always said so. Though I think the tides will turn once the events are on horseback. Coroans all excel with horses. Even my Hollis rides with speed and grace."

I leaned forward, taking in the praise. "You are too kind. And what of you, Your Majesties? Do you ride?"

"I used to," Valentina replied with a faint smile before her husband waved a hand to silence her.

"Not if I can help it," he answered quickly.

I made a face at Jameson, who understood my exasperation completely, and when he stuck out his tongue in reply, it was all I could do not to laugh.

When the spear event was finally over, the first groups of people came out for the next event: sword. After a few rounds, Silas came onto the field.

"Look there, Your Majesty." I rested my arm on Jameson's and pointed with the other. "Do you see the young man wearing no colors?"

He focused on the far side of the arena. "I do."

"It's one of the Eastoffe sons. He wanted to honor you both with his performance, so he chose no side," I explained. "He said it was for both his past and present."

Jameson considered this. "Very diplomatic, I suppose."

I frowned, a little disappointed with that assessment. "I'd thought of it as a lovely sentiment."

He laughed. "Ah, Hollis, you have such a simple view of life. I wish I had it myself."

The match began, and I saw quickly that Silas had been right: he was much better at making swords than wielding them. Still, I found myself moving closer and closer to the edge of my seat, hoping he'd somehow take the victory. His footwork was clumsy, but he was strong, swinging the sword with much more conviction than his counterpart, who, by chance, was wearing blue.

The crowd cheered and whooped with every blow, and I lifted my hand to my lips, hoping that if Silas didn't win, he'd at least walk away uninjured. I never worried about Jameson when he was jousting. Perhaps it was his skill on horseback or just the belief that it was impossible for him to fail.

Knowing that loss or injury were both very possible made me care about what I was seeing all the more. But I found my hope restored that Silas would at least be safe when I saw a hint of golden fabric peeking out from his sleeve.

He'd taken it. I felt my heartbeat fly even faster knowing that he'd scooped up my favor and was wearing it as his own. I peeked over at Jameson, hoping he didn't notice. I told myself that even if he had, plenty of ladies wove golden thread into their handkerchiefs. It was a thrilling and delicious secret.

Silas and his opponent battled back and forth, each refusing to concede. After one of the longest sword fights I'd ever seen, it all came down to the man in blue taking a few missteps and Silas bearing down with the sword hard on his challenger's back. His opponent dropped to the dirt and the round was over.

I stood, cheering with all my might and clapping thunderously.

Jameson rose beside me. "You must really support this swordsman," he said.

"No, my lord," I shouted over the noise, grinning ear to ear. "I support diplomacy."

He got a good laugh out of that and waved Silas over.

"Very good show, sir. And I appreciate your . . . statement."

Silas removed his helmet and bowed to the king. "Thank you, Your Majesty. It was an honor to fight today."

It took King Quinten a few blinks of his eyes to be sure of just what he was seeing, but once he was, he stood furiously.

"Why do you wear no colors?" he demanded. "Where is your blue?"

Jameson turned to him. "He is a Coroan now."

"He is not!"

"He fled your country to find sanctuary here. He has sworn his allegiance to me. And yet he wears no colors so as to not insult you. And you take it upon yourself to shame him?"

Quinten's voice was low and gravelly. "You and I both know he will never truly be a Coroan."

Just past them, I could see Queen Valentina clutching her stomach, her eyes flicking between Quinten and Jameson nervously. Up until now, she'd seemed above anything so common as nerves, but she was clearly worried about how this would unfold. I didn't want to see it, and my guess was she didn't, either.

"Come with me, Your Majesty. You mustn't get over-excited." I walked her down the stairs and into the shade behind the royal box. We could still hear Jameson's and Quinten's voices, but their words were muffled.

"Kings, huh?" I joked, trying to break the tension.

"I think it's just men in general," she replied, and we both laughed.

"Can I get you anything? Some water, something to eat?"

She shook her head. "No, I'm just happy to get away from the yelling. His Majesty gets upset easily, and I prefer to stay out of all that."

"I feel bad for the swordsman. I think he meant well."

"Silas Eastoffe." She looked at the ground. "I think he only ever means well."

It was funny. I was aware that Silas knew of the queen, but

I'd never considered that she knew of him.

"Has he done things like this before?"

"Not exactly. I've caught him in a few conversations where he tried to get the person he was speaking with to consider the other side of the argument. He just wants people to think."

I nodded. "I don't know him well, but that sounds about right."

A stampede of footsteps came down the stairs and Quinten was there, bearing down on his cane, pulling his wife away so quickly I didn't get to curtsy before she went. Jameson came down shortly after, hands on his hips.

"Well, the tournament's over. Quinten decided he'd rather rest than be insulted."

"Oh, no. Your Majesty, I'm so sorry."

He shook his head. "I know that boy was trying to do something clever, but he ended up causing a big mess."

"This is so ridiculous! Whatever the color, wasn't this meant to be entertainment? A diversion?"

"Yes, of course, but—"

"And doesn't one person desperately seeking middle ground set a great example of something we should *all* aspire to? Why does everything have to be a competition?"

"Hollis!"

Jameson had never raised his voice to me before. I was stunned into silence.

"You don't have to worry about this. You don't have to think so hard. All you need to do is show Coroa how good a queen you can be. And upstage that girl of Quinten's."

I swallowed. "Surely considering how to better our relationship with the largest country on the continent is part of being a good queen."

"*I'll* do that, Hollis." He shook his head. "That foolish boy. Let's hope this can be undone." He kissed my hand and went on his way.

I was left feeling small. Jameson had never been unhappy with me before. He'd never corrected me before. Then again, I'd never really shared my opinion before. Was . . . was Etan right? Was I an ornament?

I couldn't bring myself to believe that. If I was to join a long line of magnificent queens, shouldn't I be following in their footsteps? The footsteps that led to the homes of the poor? The footsteps that led to a battlefield?

I'd spent so much time being afraid of measuring up to them. Now the thought of not even trying to come close was unimaginable.

I marched over to where the competitors were milling about, hoping I'd be able to find a particular family in the mass of people. I pushed through the crowds until I, unfortunately, saw a familiar face.

"Etan!" I called.

He turned, and I waved, trying to get his attention. He tipped his head in acknowledgment.

"Where's Silas?"

Sighing, he walked over and grabbed me from the swarm. "Do you not have eyes?"

"I'm not as tall as you. Is he all right?"

"Yes, Uncle Dashiell tucked him away near the tree line while things calmed down, and most everyone is going in the opposite direction now. Here, this way."

I followed as best I could, trying to keep up with his long strides. We finally came upon them, Silas sitting on a barrel, talking to his parents with a bewildered expression on his face. Once he saw me, he stood and began attempting to atone for his mistakes immediately.

"Lady Hollis, I'm so sorry. You have to apologize to the king for me."

"Slow down," I insisted.

He took my hands, pleading. "If King Jameson revokes our permit to settle because of me . . . Hollis, my family."

His hands were rough, but those blue eyes were so gentle.

"I know." I sighed. "Please tell me you finished making the pieces I mentioned when we first heard about the king coming to visit."

He nodded. "We stayed up late to make sure they were done before he came, but no one gave us instructions on when to present them."

"Perfect," I said. "I need to get a letter to Queen Valentina."

SEVENTEEN

I stood still as Delia Grace repeatedly laced the gown, trying to get it to sit right. "This is so strange," she said. "How do your arms feel?"

"Heavy," I admitted.

Delia Grace went back to the parcel and pulled out one more thing. "For your head. We can use something of yours if you prefer."

Valentina's things were quite beautiful. The craftsmanship was not nearly so detailed as the work done in Coroa, but the gemstones were bigger, more substantial.

"If she sent it, I will wear it."

I walked around my apartments carrying books and acclimating to the weight of the sleeves and headpiece. In the middle of my seventh lap, Silas and Sullivan came in, dressed in their best and carrying their work on black pillows.

Sullivan fell behind his brother, taking in Nora and Delia Grace with trepidation. Though I longed to speak to Silas, I went to his brother first.

"These ladies are all my friends," I said, placing a hand on his arm. "And tonight, you needn't say a word. Only lift the pillow so King Jameson may take your gift."

He nodded, giving me the tiniest of smiles.

"And what are you smirking about?" I asked, turning to Silas.

"Nothing. It's just amazing to see you in Isolten blue. You could almost pass for a girl back home."

"If I grew an inch or two and spent less time in the sun, perhaps?"

"Perhaps," he replied, and then lowered his voice. "I don't know if this will mend anything, Lady Hollis."

"I know," I answered, fidgeting with my heavy clothes. "But we need to try."

After a quick knock, Valentina walked in, her single lady-in-waiting behind her. I had chosen the palest red dress I could find for her, almost bordering on pink, and as I'd hoped, it worked nicely with her skin.

"What do you think, my lady?" she asked.

"I think you should keep it. It looks far better on you than it ever has on me."

She smiled, loving the praise. Valentina was a new person when she smiled.

"My arms feel so free," she said, lifting them above her head.

"Can you please tell me why it is that the ladies in Isolte wear so much fabric on their sleeves?" I asked in exasperation.

She laughed. "One, it's a sign of status. It says you have the means to afford the extra fabric, and that you don't have to work with your hands. Ladies in the country don't wear them, or at least, not so long. And two, they keep you warm. It's much cooler in Isolte."

"Ahh," I said. It made sense, though it wasn't a practice I was planning to adopt, whether I could afford it or not.

"When she smiles, you two could pass for sisters," Delia Grace whispered beside me.

When we met, I'd been too nervous to think about anything more than making a good first impression, but she was right. Between our hair and the angle of our chins, we could pass for relatives at least.

"I was told dinner began fifteen minutes ago, so everyone should be seated," she offered. "I am ready when you are."

"Excellent. Delia Grace, Nora, if you will please take the queen's lady with you now so you can all be seated." They obeyed, and the very confused woman walked with them out of the room. "Sullivan, if you will please walk behind Queen Valentina, and Silas, please stay with me."

He nodded. "Of course, my lady." Then he lowered his voice. "It may be easier for my brother if he is with you."

I ducked my eyes before summoning the courage to answer. "But I need you with me. Please?"

He stared back at me for a long moment, as if he wanted to

say something in return. In the end, he simply nodded and our little party exited the room.

The hallways were all but empty—everyone wanted to attend the feast if only for the lavish meal.

"What are the chances your king is still mad?" I asked Valentina.

"High. He doesn't forget much."

"Do you think this will do anything?"

She considered. "Your king seems more reasonable than most, so having him back in good spirits will help. And I think if those beneath us can see our behavior, they will try to model it. A lamb will only go where its shepherd takes it."

"A very good point, Your Majesty." I looked up at Valentina. She really was quite pretty, with hair almost the shade of mine but skin closer to milk than honey. And she was so statuesque that even in my highest heeled shoes I didn't quite come up to her height. "Thank you so much for agreeing to do this. I realize I misspoke when we met, and it got everything off to a bad start. I didn't mean to offend you, and I'm so grateful to have your help."

She brushed her hand lazily at me. "You didn't offend me. Sometimes it's easier, you know? To just be silent."

I giggled. "Silence is not a skill of mine."

She pressed her lips together, seeming to already have gathered that much about me. "A few years with a crown on your head might change that."

I wanted to ask what she meant by that, but we were already at the entrance of the Great Room. A knot of dread settled in my stomach, and I feared that, just like Silas, we would mean well but make things worse. Valentina must have sensed my trepidation, because she reached out, and we entered the hall holding one another's hands.

No one noticed us at first, but I heard gasps and whispers as whole sections of the room fell into a hush to see what would happen when we reached the head table. Once the change in sound reached Jameson's ear, he looked up, eyes going straight down the center walkway. I watched as his eyes settled on the red dress, a smile almost spreading across his face before he realized the girl in it wasn't me. His eyes flicked immediately to her right, and his mouth hung slightly open as he took me in.

He spoke quietly to King Quinten, who eventually looked up from his food, grumpy as ever. Thankfully, the sight of his wife in Coroan red and me in Isolten blue was enough to stun him into silence.

We approached the dais and curtsied before them, and, as Valentina held the higher rank, she spoke first.

"Your Majesties. We come here tonight to appeal for peace between our two great kingdoms," she said.

"While the missteps of your people may be great, you are both better than your subjects, and we look to you for guidance."

"I wear red, because I have made a friend in Coroa."

"And I wear blue, because I have made yet another friend from Isolte." I gestured for Sullivan and Silas to come forward. "These crowns of gold, shaped like olive branches, are for you, Your Majesties. Made by a family born in Isolte and living in Coroa. May they be a model of our brotherhood for years to come."

The crowd behind us applauded, and I turned to pick up the first crown.

"It's so light!" I exclaimed.

"I did my best for you," Silas said quietly.

My gaze on him lingered a moment longer than I meant for it to before I reached across the table to place the crown on King Quinten's head as Queen Valentina did the same with Jameson. He was smiling, speaking to her, and King Quinten focused on me.

"I see you've become close with the Eastoffes," he remarked.

"I try to be an excellent hostess at the castle for His Majesty's sake, regardless of where our guests are from."

He nodded. "I'd suggest you take care. People in Isolte tend to keep their distance from them these days."

"I can't imagine why," I snapped before remembering I was here to mend bridges, not take to them with an axe. I swallowed, starting again. "They have been humble and most helpful since their arrival."

The look in his eyes was more of a warning than his words. "If you wish to stand next to the fire, by all means. You're the one who'll be burned."

I curtsied again to him, as I knew I must, but I hated pretending to give any level of respect to that man. I nodded to Silas and Sullivan that they could go, mouthing my thanks before turning to Queen Valentina.

"You are wiser than anyone has guessed. We will talk more tomorrow," she said into my ear before we crossed paths and went to go sit by our kings.

"What do you think?" I asked Jameson as I settled into place.

"I think if you fell off a boat in that, the sleeves would drag you straight to the bottom."

I laughed. "I had to practice walking," I admitted.

He smiled. "Teasing aside, you look beautiful in anything you're ever in." He sat back, sipping his drink. "I hear it's the fashion for brides to wear white these days. Won't that be something?"

I looked down, blushing. Of course, I was glad he still found me pretty in Isolten blue, but I wondered how he felt about what Valentina and I had done, if he appreciated our strategizing and hard work. Before I could ask, King Quinten tapped Jameson's shoulder.

"There's no point arguing. We need to get back to that contract," he urged. Out of his sight, I let out a sigh. I had no idea what they were working on, but I was pleased they weren't abandoning it over a single battle at a tournament. Even if Jameson said nothing in thanks, at least this moment had been a success.

Around the room, people were chatting and eating and laughing, and though Valentina and I hadn't walked the borders or pulled a king back from war, we'd made steps toward peace. I hoped the queens before me would have approved. Judging by the smiling faces and relaxed shoulders around the room, it seemed most people in the court did.

From his table, Silas caught my eye and lifted his glass to me. I did the same in return and took a drink. No, that boy was only good, and nothing about him could leave me burned.

The center of the floor where Valentina and I had walked down was now filling with people dancing as the meal came to a close and the music changed.

I watched with trepidation as Silas rose from his table and walked up to the dais.

"Your Majesty," he said, bowing before Jameson. "I can see that you and King Quinten are busy. I was wondering if I might ask the Lady Hollis to dance."

Jameson smiled slyly. "Only if she wishes it."

I took a breath. "Well, if I can't dance with you." I kissed his cheek and walked down to meet Silas, standing beside him while the song came to a close.

"I wanted to make good on what I said, that I'd dance with you if you ever invited me to," he whispered.

I spoke softly. "But I never got that far."

"I couldn't wait. Hope you don't mind."

I smiled. "Not at all. I've been dying to dance, and Jameson has been more interested in watching lately. I'm just so thankful to have someone ask me. None of the other gentlemen at court will now."

"Ah, I see. Well, for one song, let's forget about kings and colors and all the rest. Let's just have a lovely dance, yes?"

"Yes," I sighed.

The music began, and we lined up across from each other, moving in time with the other couples.

"I don't know how to thank you for this," I said. "You and your family saved us tonight."

He rolled his eyes. "But only after I got us into trouble."

"Nonsense. I think we all know who the real problem here is." I swung in, placing my hand in Silas's. His rough skin held my hand so delicately, and I could see the remnants of a gentleman in the gesture.

"All the same, it was the least we could do."

"Has the king compensated you yet?"

He shook his head. "We agreed there were no kings for this dance."

He was right. "Very well."

We crossed arms and spun in circles. He wasn't the best partner I'd ever had, but he was steadier than Jameson.

"I'm not sure there would be much occasion after this, but I do hope we can speak more soon," he said.

"I agree. It's been nice to have someone to talk to. Another thing I need to thank you for."

He smiled down at me, the unrestrained admiration in his gaze making me forget that there were other people in the room. "I am here whenever you need me. If anyone is in debt, it's me. You offered my family a home. You defended my actions publicly. You are quite a remarkable lady, Hollis." His face grew a little darker when he added, "You will be an unforgettable queen."

The song ended, and I curtsied to him. I turned to look at Jameson, to see if he was pleased by the dance. He wasn't even looking.

I flicked my eyes to Silas and nodded that he should follow me from the Great Room.

I went from the room and waited a ways down the hallway. I heard as the next song began, and I saw Silas's shadow before he arrived where I was standing.

"The dance is over, so now I have to say it again—if the king has not compensated you for your work, I want to make sure that happens."

Silas looked down, shaking his head. "You needn't worry about that. They were gifts."

"I insist! This whole moment tonight wouldn't have happened without your family, so I am in your debt."

"You gave us a place to live. We're in yours."

I placed my hands on my hips, which was a surprising struggle given the sleeves. He noted it and laughed at me.

"Stop! I've been trying so hard!"

"I know," he said, wiping the smile off his face. "And, wardrobe issues aside, you've done a wonderful job." He gestured toward the Great Room. "They're not just whispering about how gracefully you've behaved tonight, Hollis. They're saying they've known all along what a great queen you'd be."

The word came out a hopeful whisper. "Really?"

He nodded. "You've done beautifully."

I stared at him, at the glimmering hope in his blue eyes.

There really was something extraordinary about that blue. And the way his hair shifted when he dropped his shoulder. And how he smiled, as if he wasn't holding anything back, saving his worry and care and affection for anyone else.

"I feel so fortunate to have met you," I confessed. "Since you've arrived, I've felt . . . different."

"I feel different, too," he said, his voice dropping to a whisper. "When you're near."

It suddenly became clear to me that we were very much alone. Footsteps in these vast hallways were unmistakable, and there was no such sound.

"I should probably get back," I breathed.

"Yes."

But neither of us moved. Until we both did, meeting in the middle of the hallway for a stolen kiss.

Silas cupped my cheeks, holding me with such tenderness that I felt everything inside my body melting. I could feel the calluses on his fingers as they traced the edges of my face, and I couldn't help but compare the feeling to that of Jameson's perfectly smooth hands. There was something about the awareness of Silas's hard work, the labor that earned him those calluses, that made me treasure his touch.

I could have stayed lost in it for ages, but I heard the sound of distant footsteps.

Jerking away, I couldn't even bring myself to look into his eyes. What had I done?

"Wait five minutes and then go back," I whispered urgently. "For my sake, please tell no one."

I was already walking when he simply replied, "If you wish."

I moved toward the Great Room with my head high, trying to convince myself that if I simply looked confident, then no one could possibly suspect I'd just kissed someone who was decidedly not my intended. Who was a foreigner. Who was, by every measure I'd been taught to value, a commoner.

He'd been right; everywhere I turned, people were giving me knowing looks and thankful smiles. They'd finally come to respect me at the very moment I'd let them all down.

I walked up to the head table, kissing Jameson on the cheek. He gave me a warm look but continued his conversation with King Quinten. I was counting the minutes until that man left, taking his entourage with him. I needed everything to go back to normal.

But I was starting to wonder if there'd ever be a normal. Since the moment I'd locked eyes with Silas Eastoffe, I'd felt *something*. The string was pulling me, taut and unyielding. I couldn't help but notice I still felt that pull as he walked into the hall, eyes downcast, as if he couldn't muster the strength to fake any kind of happiness.

I'd said he couldn't burn me. I still believed that. If I was going to go up in flames, it would be my own doing.

EIGHTEEN

I INHALED DEEPLY, TAKING IN the scent of freshly blossoming flowers. Though I could have happily spent an hour by myself in the maze of hedges in the peaceful gardens of Keresken, it was surprisingly pleasant to sit by Queen Valentina as Jameson and King Quinten practiced their archery. Jameson had beautiful form, and I was sure Quinten must have at some point as well. These days, the arching of his back made pulling the bow securely a bit of a challenge. Still, I could see in his steady fingers and the sureness of his gaze that he knew precisely what he was doing.

Valentina and I took refuge in the shade of several large parasols being held above us by palace servants, and we watched as Jameson let another arrow fly. It hit very close to its mark, and he turned back to me, raising his eyebrows and clearly waiting for praise.

"Bravo, my lord!" I called, swallowing hard immediately after. It was difficult to get the words out. There was a secret kiss hiding in my throat, blocking all the words I knew I was supposed to say, halting all the actions I knew I was meant to do.

I feared that something about the set of my smile or the shade of my eyes was going to give me away. Any minute, Jameson was going to know that I'd betrayed him. And even to this second, I couldn't explain how it had happened.

I also couldn't change it. The best I could hope for was to forget it ever happened and continue walking steadily toward Jameson and the crown. I sighed, turning to Valentina.

"I want to thank you again for yesterday," I began, trying to restart our easy conversation from the night before. It was much harder when things felt so official.

"I did very little in the grand scheme. You orchestrated everything. I can see why your king favors you so much." She looked over at him admiringly. There really was no other way to look at Jameson.

Then why did you kiss someone else?

"I . . . I'm still not sure what made him choose me," I started, stumbling over the words. "Some say it's because I make him laugh." I tilted my head, still not sure what the true answer to this question was. I supposed Etan would have said it was my pretty face. "How did you meet King Quinten?"

She shrugged. "There isn't much to say. I have been at court with my parents since I was a child. The court is large, so we didn't truly cross paths until a few years ago. That was that."

I cast a knowing look at her. "That sounds close to my story. Amazing what can happen when you leave the country for a palace."

"True. The castle had all but been our home for years; we only left it to travel." A whisper of a smile crept onto her lips. "I've been to nearly every country on the continent," she boasted. "My parents wanted me to see the world."

"I envy you. You already know how small my world is."

She nodded. "Maybe your king will be more adventurous, take you to meet the princes of each land. It will serve you well; there is an education that can only be received through travel."

For the majority of my life I'd had no reason to think that I needed to see anything more than the hills near Varinger Hall or the sunrise on Colvard River as it cut by the capital. But meeting people from across the continent was enlightening, and now I ached to know more.

"I hope so. What about you? Do you hope to finish this education? Go to those final few countries?"

Her smile faded. "The king is most preoccupied with his kingdom."

"Oh." I wasn't entirely sure what that meant, but I assumed, whatever it was, it gave them cause to stay close to home. Coroa, at least, wasn't much of a journey.

"It makes me miss my parents," she said in a voice so quiet I almost didn't hear it. When I looked at her then, she didn't seem so much like a queen anymore, but more of what she was: another young girl trying to make her way in the world. "I have little trinkets from our trips. . . . This necklace," she said, touching the silver oval tied around her swan-like neck. "My father got me this in Montoth from a little gypsy woman by the side of the road. I have a feeling she didn't make it, if you catch my meaning."

I nodded, wondering whose neck it had been around once upon a time.

"She was a nice lady, though. Fiery. My father gave her more than she asked. He was kind like that."

"Then I would very much like to meet him one day."

Valentina kept her eyes on the horizon and her hand on her necklace. "I wish you could. I wish you could have met both of them."

I sighed, knowing I'd just ruined what was shaping up to be a great conversation. "I'm very sorry."

Her gaze went over to the king. "So am I."

I didn't understand the sudden tinge of anger in her tone, but I didn't have long to dwell on it. In the distance the maids were arriving, trays of delicacies in their hands.

"I've heard you have an interest in foreign cuisine. I took the liberty of having some dishes made especially for you." I gestured to the approaching army of servants and watched as her face lit up.

"You did?" Her tone was incredulous.

"Yes. I . . . I wasn't misinformed, was I? You certainly don't have to eat any—"

"No, no! I'm thrilled!" She exclaimed as tray after tray was set on our blanket. "I know this one," she said. "You usually make these for Crowning Day, right?"

"Yes. I tried to get a few things that were unique regionally and then a few associated with Coroan holy days. These pies over here? They're for the solstice and have golden syrup in them."

She picked up one of the treats and popped it in her mouth. I was adventurous with most things, but strange foods always gave me pause. I admired that, even in this, she plowed forward.

"Delicious. And these?" She went from plate to plate, asking questions and eating as much as she could stomach. When her smile was unguarded, she looked younger, more hopeful. In this tiny moment, I saw a Valentina that had not been present in the Great Room or on the jousting field. She was a clear beauty; even when she was frowning it was undeniable. There was something about this face that made me understand how she could be placed on a throne, be adored by the masses.

But then I thought of some of the comments the Eastoffes had made and realized she didn't seem to be adored in that sense. I supposed the people had never seen this smile.

"This is the nicest thing anyone has done for me in a long time," she said, basking in the sun. "Thank you."

"You're very welcome. Come visit anytime you feel the slightest bit peckish."

When she giggled, the sound flew high and danced in the trees.

"Valentina!" King Quinten snapped, motioning to his bow, as if her laughter was interrupting something of the highest importance. That bright smile disappeared in an instant, and all the light around her died. She demurely nodded her head, then picked up a pie to cover her mouth.

"He's such a tyrant," she muttered under her breath. "I swear, if he had the stamina, he'd hunt down joy itself and shoot it through." A moment later she remembered herself. "Please don't repeat that."

I picked up a small pie to obstruct the view of my mouth as well. "Don't worry. If there's anything I understand, it's the value of a certain level of privacy. Mine's dropped considerably recently, and I can't imagine yours. I wouldn't say anything. Besides, I think you're right. He's a bit of a grump."

She pressed her lips together, suppressing her smile. "So, Lady Hollis, what are our plans for tonight?"

I could feel my heart beating fast. Things were really starting to turn around. "King Jameson has recently gifted me with a set of golden dice. I'm trying to learn some games."

"I'll bring money. It's much more fun when there's something on the line," she offered, as if this were some piece of great wisdom.

"We can invite our ladies, too, if you'd like."

She shook her head. "No. I'd like to just be with you."

I smiled. "Absolutely, Your Majesty."

At the title she rolled her eyes. "All right, it was fun when I was making you grovel, but you can just call me Valentina now."

"I can always grovel for old times' sake if you get bored later."

She giggled at that, too, but pushed the sound away quickly. I could see King Quinten blow out a huff, but he took his time looking back at us. His eyes glanced off Valentina and swiftly settled on me, and I felt a chill. I may have finally gotten through to her, but I was still little more than an insect to him. I looked away quickly.

I reminded myself I was here to accompany Valentina, and if she was satisfied, I was doing my duty . . . but I knew that once I was queen, there would always be a Quinten in my life. Dignitaries and envoys would come and go, and I would be in the middle of it all, unable to hide. Some would probably like me well enough, but there would always be some who felt satisfied with ignoring me.

I pulled my chin up, and I thought of Valentina. We ladies in our gilded cage, we had to make the best of it.

NINETEEN

It DIDN'T TAKE LONG FOR Valentina to tire, which worked out just fine for me, as I had business of my own to attend to. The parcel was light, and, thanks to the painting outside their rooms that Lady Eastoffe had told me about, I knew where I was heading.

I was technically there to see Scarlet, but there were butterflies plotting a riot in my stomach. I felt too many things at once to know what they truly were. Would Silas be there? Would he try to talk to me? Did I want him to?

The kiss had been a surprise. No, not a surprise, a mistake. Certainly, Silas was easy to talk to, easy to understand. There was an undercurrent of goodness to everything he did, and the way his family so clearly valued each other made me want to be closer to not just him but all of them. And he was his own kind of handsome, with those blue eyes and that angelic smile. Yes, there was something very charming about Silas Eastoffe.

But seeing as he was not Jameson Barclay, it really didn't matter. Charm wouldn't give me a crown or bring hope to a kingdom. Charm was nice, not necessary.

I squared myself in front of the door, bracing myself for whatever—and whoever—might be on the other side, and I knocked.

"Lady Hollis! How nice to see you!" Scarlet greeted me, opening the door wide.

"Just the person I was looking for," I said, ignoring the pang in my heart. "I hope I'm not interrupting anything."

"Not at all. Please, come in." She motioned that I should enter, and I walked in, taking in the space.

There was a small fireplace and a table that was maybe big enough for four with six chairs crammed around it. There wasn't much for decoration, but they did have some flowers on the set of drawers beneath the window. Two doors led to where their sleeping quarters must have been. I felt a little bad for Scarlet, as she must have been sharing a room with her brothers, with no space to herself.

The only thing that saved the apartment was that one window. It was large, matching the size of all the others down that particular outside wall, so that every chamber in the palace, regardless of size, had a wide pane of domed glass letting light in. I stared at it, thinking her view was so very different from mine.

"You see that building over there?" she asked, pointing to

a small stone structure with a thatch roof and a large chimney that was expelling smoke even now. "That's where Silas and Sullivan are working."

"Really?" I asked, coming close to the window to inspect.

"Yes. And if Sullivan needs my tiny fingers to finish off a piece of jewelry or Silas needs me to polish a sword, they put a blue handkerchief in the window. I'm always keeping my eye out for it."

"That's such a remarkable skill they have," I commented in awe. "I can sew, but that's where my talents end."

"Not so!" she protested. "You dance so well, and you are twice the conversationalist of anyone in Isolte." I didn't want to tell her that was hardly a compliment. "But I admire my brothers, too. It's unique for anyone in Isolte to pursue something that might be considered artistic. And even between the two of them, what they do is so different."

"How?" I asked, looking at the glassless window of the outbuilding, trying to make out if that was Silas or his brother moving across it.

"Sullivan's work . . . he needs fire, but it's much more delicate. The amount of metal he uses at one time is much smaller, so, all things considered, it's much safer. He could probably do it indoors if he chose."

"It looks like he sticks close to Silas as much as possible."

She nodded. "Always has. I don't think any of us understand him the way Silas does. People think he's distant, but he's not. He just doesn't know what to say."

I gave her a sad smile. "I know that feeling all too well. So what is it that Silas does out there, then?"

"It's far more dangerous. He's plunging huge chunks of metal into fire, pulling them out, and then hammering them until they bend into the right shape. He's burned himself a few times, and at least twice we worried he'd really damaged his arm. Thankfully, we know how to stave off infection, so he's been fine."

"Thank goodness." It was well known that healers in Isolte had made far more medical advancements than we had in Coroa. If Isolte could use our dances and music and art, could we not use their knowledge about medicine and herbs and the stars? I had a feeling that, if we asked, we could send people to study. My guess was both Jameson and his father would never have let their pride down long enough to make the request. "He seems to be good at what he does, though."

"One of the best," Scarlet bragged.

I smiled. "Well, his sister is an excellent teacher and friend, so this is for you. A thank-you for agreeing to help with Crowning Day."

She took the parcel and walked over to the table. "For me?"

"Yes. And I want you to know that I'm trying to pre-emptively set at least part of my household. I'd happily have you in it, but I'm going to need some time with Delia Grace before I can convince her of your many virtues. I hope you won't mind waiting until I can talk her into being a bit more . . . open-minded."

She looked at me over her shoulder. "I mean this in the

nicest possible way, but I don't see Delia Grace ever being open-minded."

I chuckled. For how little time she'd spent with her, Scarlet already understood Delia Grace better than most. I thought of her searching eyes that first day she'd walked into the Great Room; I wondered just how much this girl knew about life in the castle.

"Besides, I'd have had to turn you down anyway," she went on. "We're hoping to settle out in the country soon, somewhere with a lot of land and quiet."

I wasn't sure how to take that news. I certainly felt a twinge of sadness, but there was also a rush of relief. At some point, I wouldn't stand a chance of running into Silas down these hallways, of seeing him awash with the colors streaming from the stained glass. I really didn't have room for more surprises—or mistakes—in my life. I could be free of them once he was out of the palace for good.

I snapped back to the present, trying to carry on a normal conversation.

"Coroa has some fine lands. I'm sure you'll find something suitable."

She unwrapped the gift and gasped in delight. "Hollis, I love it!" She hugged the dress to her chest.

"I left material in case we need to make it longer. You're very tall."

She laughed. "I know. And look at the sleeves."

"I just thought you'd like to match everyone else when we finally get to do this dance, and I did so appreciate your help. Though Saul *was* my favorite dance partner of the day."

"He hasn't smiled that much in ages. That alone was a gift for all of us."

Something about the wistful tone of her voice almost made me want to cry. I wondered if I'd ever understand all that they'd been through.

"Good," I said, not sure what else there was to say. "Well, I'd better be off. *Someone* has a private meeting with Queen Valentina today, thanks to the insight of a certain new friend," I said, eyeing her.

"The food?"

"I stuffed her full of Coroan treats. She loved it. Thank you."

"Anytime, Hollis. Genuinely."

She was still holding up her dress, pressing it against her to see how it would fit.

"Good day, Lady Scarlet."

Her eyes changed. She must have abandoned hope of being called a lady ever again. I pulled the door shut behind me, making my way back to the queen's rooms and thinking of how I'd laughed at Scarlet under my breath that first day in the Great Room. I felt so silly for not understanding then what I did now: we weren't that different. Not her, not Valentina, not Nora. In the end, we made enemies with our heads, but we unmade them with our hearts.

TWENTY

I SAT IN FRONT OF my vanity, playing with my hair. As per Valentina's request, I'd dismissed my ladies for the evening, so, for the very first time, I was alone in my new rooms. I took a moment to close my eyes and appreciate the aloneness. The palace was never really silent, and I supposed that was one of the things I'd come to love about it. The fire was making crackles and sparks, and I could hear the distant click of footsteps above me. Outside the window, the city that came right up to the castle was far from settling. I heard horses on the streets, men calling out orders, and people laughing in the open evening air. If I focused, I could even hear oars slapping the waters of the river. Unlike the noise in the Great Room, these sounds were a welcome song.

My whole life, I'd found so much delight in dancing and tournaments and company that I never realized how lovely a moment of stillness was. I'd discovered it far too late.

I opened my eyes to the knock at the door and paused a second before realizing I had to tend to it myself. Valentina was smiling, wiggling a small leather purse.

"I hope you're prepared to hand over your fortune, Lady Hollis. In my day I'd rob the gentlemen of court blind." She walked past me without waiting for an invitation. While it irritated me to no end when my mother did that, it felt quite natural from Valentina, and I couldn't help but feel it added to her charm.

"Not anymore?" I asked, taking a seat at the table in the greeting area.

She shook her head. "No. The men of court keep their distance now. The ladies, too." She threw her little bag down and surveyed the room, peeking around the wall into the bed space before coming to sit. "You have beautiful rooms."

"Well, they should be beautiful. These are the queen's apartments."

She looked around again, eyes wide. "Already?"

I nodded. "If I was to meet a queen, His Majesty wanted me to be dressed and jeweled and roomed to equal her," I commented with a smile. "I suppose it's only a matter of time before an official proposal."

Her face was colored with surprise yet again. "He hasn't given you a ring?"

"Not yet. He wanted to be cautious. But now it seems everyone knows his intent, so it should be happening soon."

She seemed tickled by my situation as she reached over for

my golden dice. "Your relationship with your king is most amusing. He seems to enjoy that you are . . . a free spirit, let's say."

I shrugged. "I wish everyone felt the same way, but I'm glad Jameson appreciates me. What is it that drew King Quinten to you? You didn't really say much about it earlier."

Her eyes were instantly distant. "I don't talk about it much," she admitted.

"Oh." I squinted, confused. "I'm sorry if—"

"No, no. Not many people understand; it might be good if someone else finally did." She sighed, toying with the dice but not looking up at me. "After Queen Vera died, most everyone at court assumed Quinten would remain single. He had a male heir, and as far as anyone could tell, he had no interest in remarrying. I think . . . I think it was possible he really loved her. Queen Vera, that is. I caught him smiling at her a few times when I was very young.

"I'd been planning to marry Lord Haytham. He liked me very much, and my parents approved of him wholeheartedly. And Quinten's focus was entirely on making a match for his son. But it seemed reports of Hadrian's fragile health spread farther than anyone thought they would. The few girls who were approached by the king were quite suddenly engaged. One of them, Sisika Aram, was a dear friend of mine, and I know for a fact her arrangements were made the *very day* her family was called to meet with Quinten."

"Why?" I asked. "At the very least, these girls had an opportunity to be royal."

"I asked the same questions myself then. Now I know they were very smart." She was still looking away, her bitter tone making me think her love story had little to do with love. "Eventually, Quinten reached out to other countries, which he wasn't keen on; he was positive he'd find a quality family in Isolte for his son. But he finally found someone for the prince, and their wedding is set for the winter."

I smiled. "Snow is lucky in Isolte, right?"

She nodded. "We're hoping for a thick blanket of it to bless them."

That was sweet. Snow meant nothing here, nor did rain, nor did the breeze. But I would wish for snow for Hadrian's sake.

"Wait. That doesn't explain anything about you and King Quinten."

"Ah," she said, her smile humorless. "I knew less about the royal family than others did. As I said, I traveled frequently, and I kept to my own group of friends. But most of those friends got married, and I lost them as they left to go inspect their new households, start families—the things young brides do."

"Yes."

"So when it became clear the king was looking for a new wife, I was one of the few younger women at court who was eligible. I was charmed by the idea of a crown, by the image of a man in full regalia, and when my parents were made an incredibly generous offer for my hand, I was flattered.

"What I didn't know until later was that Hadrian had a

very scary bout of a fever a few weeks prior to my proposal. He was unconscious for three days. Quinten realized he needed another heir, and I was chosen, not for my wit or my singing or my pedigree. I am a healthy young woman, and I ought to be able to provide a child." She sighed. "I *ought* to."

I was stunned into silence. Valentina, who looked to me to have so many qualities worth loving, was maybe not really loved at all.

"Don't look like that," she said, rolling the dice for no reason except to watch them fall. "Most marriages in the crown work this way. If you like your husband, that is desirable. But what is necessary is keeping the line. And a state bed is as comfortable as any."

I swallowed. "Can I ask you the rudest question I can possibly think to ask at the moment?"

She smirked. "I like you, Hollis. Yes, go ahead."

"What happened to Lord Haytham?"

"He left court. He's living in the country these days, and I've not seen him in three years. I have to assume he's married by now, but I don't know." She looked down. "I wouldn't mind so much if he was. But it'd be nice to know one way or the other."

For a flicker of a second my thoughts went to Silas. His family would find property. They would make a name for themselves with the impeccable work they were producing. He'd catch the attention of some girl, and he'd break through her preconceived notions with those piercing blue eyes. He'd marry her.

Or maybe he wouldn't.

How would I ever know?

"Can I ask you a rude question myself?" Valentina ventured.

My eyes fluttered as I focused back in on her face. "You've certainly earned the right to it."

"You must tell me the truth. Your king . . . has he ever been unkind to you?"

"Unkind? Unkind how?"

She made a noncommittal gesture with her hand. "Just . . . *unkind*."

I searched my memories. Maybe he'd been inconsiderate, but never unkind. "No."

She pressed her hand against her stomach, on guard.

"Valentina?"

She shook her head. "It's nothing."

I reached across the table, holding her free hand. "Clearly, it's not. If anyone can understand the pressure of going from court girl to queen, surely it's me. Speak to me."

Her pressed lips started trembling and suddenly parted in quick, shaking gasps. "Everyone keeps watching me. They're waiting for me to give them another heir, and I know they whisper about me. But it's not my fault!" she insisted. "I've been so careful!"

"What are you talking about?" I asked, looking down at that delicate hand across her stomach. "Are you pregnant now?"

"I'm not sure. I haven't bled in two months, but the

symptoms . . . I've already been with child twice before now and lost them. This seems different. I feel . . . I feel . . ."

"Shhh," I urged, reaching out to hold her. "I'm sure you will both be fine."

"You don't understand." She sat up, trembling and wiping wildly at the tears on her face. I thought she must be having some sort of fit, because her sorrow quickly shifted to anger, and she never stopped shaking. "If you speak a word of this, I will end your life, do you hear me? If it comes down to your life or mine—"

"Valentina, I've already told you how much I value privacy. I will keep anything you say between the two of us."

The fight seemed to go out of her, and she slumped, propping herself exhaustedly against the back of her chair. Her hands were clutched across her stomach, not so much protective as prayerful. I'd never seen such haunted eyes.

"They think I think I'm above them," she began. "All the women at court. They think I don't speak to them because I've been elevated, and so I must assume I'm too good to associate with them. But that's not true. It's Quinten. He likes me to keep to myself."

I thought of what Scarlet had said about her being in isolation for six months. I wondered if anyone knew her solitude wasn't self-imposed.

"I'm sorry. Is that why you only have the one lady?"

She nodded. "We don't even speak the same language. She brings me what she knows I need, and we're managing to understand each other more, but she's not exactly a confidante. I have no one to talk to, no allies, and I'm afraid."

"Afraid?" For goodness' sake, she was the queen. "Afraid of what?"

I could see the terror in her eyes, and she started shaking her head very quickly. "I've said too much. I . . . you can never tell."

"Valentina, if you're in danger, you can claim sanctuary in one of our holy buildings. No one is allowed to take you from there."

"Maybe here," she said, rising clumsily to her feet, "but not in Isolte. And they won't care."

"Who won't care?"

"They always come. If you're in the way, they always, *always* come."

"Who?"

"They took my parents. And if I don't produce an heir, it's probably only a matter of time. . . ."

I grabbed her by the shoulders. "Valentina, what are you talking about?"

Something in her eyes shifted again, and now her face looked calm, resolved. I'd never seen anyone's emotions bounce in so many directions so quickly.

"Be thankful for your beautiful little life, Hollis. Not all of us are given such a luxury."

Wait . . . what was she trying to say? And who were *they*? Before I could figure out how to form my next question, she was standing, straightening her robe, and walking from the room.

I was left sitting in my hard chair, stunned. What in the world had just happened?

I tried to slow my thoughts down and go back through the conversation. Valentina may or may not be pregnant, and she'd already lost two babies since she'd been married to King Quinten. She was alone in Isolte. She had lost her parents through some dark means. And she feared for her safety.

I didn't think I could go ask Valentina for any more answers, and even if I dared, I wasn't sure she would be able to answer in her state. I knew who I could ask, but after last night, I didn't know if I could face him.

I couldn't help myself. I had to know more. I tore from the room, making my way to the back of the castle. The hallways were mostly empty, but even if they hadn't been, I would have run through all of them. I hesitated in front of the Eastoffes' door. For the sake of so many people, it would be wiser to walk away.

But if I did, there was no way I could help Valentina.

Behind the door, people spoke in low tones, but all noise came to an abrupt stop when I knocked. It was Lord Eastoffe who answered.

"Why, Lady Hollis. To what do we owe the pleasure of your company?" he asked cheerfully. Over his shoulder, I saw his wife smiling, as well as their guests, save for Etan, who rolled his eyes and moved from the table. He wasn't alone in his feelings, though. I was surprised to see even Scarlet looked skeptical and Sullivan lowered his gaze. Silas seemed unsure of how to respond to my unexpected arrival.

I could have spoken to any of them, I supposed. Scarlet was a girl; maybe she'd know more. But there was only one person in that room I could have trusted with such a secret.

"I've found I have a very specific question about Isolte, and I was wondering if I could borrow Silas for a few minutes. I promise not to keep him long."

Lord Eastoffe looked over his shoulder. "Absolutely. Son?"

Silas stood and followed me into the hallway, his expression somber.

"I think there's a door just over here?" I offered, finding it very difficult to look him in the eyes.

"Yes. That's how we walk to the outbuildings." I trailed behind him, thankful that the moon was still nearly full, as we made our way to the path outside the castle. We didn't make it very far before he turned around.

"I'm sorry."

"What?" I asked.

"For last night. I don't know what came over me, and I'm very sorry to have offended you."

"Oh." I blushed remembering that rather dazzling kiss. "You didn't offend me."

He raised a single eyebrow. "You bolting from the hallway indicated otherwise."

I laughed. "I could have responded better."

"You could have stayed," he offered, a slight smile on his face.

The wind rushed out of me. "I think we both know I

couldn't have. I hardly know you, and even if I did, I'm betrothed."

"I thought you said the king hadn't proposed."

I sighed. "No, he hasn't. He can't just yet, but—"

"Then what promise would you be breaking?"

I stood there, fiddling with my hands, trying to come up with an unshakable reply. I had none.

"I've been working so hard to convince people I'm worthy of the position I've found myself in. It feels like I've gotten so close, and I don't want to fail. I'm afraid of what would happen if I do," I admitted. "I didn't always respond to things with fear. Now it seems to hang over every choice I make. Even the one to come here tonight."

Silas stepped closer, and my breath temporarily departed from my lungs. It took me a moment to miss it. "What's wrong?"

"It's Valentina," I confessed, trying to focus on why I'd come in the first place. "She came to visit me tonight, and she seemed fine at first, but we were talking about her family and the king, and she suddenly broke down and started telling me things that didn't make sense." I took a deep breath. I couldn't break Valentina's confidence, so I had to be careful how I phrased everything.

"I was wondering if you knew anything about her parents. She kept saying 'they always come' and then whoever these people were took her parents. Do you have any idea what she means?"

At that he looked at the ground. "I'm afraid I do. Valentina's parents were"—he paused, looking for the right word—"*opposed* to certain things happening in Isolte. They became a little too vocal about it, and they caught the attention of the Darkest Knights."

The very words gave me prickles up and down my arms.

"Who are the Darkest Knights?"

"We don't know. Some say they are nobles, others say they are gypsies. Some are convinced they're members of the royal guard, but no one can be sure. Their identities have been carefully protected, which is a necessity, because when they come, their destruction is absolute. It's inspired rage of the most acute nature in my homeland. I knew a man who lost everything in a fire supposedly started by them, and he went out to take revenge against someone he believed was a Darkest Knight. Killed an entire family."

Silas paused, shaking his head. "He was wrong. Everyone knew Lord Klume to be a good man, but his rank and closeness to the king made some believe otherwise. To keep the peace, King Quinten had Lord Klume's murderer killed so no one would be tempted to take the law into their own hands again. But many people live in fear that if they say or do the wrong thing, these men will come for them. And as no one can be sure of their identities, it's hard to know who you can trust."

"So Valentina's parents trusted the wrong people?"

Silas shrugged. "Possibly. Either way, when the queen's parents disappeared, it put most people in their place."

"Disappeared? Are they still missing?"

"No." Silas looked into the distance as if he could still see it all. "Their bodies were left in front of the castle gate. Everyone saw them. *I* saw them. It was very . . . deliberate. And Valentina . . . when she made her way to their bodies, she made a sound that I've never heard come out of a human before. I still can't imagine her grief."

I shook my head. "No wonder you all chose to leave."

"My parents just wanted to give us a chance," he said simply. "Peace has felt like an unattainable dream for us most of our lives."

I appreciated his hope, and I was pleased that living in Coroa would allow him a chance at a happy life. But my thoughts were still with Valentina; she didn't have the option to stay. I placed my hand over my heart, thinking of her words. "Do you think the queen is in danger?"

Silas was quick to answer. "No. The king needs her. She's the only path he has to another heir. You've seen Prince Hadrian. Every day that he still lives feels miraculous. Yes, he's set to marry this winter, but . . ."

I considered this. "I don't know. She seemed so . . . I don't even have the proper words to describe it. Desperate and scared and anxious and tired. All of that at once and then some."

Silas reached out, touching my arm. "She's probably one of the loneliest people I know. The women at court won't associate with her, there isn't a man in his right mind who would so much as look at her, and now her parents are gone.

I'm sure she's feeling a lot of things. I don't much care for her as a queen, but I'm glad she at least had you to talk to."

All I could think about was the warmth in his touch, the tenderness in his voice. It was getting harder and harder to remember I was here for Valentina.

"I would always be willing to listen to anyone in need of a friend."

"I know," he said softly. "It's something that makes you unique. I have a sense that even those you weren't sure you could trust could always trust you regardless."

I nodded. "Which is why I have to go now. I've said more than Valentina would have wanted me to. I'm hoping you will do me the kindness of keeping her secrets."

"I would do anything you ask."

I bit my lip, choosing my words carefully. "And there are others counting on me. . . . I'm afraid I'd let them all down if I stay much longer."

His hand was still on my arm. "I wish you would all the same."

Tears were prickling at the corners of my eyes, and a hard heaviness settled in my throat. "I don't understand what this feeling is, why it is I can't bring myself to stay away from you . . . but I *have* to. There's so much riding on me marrying Jameson, not just for me, but for you, too. Jameson could choose to send you and your family back to Isolte if you offend him, and if things are as bad as you say, I don't want to put your lives in danger. Scarlet means too much to me."

"Just Scarlet?" he asked softly.

I paused. "No. You. *You* mean too much to me."

In the little light the stars were granting us, I could see his eyes were glassy. "And anything that could hurt you would pain me. It seems we lose either way."

I nodded, tears spilling over. "I believe life will give us happiness that we can't see just yet." I gestured to the sky. "There are stars now, little glimmers of light. But soon, the sun will come. We need only wait."

"But *you* are my sun, Hollis."

It was different from what Jameson had said about me a dozen times before. He'd said I was *the* sun, bright but distant, shining on everything in reach. Being Silas's sun alone made me feel like I had a reason to rise in the first place.

"I promise to keep my distance. I won't seek you out or speak to you anymore. And I'm sure you won't need any more jewelry made for emergency royal visits."

I nodded.

"Good. That will help." He swallowed. "Before I never speak to you again . . . could I kiss you one more time?"

I didn't even question the desire. I flew at him.

It was so easy, like falling into the rhythm of a dance or taking a deep breath. Kissing Silas was like something that had always been waiting for me, something I knew to do without thinking. His hands went up into my hair, holding me tight, and his lips moved feverishly, knowing we'd never be alone like this again. I gripped his shirt, pulling him in close, wanting to remember how he always smelled faintly of dying embers.

Too soon, he pulled away, looking into my eyes. "And now I must get back to my family."

I nodded. "Goodbye, Silas Eastoffe."

"Goodbye, Hollis Brite."

He stepped back, falling into a deep bow, and using every last bit of willpower I had in my body, I turned and walked away.

TWENTY-ONE

"Hollis," Delia Grace whispered, pulling me from sleep.

"Mmm?"

"There's a message for you." I glanced up to find Delia Grace standing over me, concern flashing across her face. "Goodness, your eyes are red. Have you been crying?"

In an instant, visions of the night before flooded through me.

It had taken hours for exhaustion to silence my head and even longer for it to steady my heart. I had no idea how much sleep I'd gotten, except to say it wasn't much.

"No," I said firmly, trying to smile. "I think something must have irritated them last night."

Delia Grace set herself on the edge of my bed, lifting my chin so she could see them better. I didn't like her looking so deeply into my eyes; I kept getting the feeling she knew my thoughts better than I did.

"I'm going to soak a towel in cool water, and you're going to gently press it against your eyes. We can't have you meeting with the king and queen like this."

"What?" I asked.

"Sorry," she said, shaking her head, standing to fetch a towel. "That was the message for you: King Jameson *demands* your presence for a meeting with King Quinten and Queen Valentina this morning."

"Demands?" I asked, swallowing. Immediately, I thought that someone knew something, but I'd been very careful with Silas, and it was all over now. No, it must be something else.

"I think the black dress today, Delia Grace. The one with the red in the sleeves?"

She nodded. "Very nice. That's a much more serious look. And I think we have a headdress that will do nicely. You lie down with this," she said, bringing over the wet cloth. "I will have everything ready in no time."

I shook my head. "What would I do without you?"

"We've already been over this, Hollis. You'd drown."

I pressed the cloth onto my eyes and managed to get the swelling mostly gone. Once I put myself together, no one would even notice. I had to do little more than stand still while my hair was brushed and my dress was tied on. When it was time to head out, Nora and Delia Grace lined up behind me, my own little army. I had to admit I felt better with them by my side.

People milled about the hallways and the Great Room, and I walked up to the guards by the king's door without hesitation. "I have been summoned by His Majesty."

"Yes, my lady," the guard replied. "He's expecting you."

He held the door for me but stopped Delia Grace and Nora before they could follow.

"This is private, ladies," he said, and I watched helplessly as we were separated by the large wooden door.

I steadied myself with a deep breath as I walked in to find Jameson and King Quinten sitting at a table with papers laid out before them. A few others stood against the wall, holy men and members of the privy council, all poring over books of the law or other notes. The most surprising addition to the party was my parents, who hadn't spoken to me since my lessons the other day.

I briefly took in their smug expressions before Jameson leaped to his feet to greet me.

"My own heart!" he sang, holding out his arms. "Are you well today?"

"I am." I hoped he couldn't feel my trembling hands. "I feel I've scarcely gotten to see you these past few days, so merely being in your presence brings me joy."

It used to be so easy to flatter Jameson, to say the words I knew would cheer him. Now it felt like chewing gravel to get those lines out.

He smiled, caressing my cheek. "You are right; I've been very occupied, and I promise to make it up to you once our guests leave. Come, stand by my chair."

I followed and dutifully took my place. It was difficult to feel comfortable, however, with King Quinten sneaking disapproving glances at me.

"At least yours arrives on time," he muttered.

Not a second later, the last member of our party, Valentina, dashed into the room. She kept her hand positioned over her stomach.

"My deepest apologies," she began calmly. "I was . . . indisposed."

King Quinten seemed satisfied with that and turned his attention back to Jameson. "So you say your wedding will be when?"

Jameson smiled. "I didn't. There are some details I'm finalizing," he said, raising his hand to touch mine where it rested on the back of his chair. "But you will be getting news of my plans soon enough."

Quinten nodded at this. "And you're sure she is from good stock?"

I tried to keep my face steady. I didn't like being spoken of like a horse—a horse who was clearly in the room, at that.

Jameson straightened in his chair. "Are your eyes failing? All you need do is look at her."

Unimpressed, Quinten nodded toward my parents. "Didn't they say she was the only one? What if she is barren? Or only gives you a single child?"

I saw the skin above Jameson's collar turning a disturbing shade of red. I placed my hand on his shoulder and addressed the king myself.

"Your Majesty, you yourself ought to know that a man with a single child is not diminished in any way. He is merely . . . focused on that single heir."

Jameson smirked up at me. None of us could call Hadrian a smashing success, but who did this man think he was, coming after children who hadn't yet been dreamed up when his was knocking on the door of the Reaper?

Quinten's eyes were cold, obviously displeased. "You were not invited to speak."

"I value all opinions of the Lady Hollis," Jameson insisted, though this was contradictory to what he'd told me the other day. "Her joy in life and curious mind are some of her most treasured attributes."

Quinten rolled his eyes. Valentina had told me to be thankful for what I had, and I tried to appreciate that Jameson at least had the kindness to lie about how important I was.

"Her reply alone ought to be proof enough of her health, not just in mind and spirit, but in body as well." Jameson spoke with such passion, it was easy to see how I'd fallen for him. I hoped it would be enough to make me do it again. "I trust that Hollis will produce a fine heir for Coroa with a half dozen to spare."

I looked away, tucking my hair behind my ears. What had been insulting a moment ago was now agonizingly personal. And of all the things to be discussing, why were we talking about my potential for bearing children?

Quinten kept looking me over, measuring me in his mind as if I were for sale. "And your choice is unswayable?" he asked as if he hoped Jameson had another lover hidden in the North Wing somewhere.

Jameson looked up at me, his dark eyes so adoring. Pangs of guilt flooded my heart, because there was a part of me wishing he'd had a lover as well. "My affection for Hollis is fixed and irrevocable. If you want me to sign this, then you need to know her signature will be beside mine."

The shame came in waves, crashing again and again. He'd put me in the queen's rooms, and he'd let me wear jewels reserved for royalty, and here he was, ready to put my name on a matter of state.

A holy man raised his hand, and Jameson nodded at him to speak.

"Your Majesty, while you have made your intentions clear as regards Lady Hollis, by law you cannot put her name on the document before you are married."

Jameson huffed. "This is a ridiculous triviality. She's as good as my wife."

My stomach roiled, and I was grateful I hadn't eaten yet.

You already knew he was going to marry you, I told myself. But still . . . he had never said it like that before. Like there was no way out.

I waited for the voice in my head to tell me I was wrong, that there was a way I could still please my parents, still elevate Delia Grace, still protect the Eastoffes, and still be a faithful subject to Jameson without a ring and a crown. It never came.

"Your ancestors had good intent," the holy man insisted,

"but if we wished to change it, by law we would have to wait for the next meeting of the lords and holy men, and that wouldn't be until early fall. For now, we must obey the law. For if we undo one . . ."

"We undo them all," Jameson huffed. It was the same rhyme I'd learned as a child, the reason we studied every little rule passed down, not wanting to break a single one, because it was as good as breaking all of them. "If the law says to wait, then we shall wait."

"Agreed," King Quinten added, for the first time adding a hint of reverence to his tone. Isolte was a land of many laws itself, though I didn't know theirs at all. At least to this, we all consented: the law was the law. "Let it have our names only, so the treaty is set. Once Hadrian is married, he and his wife can sign it, along with you and yours, in an amendment added, say, this time next year."

Jameson nodded heartily. "Agreed. And seeing as it's your line this affects most directly, the contract should go with you. We will make the journey to sign it next year."

I squinted. What arrangement was being made that it involved Prince Hadrian?

"So let us both be in agreement," Jameson stated firmly, looking directly at King Quinten. "Our eldest daughter will go to the eldest son of Prince Hadrian, but only if we also produce a son to have a direct male heir. But because girls are not passed over in succession in Coroa, if we only have girls, our second-oldest daughter shall be his bride instead. Is that acceptable?"

I felt my knees go weak. He was signing away our children? He was giving them to Isolte? I gripped the back of his chair tightly, trying to keep myself upright.

King Quinten grimaced, as if weighing whether he could make a better bargain, as if him taking my daughter wasn't enough. Finally, he pushed forward, reaching for the quill.

Valentina and I stood by quietly as the contract was signed, and I realized that, even though my name wasn't on the paper, it bound me to Quinten, Valentina, and Hadrian as family.

He had our daughter. And so, he'd taken a part of me as well.

Everyone in the room applauded, and as Jameson and Quinten shook hands, I walked over to Valentina, embracing her.

"Did you know?" I whispered.

"No. I would have warned you. I hope you trust me enough to believe that."

"I do. You're the only one who knows what it's like to be me."

She took me by the hand and pulled me toward the wall. "About last night," she whispered in a rush. "I was very out of sorts. Sometimes when you're carrying a child, your mind feels strange, and I—"

"You don't have to explain."

"I do," she insisted. "I wasn't speaking clearly, and you mustn't take any of what I said seriously. Besides," she said, stroking her stomach, "I was sick this morning. That's why I was late. That's a very good sign."

I put my hands on top of hers. "Congratulations. . . . But are you quite sure you're safe?"

She nodded, holding my hands. "I am now."

"Promise me you'll write. I am going to need so much guidance. Like how to survive my children being used as pawns." I felt a biting sting at the back of my nose, and I worked hard to suppress it.

"I know. Imagine the pressure I feel. But I will write when I can . . . though you may have to guess at my meanings sometimes. I don't think my correspondence is entirely private."

"I understand."

"Take care of yourself, Hollis. Keep your king smiling, and all will be well." She reached over and kissed my cheek. "I have to go oversee the packing. And rest," she added, smiling.

I curtsied. "Your Majesty."

"You write first," she insisted quietly, "so I have an excuse to write back."

And she was on her way out, joining with King Quinten, who gave me a final condemning look before he passed through the door.

Jameson walked over, rubbing his hands together as if he'd just delivered the finishing blow at a tournament, and I gave him what I hoped was a winning smile. "My father never could have done *that*," he said with a laugh. "And I'm glad you spoke up when you did. Saved me the trouble of charging at an old man."

"It would have been no contest there," I remarked, and Jameson laughed again. I'd once considered a laugh from Jameson something like a prize; now it was so frequent it felt like noise. "I'm curious why he was trying to get an arrangement for Prince Hadrian's children and not the child I suspect Valentina is carrying."

"Like they say, no one can guess at that old man's motives. What else is strange is that he even approached us at all," Jameson commented, taking my arm to lead me toward the Great Room.

"What do you mean?"

"Most Isoltens prefer to marry their own kind, and their royal line has been completely pure from the onset. If he wants another princess to marry his grandchild, he must have a remarkable reason."

"Interesting. Valentina told me Hadrian is marrying another royal as well," I commented, too overwhelmed by my own feelings to really care one way or another. I smiled up at Jameson, trying to hide my sorrow with jokes. "Either way, next time you plan to sign away our children to another kingdom, could I have warning before I walk into the room?"

He scoffed. "Oh, Hollis, they aren't *our* children. They're *mine*."

"What?" I forced myself to keep a smile on my face.

"Any children we make are arrows in my quiver, and I will aim them wherever I must for the sake of Coroa."

He kissed my cheek as the door opened, letting me go into the company of my ladies. Delia Grace could read the horror on my face as we turned to go, but it was Nora who took my hand as we walked. For the sake of appearances, I kept my feelings pushed down, nodding my head at those we passed. And I managed to do just fine until I saw the Eastoffes.

The Northcotts were with them, perhaps saying their goodbyes, and I was thankful to know at least that Etan was leaving the country. But I caught sight of Silas's blue eyes, and my mind jumped forward, imagining children with those perfect eyes and my olive skin. Those children . . . they would have been mine. . . .

I hurried from the room before anyone could see how violently I was crying.

TWENTY-TWO

After the Isolten court left, I found it nearly impossible not to look into the eyes of every child I passed, curious about their families, their futures.

Funny enough, it was the boys who always stood a little closer to their parents, either looking apprehensive or standing tall as if they were on guard. Most of the girls did as Delia Grace and I had done: find a friend to hold close, take in the excitement together, and wait to see what adventures life at court brought for you.

That was how it always felt when we twirled around each other on the dance floor or paraded around the palace on the holy days; it was a marvelous adventure. And I had pitied those girls in the country, the ones out working the land owned by our families, who would never know the feeling of satin or be lifted off their feet in the middle of a volta. After the shock of being given the queen's apartments wore off, I'd felt untouchable, like I'd finally proven wrong everyone who'd ever doubted me, showing my worth to the world as it was measured by the love of a king.

I had it all.

And yet, when Jameson placed a ring on my finger and a crown on my head, I knew it would feel as if I'd lost everything.

"My lady?" a concerned voice asked. I looked up to find Lord Eastoffe and his entire family crossing down the hallway toward the Great Hall. I realized I'd stopped to study a family as a father pointed out a beautiful arch in the castle ceiling. I shook my head, blushing as I stepped out of the way. "Are you troubled?"

"No," I lied, trying to keep my eyes from settling on Silas too long. "I suppose after all the excitement of the recent company, I'm just a little low."

He smiled. "In my younger years, I experienced that feeling more than once," he commented, sharing a knowing look with his wife.

Lady Eastoffe looked at me warmly. There was something about her that made me want to rush into her arms. She'd fled her country presumably for the sake of her children. If I told her mine would be used as pawns in state affairs, she'd understand my pain. "Don't worry, my Lady Hollis," she said. "Crowning Day is on the horizon, yes? Scarlet's eager to come and practice the dance soon. So there are still celebrations to look forward to."

I forced a smile and nodded. "Thank you, my lady. There is a lot of preparation for Crowning Day yet to do. I will send word soon, Scarlet. I think some dancing would do us all good."

Between Scarlet's all-seeing eyes, Lady Eastoffe's concerned smile, and Silas's continued gazing at the floor, I guessed at least half of the family knew I was drowning in sadness and none of us could really talk about it.

"I'll be waiting," Scarlet said with a brief curtsy. I nodded in reply and continued on my way.

I fought the urge and lost. Halfway down the hall, I looked back.

Silas was watching me.

He gave me a small smile, and I did the same in turn. And then we both kept walking.

Dear Valentina,

You have been gone only a few days, and I already find myself longing for your company. I'm still quite overwhelmed by that contract. It made me aware of just how true everything you'd said was. Love might have gotten me to Jameson, but this life will not be as easy as I'd first hoped. After hearing how you came to the crown, I can't imagine anyone gave you lessons in being queen. But if so, could you pass any of that wisdom on to me? Since you've left, I feel like I'm sinking in

"What are you writing?" Delia Grace walked past my desk, a little too close for comfort.

I crumpled up the paper. "Nothing." I couldn't send that to Valentina. I knew she'd understand, but I needed a way to ask that wouldn't sound so pathetic if someone else got ahold of it.

"Are you well?" Delia Grace asked. "You look as pale as an Isolten." She smiled at her own joke.

"I feel a little tired. Perhaps all those days of entertaining finally caught up with me."

"You can lie to anyone else you like, Hollis, but you're wasting your time when it comes to me."

I looked up at her, and she was standing there with an eyebrow raised and a hand on her hip.

"Fine. It's just . . . I thought I could turn being queen into something beautiful and fun. It seems being queen is twisting me instead. I don't think I care for it."

She lowered her face to mine. "You are going to have to find a way to deal with it. You've got it better than so many others. Your marriage isn't arranged to some stranger, your parents aren't sending you to a different country, you're not twelve, for crying out loud!"

I sighed. I knew that others had it worse than I did in the husband department, but that didn't make my own ache any less real.

I toyed with the golden dice sitting out on my table. "Did you feel sad for Valentina, then?" I asked.

She spurted out a laugh. "Didn't you? With that old prune for a husband?"

"But was that all that made it so bad? Didn't you see that, for all she had, she was lonely? Sad? Jameson loves me, and he will treat me better than Quinten treats her, but there are so many other little things I never considered. I'm just . . . What if, once he's older and his love has cooled, all I'm left with is feeling like I'm another possession of the state? A crown jewel locked up in a room with no windows, only taken out when the people need their spirits lifted and good for little else?"

After a long pause, I turned to look at her, to gather her assessment of the idea, but all I found were her accusing eyes.

"Don't do this," she said. "If you fail, you drag me down, too. I can't stand for it, Hollis, I won't."

"Would you ask me to be miserable so you could marry some reputable lord you don't even care about so people will finally shut up about you?"

"Yes! It's exhausting!" she lamented, bordering on tears that she refused to let fall. "I've lived an entire life with people whispering behind my back. And that was if they weren't brazen enough to insult me to my face. Now I'm the principal lady for the queen, and that gives me a chance at being respected. Wouldn't you take it if it was all you could get?"

"What if we could get something better?" I proposed.

"Better than a *king*? Hollis, you can't do any better than that! And *I* certainly can't do anything if you don't follow through." She was quiet for a moment. "What in the world has happened to you? What would make you think . . . . Is there someone else?"

"No," I replied quickly. "It's the thought of losing . . . myself. The benefits of being queen are not lost on me. But neither are the ones of being a private person. First it was the lords and their many complaints. And then it was dealing with visiting royals. And now . . . Jameson's promised our first daughter away." I swallowed, hardly able to speak of it. "He could give *all* my children away. To anyone. To people who don't even care about them."

She inhaled deeply and allowed me to calm myself.

"Each challenge on its own is nothing too much to bear, but piling them on, one after another? I don't know if I can take it."

She shook her head and started muttering. "It should have been me."

"What?"

She stood there, glaring at me with dark eyes that managed to look icy. "I said, it should have been me!"

She started walking away, deeper into the apartments as if they were hers. I hopped up to follow her. "What are you talking about?"

She rounded back on me, leaning forward, as angry as I'd ever seen her. "If you had been paying attention to anyone but yourself, you'd have seen that I was watching Jameson very carefully. I could see he was getting bored with Hannah. I knew he'd be ready for someone new soon. All these little rudimentary lessons you were taking to prepare for Quinten's visit? I've already learned it all. There are plenty of books in that castle to teach you about Coroan history or relations with Isolte and Mooreland and Catal. You were just too lazy to ever go look." She shook her head, gazing at the sky before coming back to me. "Did you know I can speak four languages?"

"Four? No. When did you—"

"Over the last several years while you were off making dances and whining about your parents. All you ever had to do was *try*, and you didn't. But *I* did! I was perfecting myself. You don't even look like a proper Coroan," she shot out.

"Excuse me?"

"Everyone talks about it, about your wheat-colored hair. You've got Isolten in your blood. That or Bannirian. That's part of why the lords complain. If he is going to marry a Coroan, she ought to look the part, and if he's going to marry a foreigner, he ought to marry someone who could offer something to the crown."

My eyes were stinging. "Well, there's nothing you can do about it," I spat. "It was destiny that made me fall into his arms."

"Ha!" She countered. "No, it was my bad timing. I let go of your arms that night, Hollis."

"No . . . we both—"

"I was trying to make you fall on your backside so I could rush over to your aid. I saw the king coming behind you and was intending to arrange a memorable meeting, one where he might be able to tell me apart from the scores of girls fawning over him. I thought if I could make an impression, he'd at least *see* me. But I let go at the wrong time, fell myself, and he caught you." She said this with a bitterness that stung like arrows. "I made a mistake and erased myself from his thoughts completely."

She raised a hand to her mouth, still looking like she might cry but never actually allowing the tears to fall. I was too stunned to respond. I knew she had designs for a better life, but I didn't know how high they went. I didn't know they meant to bypass me entirely. But then her eyes met mine, softer than before. Sad, desperate. I found myself feeling sorry for her more than angry at her.

"Why didn't you say anything? You're clever enough that we could have turned his head."

She shrugged. "I thought I'd have my chance when he got bored with you, as he seemed to do with all the ladies before. But then, the way he kept looking at you . . . I could tell something was happening, and then what could I have said? You have been my closest friend. . . . When everyone was muttering that I was a bastard, you ignored them; you stayed with me. It was the least I could do for you. I told myself that helping you would be like winning myself. That's why I worked my way into place as your lady as quickly as I could; it would be my only chance to rise up with you. But you don't even want it. And watching you be exalted while I've become your attendant is harder than I thought it would be."

"I never meant to exalt myself," I replied sincerely, finally understanding why she'd been so on edge these last weeks. I crossed the space between us, taking her hand. "And you aren't a servant to me. You are my oldest, truest friend. You know more about me than anyone, and I trust you with all my secrets."

She shook her head. "Not all of them." Again, her eyes were searching mine, going deeper than most, trying to see what I was too frightened to show. "I know you've been hiding something, and I can't figure out what's made you suddenly want to abandon the goal every eligible woman in Coroa was aiming for."

"If you were standing where I am, you would understand. It's terrifying to discover that freedom is not what you thought. That love is not what you thought."

When she spoke next, I couldn't pinpoint her tone. Something between sympathy and anger, never really falling into one or the other. "But isn't this worth it? Would you rather be the scandal of court? If you leave him now, you will ruin me, and worst of all, you will destroy Jameson."

I stared off, weighing everything in my head, knowing there was no real way to win. Either I had what I wanted, or everyone else had what they did. . . .

"You're actually considering—?" Delia Grace shook her head and went to leave.

"Wait," I commanded her.

It was a credit to Jameson's taste in women that I possessed the tenor to make her obey. She turned around with a huff.

"Of course I'm marrying Jameson. For a long time now, there's been no other choice for me. So, if Jameson has settled upon me, then you must already have an alternate in mind. You've planned everything else. So give me a name."

She squinted at me. "What do you mean?"

"Who do you want?"

She didn't have to think. "Alistair Farrow. Good estate, a respected name, but not so high up that he'd be in a position to turn me down should you arrange something."

"Do you love him?"

"Don't be stupid, Hollis. Love is the final course at a feast that I'm still waiting to be invited to."

I nodded. "Then it's done." I pressed nonexistent wrinkles out of my dress and went back to my stack of papers, still unsure of what to say to Valentina.

"Wait, Hollis?" I looked to Delia Grace, who was standing there bewildered. "What about Jameson? Do you love him?"

"In a way," I admitted. "I love that he is happier when I'm near. And even if my parents are disappointed in me, I love them. And even if you're angry with me, I love you. With everything that's happened, I love you."

There was silence and a decade of memories floating between us. Beyond anyone, Delia Grace had supported and cared for me through every moment of the last ten years. She had a most precious place in my heart.

"So it's time to let everything else go. And when Jameson proposes, I will marry. For love."

TWENTY-THREE

"CROWNING DAY," NORA SAID, BURSTING into the room later that same afternoon. "He's proposing on Crowning Day, after the ceremony."

"Are you sure?" I asked.

She nodded, crossing to Delia Grace. "Lord Warrington's wife said her husband has been whining about it in private. She's quite supportive of you, actually, but Lord Warrington thinks that Jameson should marry for international advantage."

"Well, he's in the minority now. Ever since that stunt with Valentina and the crowns, everyone's started backing Hollis." Delia Grace's words were tinged with sadness, though nothing that sounded bitter. It was much easier to be around her now, knowing everything. "The sooner the king proposes, the better. Once you're queen, no one in their right mind will oppose you," she said to me, adding a tiny smile at the end.

Nora came over and grabbed my hands. "Congratulations," she said, tilting her head.

"That's very sweet, but maybe let's wait for the actual ring."

She laughed, then sighed, pulling her hands back. "So that's two days away. We need to finally get the dance together, and put the finishing touches on your dress. . . . I wonder if the king will send more jewels for you."

I turned back to the mirror as she went on with her list of wonders and concerns. I sat as Delia Grace brushed my hair out, neither of us quite able to muster any excitement.

"And one, two, three, turn!" Delia Grace called, spinning back to back with Nora. With all that we had to do for the recent visit from King Quinten, there was no time left to prepare for Crowning Day the way I would have in the past. In the end, the dance was mostly pieces from ones we already knew but arranged differently; not even Delia Grace, with all her skills, could combat time. Still, it would be pretty, and everyone was moving together so nicely. Scarlet was with me, turning to the bright sound of the violin.

"Are you having fun?" I asked, though her wide smile gave her away completely.

"I am. I miss many things about home," she began. "The food, the scent of the air. But I do love that you all dance here almost nightly. Back in Isolte, we only dance on special days, for tournaments and things."

"Well, you're a Coroan now," I said, touching her wrist to mine and walking in a circle. "We'll have to catch you up on years and years of dancing. Though maybe Delia Grace would be a better instructor. She's always been the superior dancer."

Delia Grace gave us a thin smile before doing her next steps. "Not quite good enough," she mumbled.

Scarlet looked at me with questioning eyes, but I just shook my head. It was far too much to explain, especially considering the role her brother played in it all.

We went through, step by step, making sure everyone knew the moves by heart; all eyes would be on us, so we couldn't make a mistake.

Luckily for us, Scarlet was a natural. Though we had to go over steps multiple times for her to commit them to memory, when she performed them, there was an easy grace to the movements.

"So beautiful, Scarlet. You made me think you danced so rarely that you might struggle. The way you move your hands is particularly lovely."

"Thank you," she said as we moved. "Honestly, I think it may come from using a sword."

"Your brother didn't mention your skill with a sword," I commented, still going through the steps. If he had, I would have remembered. I'd been working hard to banish Silas Eastoffe from my thoughts, but I couldn't forget all our tiny moments together, all the things he'd said. If pressed, I could recall the entirety of our conversations.

"Practicing moving in a gown with a heavy piece of metal in your hand will make you light on your feet."

I laughed. "I suppose. Come to think of it, Silas danced with me recently, and he did a wonderful job." *Stop talking about him, Hollis. It isn't helping.* "Perhaps it's also a family trait."

"Perhaps." She spun around. "My family is very important to me. We're all we have left now."

There was something slightly accusatory in her tone. "That's not true. You're doing so well."

She shook her head as we went through the moves a final time. "You must realize we are not completely welcome here. Our former king views us as traitors, we have to work now, which is fine but new. . . . No one outside our family truly understands what we're going through. I wouldn't want anyone hurting my family . . . even if it came from a place of love." She looked up at me from under blond lashes, her eyes pleading.

I swallowed. I wondered if he'd told or if she just knew. Scarlet and Delia Grace seemed to have a skill for that, for *knowing* things. I spoke softly, hoping the violin would mask my words. "Please believe me when I say, I would never intentionally hurt your family."

"Intent doesn't matter if it happens anyway."

I inhaled sharply, looking around to make sure no one was

within earshot. "You have nothing to worry about. Besides, I've learned that Jameson plans to propose at the celebration for Crowning Day."

She sighed in relief. "Well, that's good. And we'll be leaving soon after, anyway."

I dropped my hands. "What?"

Delia Grace and Nora went through the moves, though their eyes were decidedly fixed on us. Scarlet looked at their curious faces before turning back to me.

"I . . . I told you," she began quietly. "That was always the plan. We want to live a quiet life, a life that belongs to us. Finally." She breathed the last word as if she were very tired. "Since we arrived, we've been making inquiries for property, and we've found a manor with good lands out in the country. We've been receiving commissions for work, and it looks like we'd be able to support ourselves, with or without income from the land. We're leaving."

I clutched my hands in front of me and worked to pull a smile to my face. "Valentina made me aware of how . . . strenuous court life in Isolte can be. It's no wonder you long for the peace of the country. How lucky am I to get to show you off at least once before you go? Come, let's finish our practice."

I was exhausted, unable to put anything into the dance beyond the basic moves. And once we finished, I wordlessly walked through my apartments to the back rooms. I'd never done anything like that before, and everyone was wise enough to understand that meant I didn't want to be followed.

Settling in on a seat beneath a window, I looked out over the river, over the sprawling city, to the plains in the distance as far as my eyes would reach. Somewhere past that line, the Eastoffes would make their home. I told myself this was a good thing. If Silas left, it would remove all temptation to speak to him, to ruin the brightest thing in my life. It would make it so much easier to see Jameson anew, to remember how he loved to lavish me with gifts and affection.

This was someone removing my shoe and taking the pebble out; I would walk steadier from here on out.

So it made no sense that I sat there, taking in the best view the palace could offer, crying until my tears ran dry.

TWENTY-FOUR

When I woke up on Crowning Day, it didn't feel like it usually did. It was so very average. Plain weather, plain sun, plain me.

"Hollis," Delia Grace said quietly, pulling back the curtains on my poster bed. "You have a delivery."

"What?"

"My guess is it's for tonight. No ordinary old headdress would do for you, would it?" she said, a pang of longing bleeding into her voice. With a sad but resolute smile, she held out a hand to help me from the bed.

"Have you opened the box yet?"

She shook her head. "It's only just arrived, and we'd never open something for you, my lady."

I gave her a weak smile. "Very well." She held out a robe, and I stepped into it. "Let's go take a look," I said as I marched over and opened the box.

The sight of three perfect crowns set in black velvet was enough to leave me breathless. I ran my fingers over them, taking in how unique they were. The first was mostly gold and looked similar to the Crown of Estus, while the other two were much more bejeweled. The second was primarily covered in rubies that suited Coroan red, and the final was much more pointed and covered in diamonds.

"The third is my favorite," Nora insisted. "But you'd look stunning in any of them."

"What do you think, Hollis?" Delia Grace asked. "The first one looks like—"

"The Crown of Estus," I finished. "I thought that, too."

"You'd match. That sends a message."

It certainly would. But I smiled to myself, remembering an old conversation with Silas. There was a language to our clothes, our choices, one others could choose to listen to or ignore.

"I won't be wearing any of these. Don't send them back, though," I ordered. "I want my choice to be a surprise."

"The jealous side of me is reluctant to admit this," Delia Grace began, "but I think you may stop hearts tonight."

"Do you like it?"

"It suits you. Better than any of those stuffy crowns would have, for sure." She moved beside me to look in the mirror, and I couldn't help but think she was right; this was me.

Silas had once made a joke about me belonging in a crown

of flowers, and now I was wearing the biggest and most fragrant blooms I could find atop my head. I'd even managed to stick a few pins with jewels on it to hold it to my hair, and they caught the light, making it all the more special.

I didn't think I'd ever love a crown as much as this one, and I'd only be able to wear it once.

Beside me, I could see Delia Grace's shoulders sinking. She, too, had flowers in her hair, though none quite so dazzling as mine. It was yet another instance where Delia Grace was forced to accept having things one step below mine. I thought it must really be bothering her now, in the moment she had to accept her hopes for the crown were truly over.

"I need you to know," I said, "that if your plan had worked, if it had been you, I'd have done my absolute best to attend you. Though I don't think anyone could have done what you have in these last few weeks. Honestly, Delia Grace, I'll never be able to thank you enough."

She rested her head against mine. "Just wrap Lord Farrow up in a nice big ribbon, and that'll do."

I giggled. "Absolutely. If I can, I'll see that you are married before I am."

"You will?"

"You've spent a long time waiting for things to happen. So long as you're pleased with him, I can't see a reason to wait."

She crushed me in a hug, her eyes welling up. I hadn't seen her cry since we were thirteen, after a particularly terrible bout of being teased. She vowed after that no one would see her cry again. If she'd ever so much as let a tear slip, I never knew about it.

The moment was broken by Mother marching through the door, still refusing to knock.

"What in the world are you wearing?"

My face fell instantly. "What's wrong?" I looked back at the mirror, turning to take in every angle.

"Take those flowers off your head. You're a lady; you need to be wearing a proper crown for Crowning Day." She pointed to her own head, where she was wearing a small crown that had been passed down through the generations of the Parth family. It was not so grand as the one she'd lost, but it was old, and that would do.

I sighed. "Oh, is that all? I chose these on purpose."

"Well, take them *off* on purpose." She walked back to the receiving area, knowing exactly what was in the box on my table. "King Jameson sent you perfectly gorgeous crowns. Just look at this!" she said, holding up the one encrusted with rubies.

"It's beautiful, Mother. But it's not for me."

She set it back down. "No, no. Come and look again. The lords won't like this at all." She grabbed me by the arm and pulled me over to the box.

"I don't care what they think of me." And I didn't say it, but I didn't care much what Jameson thought, either.

"You should. The king needs them, and you need the king."

"No, I don't. I just can't do—"

"Hollis, you will listen to me!"

I took her by the shoulders, forcing her to look into my eyes and speaking with a calm, steady voice. "I know exactly who I am. And I'm content with it." I touched her cheek. "You're my mother. I wish you could be content with me, too."

Her eyes darted all around my face as if she were seeing me, truly seeing me, for the very first time. Maybe I only imagined the tears in her eyes, but her tone was much softer when she finally answered me.

"I suppose they look right on you. Oh . . . are there jewels in there, too?"

"Yes! Do you like them?" I did a turn so they could all catch the light.

She nodded, a whisper of a smile on her face. "Yes, I think I do."

Delia Grace clapped her hands. "Come on, ladies. We can't have our future queen arriving late."

"Are you staying with me or going with Father?" I asked.

Mother still looked stunned. "I'll be with your father. But we'll see you in there."

I nodded as she made her way from the room, and I turned to make sure my dress was straight.

"We are ready when you are, my lady," Delia Grace said. And with a nod, I marched us toward the Great Room.

The feeling of entering the hall on Crowning Day was similar to that of the day King Quinten had come, with so many people sighing and staring as I sauntered past. I did feel beautiful tonight, the most like myself I had in ages. I think it showed.

I made my way to the front of the room, as I knew Jameson would expect me there for the ceremony. I supposed most kings didn't have their fathers present for their own Crowning Days, but he also had no mother, no siblings. He was the last of his line until he produced heirs, and that was all dependent upon me. I made sure to stand where his family would have been if they could have been here. Maybe it didn't quite feel that way yet, like we were family . . . but we would be soon.

Tonight, Jameson would be symbolically recrowned with the same ancient crown used on Estus. The nobles who had their own crowns were wearing them, and most women were bedecked with jewels to mimic the appearance. After a short ceremony, we would celebrate with dancing. It was easily the most exciting night of the year because it didn't end until dawn. Crowning Day had its roots in something very sacred, but it was more like a free-for-all for as long as I'd been alive. Of course Jameson would want to propose today; it forced the entire country to celebrate it, too, whether they intended to or not.

The trumpets played, and I pushed my cynicisms aside, ready to be as queenlike as I could.

A hush fell over the room as the boys in red robes came out ringing their bells. Jameson followed, wearing a heavy fur robe that trailed ten feet behind him. He was followed by the holy man who was gingerly holding the Crown of Estus.

The boys parted, and Jameson walked up the center aisle they created, taking a seat on the throne. The holy man stopped at the base of the throne, holding the crown aloft. In perfect unison, the bells stopped.

"People of Coroa," the holy man intoned, "let us rejoice. For one hundred and sixty-two years, we have had one faithful ruler, a descendant of Estus the Great. Today we honor King Jameson Cadius Barclay, son of Marcellus, son of Telau, son of Shane, son of Presley, son of Klaus, son of Leeson, son of Estus.

"Above all people, we are the happiest, for we celebrate a long and happy reign of the most powerful family on the continent. Let us today renew our devotion to King Jameson and pray for his life to extend for many years, and for his heirs to be plenty."

"Amen!" the room chanted as Jameson looked ever so slightly to his right, knowing I would be there.

The holy man set the crown upon his head, and the room erupted in applause. Once that was done, Jameson smiled at the holy man, murmuring words of thanks before standing and raising his hands to silence the room.

"Good people, I thank you for trusting me to lead you. I know I am a young king, and my reign to date is short. But above any king on the continent, I am devoted to your happiness and the peace of our land. I pray for our kingdom to prosper. I will continue living my life for our country, which is growing not only as our own people make their families, but as others choose to join us," he said, gesturing to the back of the room. I followed his hand, and many of the families who'd come from neighboring countries were gathered together there, including the Eastoffes.

"And for tonight, that is certainly a reason to celebrate!" he cried. "Music!" And the people cheered, and the musicians began to play.

And while the lords enveloped the king, I stared at the back of the room.

TWENTY-FIVE

MY EYES STAYED LOCKED WITH Silas Eastoffe's as the room swirled to life around us. I'd seen him dressed in his best before, but he seemed particularly handsome tonight. The Eastoffes, understanding the occasion, were wearing crowns of their own, and I couldn't help but wonder if they were heirlooms of their long family lines or creations they'd made themselves.

Around me, people embraced and complimented each other's gowns. People cheered, already managing to find large cups of ale to toast the king, the country, the night . . . anything, really. But my eyes were only for Silas, and his were for me. He swallowed, looking outwardly how I felt inwardly: decimated with longing for something I could not have.

"Hollis!" I finally snapped at Delia Grace calling my

name. "There you are. We've been looking for you."

Had I moved? How much time had passed?

"The king is asking for you," she said pointedly.

I took some deep breaths, trying to bring myself back to my senses. "Yes, of course. Lead the way, won't you?"

I slipped my hand into Delia Grace's, and she walked me to the front of the room. I could feel her eyes coming back to me, inspecting. She knew my reservations, of course, and I sensed she could tell there was something more happening. There were so many people around us that she didn't dare ask, but instead faithfully delivered me to Jameson.

"You are perfection brought to life," the king said, holding out his arms to greet me. I noted the chalice in his hand, amber ale spilling from one side. "I absolutely love the flowers. Are they glittering?"

"Yes."

"Amazing. Lord Allinghan, did you see sweet Hollis's flowers? Aren't they beautiful?" He didn't wait for an answer but lowered his voice to continue talking to me. "We'll have to do this for the wedding. Don't you think?" His tone was higher than I'd ever heard it before, trilling into a frenzy.

"You are giddy, my lord."

He laughed wildly. "I am! Ah, I'm having the best of days. Aren't you?"

My lips may have been trembling when I answered. "Every day is the best one I've had until I meet tomorrow."

He gracelessly brushed my hair back. "For you, I believe that's true. So beautiful. You will look so lovely with your face printed on a coin, don't you think? I've decided you will be on a coin, by the way. Are you well? You seem out of sorts."

I couldn't guess how my face looked, but it clearly wasn't as happy as he was expecting. "Perhaps it's the heat. Might I step outside for a moment? Catch my breath?"

"Of course." He bent to kiss my cheek. "Come back soon. I want everyone to see you. And"—he chuckled, the sound coming across ever so slightly mad—"I have an announcement when you get back."

I nodded, thankful for the many lords who always clung to the king like bees to honey. It made it easy to turn and run. I must have looked ridiculous, dodging elbows and weaving through couples, but it felt like my lungs were about to burst and I had to—*had to*—get out of that room. I wasn't sure where to go. My ladies would find me in my rooms, or even my parents' quarters. I could wander the castle, but there were still too many people here, with nobles coming into the palace just to be present for this feast. I turned then, making my way to the side entrance where dozens of carriages were waiting to take their masters home once the festivities had died out. I propped myself up against the side of one such carriage and allowed myself to cry.

I told myself to get it all out now. Jameson would expect smiles when I returned, smiles for the rest of my life. But how would I ever stop crying, knowing I was going to marry one man while ignoring the distinct calling of my heart toward another?

"Hollis?"

I turned and saw, under the light of all the torches, that Silas was hiding out here, too, and that he had been crying as well. We looked at each other for a moment, both shocked and amused, and then laughed to find one another out here.

I wiped at my eyes as he did the same. "I'm a bit over-whelmed by the celebration," I lied.

"As am I." He pointed up. "A flower crown."

I shrugged. "You're leaving soon. I thought . . . I thought this might be the way you want to remember me."

"Hollis—" He broke his words off with a shudder, look-ing as if he was building up courage. "Hollis, even in the night, you are still my sun, bringing light to my world."

I was so thankful for this brief moment of privacy. "I hope you and your family finally find peace. And know you will always have a friend at court, should you ever have need."

He stared at me for a long time before reaching into his pocket. "I made you something," he said, unfolding a piece of fabric.

"Not a sword?"

There was a small chuckle. "One day. But for now, I thought this would be fitting."

He pulled out a broach with a huge golden stone that glimmered in the firelight.

"What is that?"

"It's called a citrine. If you, Hollis Brite, were a star, you'd be the sun. If you were a bird, you'd be a canary. And if you were a stone, you'd be a citrine."

I looked at the gem, unable to wipe the smile from my face. It shone even in the darkness, with tiny pears surrounding the base of the whole stone, all set in gold.

"May I?"

I nodded.

He reached up, taking the bodice of my dress in his hands, the backs of his fingers against my skin. "I wish I could give you so much more."

"Please don't go," I whispered even though we were alone. "At least stay at the castle so I can talk to you from time to time. The king doesn't want me to speak or to think or, perhaps, even to care. I don't want to be an ornament with no one to turn to."

"I have to go with my family," he vowed. "We're stronger when we're together, and, though I'm sure I will ache for you until I die, I could never live with myself if I abandoned them."

I nodded. "And I could never live with myself if I was the cause for you abandoning them."

He brought his lips close and spoke in whispers, raking his fingers through my hair. "Come with us," he pleaded. "I would love you without condition. I cannot offer you a palace or a title, but I can offer you a home where you will be treasured for exactly who you are."

I was left so breathless it was hard to get the words out. "And who exactly am I?"

"Don't be silly," he breathed with an easy smile. "You're Hollis Brite. You dance and sing, but you ask questions, too.

You battle with ladies on boats, but you provide for those around you. You love to laugh, but you're learning about sorrow. You are loved by a king but can see him as a mortal. You met a foreigner and treated him like a friend. In a short time, that's what I've seen. To know everything you are would take years to study, but you are the only person in the world I truly want to know."

Tears came again then. Not because of sadness or fear, but because someone had seen me. He saw me and took me as I was. He was right, there was so much more, but good or bad, he was willing to take me.

"I want to go with you, but I cannot. Surely you understand that. If we were even seen now, my reputation would be ruined! I could never come back to court."

"Why on earth would you want to?"

And in that instant, I realized I never wanted to be within an arm's length of a crown so long as I lived. Everything that had been constant in my life now was vividly superfluous. It was intoxicatingly freeing to see it now for what it was: a bunch of empty nothing.

"Come away," he asked again. "Even if your reputation is ruined, you will be beloved by my family. You would make losing my country, my home, everything, all worth it. To know there was one good thing I could dedicate my days to, to live with and for . . . you would change my world."

I stared deep into the eyes of Silas Eastoffe . . . and I knew. I had to go with him. Yes, love was a part of it—a huge, sweeping part that I'd been terrified to own up to—but that nameless thing drawing in my chest calmed when I decided I would go wherever he did.

"Ready the horses," I said. "And tell your family. If I'm not back in thirty minutes, you should run without me."

"Tonight?" he asked, in shock.

"Yes. There's something I have to do. If it doesn't work, I'm trapped, and you should go for your own safety. If it does, we need to leave now."

Silas nodded. "I'll be here in thirty minutes."

I reached up, kissing him quickly, and turned to go back into the Great Room. I couldn't think of anything I'd experienced in my life as frightening as what I was about to do, but there was no way to get around it.

I needed to speak to my king.

TWENTY-SIX

In the short time I'd been gone, the courtiers had already gotten swept up in the festivities. I had to press myself up against the wall to walk to the head of the room so I didn't get trampled. Jameson was poking one of the lords in the chest, laughing at a joke or comment, loving the mood of the room and the adoration of his people.

"Hollis!" he called out upon seeing me return. "I have something I must take care of."

He moved to get the attention of the room, but I pulled his hands down.

"Please, Your Majesty. Before anything, I must speak to you in private. It's urgent."

He squinted his eyes, as if he couldn't believe I might have any need that could be considered urgent. "Of course. Come with me."

He ushered me into his private rooms, closing the door and locking out the fray.

"My Hollis, what is so imperative that we had to speak now?"

I pulled in a breath. "It has come to my attention that you intend to ask me to be your queen tonight." He smiled, knowing this was no secret to anyone anymore. "I had to tell you that I am not prepared to say yes."

The excited fidgeting he'd been doing all night came to an abrupt stop. He stared at me as if I'd taken an axe to the stained-glass windows, as if the shards were showering down around us now. Very carefully, he reached up and took off the Crown of Estus, setting it on the nearby table.

"I don't understand."

"It's difficult to explain. You have shown me such respect and care, but I'm not ready to live this life." I held my hand out. "You once said yourself that this role could change people, and I've found . . . I've . . ."

Jameson's demeanor changed, and he came over, taking me by the shoulders. "Hollis, my love. Yes, I wanted to announce our engagement tonight, but that doesn't mean we have to rush into a wedding. You can take your time, adjust. That won't change my feelings for you."

I swallowed. "But . . . but what if *my* feelings . . ."

His face grew darker. His mouth hung slightly open, and I watched as he menacingly pushed his tongue against the back of his teeth, looking me over.

"Have you been lying to me, Hollis?"

"No. I did love you."

"*Did?* And now?"

"And now . . . I don't know. I'm so sorry, I just don't know."

He turned, walking in a circle as he rubbed his hand against his chin. "I signed a treaty with you in mind. I've sent off drawings for your coin. As we speak, our initials are being embroidered on tapestries to be hung across the castle. And you would leave me?"

"Jameson, please. I don't want to hurt or offend you, but—"

He held up a hand to silence me. "So what do you propose?"

"I need to leave the castle. If I have shamed you, then you may make up any story you please about me. I will bear it without complaint."

He shook his head. "I wouldn't do that. I've fought too hard to preserve your name to tear it down with my own hands." After a moment of quiet thought, he looked up at me, his face decidedly softer. "If you must take your leave of the castle, then do so. I have no fear. You will come back to me, Hollis. I know, without a single doubt, that you will be mine. In the end."

He didn't know that Silas was waiting with a horse. He didn't know that I'd be married as soon as I could arrange it. He had no idea I wanted to distance myself from him and the crown for the rest of my life.

And now was not the time to correct him.

"I will always be your faithful servant," I said, sinking into a deep curtsy.

"Oh, I know you will." When I rose, he nodded toward the door, and I took my leave without hesitation.

In the Great Room, the festivities were in full swing, with roaring laughter and jovial conversations marking the night. I pulled up my skirts, moving as quickly as I could. When a tray passed with cups of ale, I took one and downed it in a gulp.

"There you are!" Delia Grace ran up to me, grabbing me as I was trying to move. "Did he do it? Do you have a ring?"

"Now's your chance," I told her.

She dropped my arm. "What?"

"Now's your chance. You can do it, with or without me," I assured her as I rushed from the room.

Out among the carriages, Silas was waiting with two dark horses and a furrowed brow. He'd managed to gather a few things quickly and put them in bags across the horses.

"I hope you're ready to go," I told him. "I don't want to wait and see if he changes his mind."

"Wait, you told the king?" he asked in shock.

"I told him . . . something. I can explain along the way. Let's go."

"Let me help," Silas offered, hoisting me up on my horse. Grabbing a torch and reins of his own, we set off.

"Where are we going?" I asked.

"You're going to laugh when we get there," he promised.

He took off and I followed suit, already laughing with excitement, lacing through the streets of town, rushing past people as their celebrations poured out of the taverns and into the walkways. Every moment I placed between the palace and myself, I found that my breaths came easier, that my smile grew bigger. I knew what I wanted, and he was within my grasp. I would follow Silas Eastoffe into oblivion.

A minute down the road, my flower crown flew off behind me and landed somewhere in the dark.

TWENTY-SEVEN

Dearest Valentina,

Before you read another word, please make sure you are sitting. I have no time for codes or intrigues, and I wouldn't want to startle you or the precious baby you are soon to bring into the world.

I have left the castle.

When you trusted me with information that could have ruined your very existence, I ought to have told you I had my own dangers unfolding in the wings.

It's quite possible that I have loved Silas Eastoffe since the moment I laid eyes upon him. I didn't know it at the time, but this morning, I find myself at his family's new manor in Dahere County, waiting for the rest of the Eastoffes to arrive. Seeing as we left by night on horseback without informing a single member of the court—not even my parents—and the rest of the Eastoffes left calmly on their own, their journey is taking slightly longer than ours.

The manor here is in need of attention, but it has several outbuildings for Silas and Sullivan to continue their work in, and they even have a beautiful garden. It is in disrepair, but I'm sure Lady Eastoffe won't mind me helping tend to it. She is, after all, soon to be my mother-in-law. Yes, that's right! Silas and I plan to marry as soon as possible, which will be within a few weeks if we can manage it. My next letter will be to my parents to inform them that I am at Abicrest Manor, which happens to be a short ride from my family's own lands. Once my parents are here, I intend to make myself an Eastoffe before Jameson can decide he'd like to attempt to woo me back. When I left, he made it clear he would try, and I didn't want to disappoint him. I feel confident that he will find a suitable replacement quickly. I'd wager money on it.

I hope you are not too disappointed in my choice. It didn't seem like the Eastoffes were too friendly with the royal family of Isolte, and King Quinten made his feelings for them quite apparent. I have kept our friendship a secret from my soon-to-be family for now, but I would like to tell them of it if that would be acceptable to you.

As I said, I know this news will be a surprise for you, but I'm sure it will be a great comfort to your king, who didn't seem too delighted at my place in Jameson's life. I know that I am now only a private person, but I am still hoping you will find time to write to me. Of all the things I've said goodbye to recently, you are the one I miss the most.

Please write to me as soon as you're able and tell me all your news. You will always have a trusted friend in me, and I hope that I shall always have one in you. Send all letters to my family's manor: Varinger Hall, Dahere County, Coroa.

Your dear friend,

Hollis

"Who are you writing to?" Silas asked as I pulled out a new sheet of paper.

"Friends, family. My parents are next on the list so they'll know to come home."

He shook his head, looking around the empty, dusty manor that his family was going to make new. "You left a palace for this. . . . I'd be lying if I didn't say I felt a little embarrassed. I want to give you more, Hollis."

I stood, walking over to him in my mud-stained ball gown from the night before. "I would live in a shack if it meant you would be there with me, Silas Eastoffe. I don't want that life, not in the least."

"All the same," he said, wrapping his arms around me. "When I said I didn't want you to worry about your reputation, I didn't know exactly how bad this could be."

"It's not as if I eloped," I protested.

"No. You simply left the castle with no chaperone to go with a man who is not your intended to live in the country while your would-be fiancé—who happens to be the king—deals with the aftermath of your humiliating departure."

I grimaced. "It does sound rather bad when you say it like

that, but I've lived in Keresken Castle for years. Trust me, within the week, there will be a new scandal so outrageous that I will be a whisper of a memory forgotten in time."

"Do you really think so?"

I tilted my head up, thinking. "Hmm, maybe a week is too soon. Let's start counting. This is day one. If something entirely new hasn't swept up the attentions of court in, let's say, fifty days, then you can choose your reward."

"Deal." He sealed the bargain with a kiss, and it was the most beautiful thing, to be free and alone with Silas.

We heard the unmistakable sound of horses in the distance and ran to the front of the manor to see. Coming down the weathered path, Lady Eastoffe poked her head out of the carriage, waving. Silas and I stood on the front steps, ready to welcome our family to their new home in Coroa.

TWENTY-EIGHT

"LET ME DO THIS FINAL knot, and you'll be ready." Scarlet laced me into one of her dresses with slightly less extravagant sleeves so I could brave the trip to Varinger Hall. It had taken a day for my letter to reach the palace, another for a reply, and now it was time to face my dragons.

"Did you all intend to buy a home so close to mine?" I asked, still nervous about my mission.

"Not at all," she answered with a laugh. "We had four replies for estates, and this was the least expensive one."

I looked around at the ragged room we'd been sharing the last two days for the sole purpose of improving one room at a time. "I can't imagine why."

"Silas made me swear I'd never tell you where we were settling. He said you would be living at the castle forever now anyway, so you'd never know. Personally, I thought it was fate."

She turned around so I could line up her laces, quite content with her assessment. "Fate, you say? I'll ask you about that again when we're sweeping cobwebs from the corners this afternoon," I teased.

She giggled as I pulled her in tight, and I was pleased to see I hadn't lost my talent for tying a gown.

"There. Pretty as a picture."

"Do you want me to come with you?" she offered.

"No, I think your mother will suffice. Besides, I'm not sure how the staff will behave when I show up without my parents."

"I'm sure it will be fine." She kissed my cheek. "Come visit soon, all right?"

"I don't think Silas would let me stay away too long anyway. You have my word. I'll bring your dress back by the end of the week, at least," I promised, going to find Lady Eastoffe.

She was waiting in the entryway, sliding her gloves on. It was a move remarkably reminiscent of my own mother, the final touch to make sure she looked like a lady. She walked over, giving me a warm embrace.

"All ready?" she asked.

"Yes. The dress is a bit long on me, but at least it's not a muddy ball gown. Thank you all again."

She laughed. "Anything for you, darling girl. Let's get

going. Your parents will have a lot to say to you, and I don't want to keep them waiting. I'm sure they've got enough to dislike me for at the moment," she added with a wink.

I followed obediently into the coach, and we sat in comfortable silence for most of the ride to my house.

"Silas says you two would like to be married quickly. Are you quite sure about that? You were just in a very serious relationship," she offered.

"No, I wasn't." I looked away, going through the memories in my head. "It was short. And manipulative. And one-sided. I was so caught up in the fun of being elevated that I didn't see for a long time how Jameson was treating me. I hate to admit this, and you must *never* tell him I said it . . . but Etan was right. Jameson wanted me to be pretty and entertaining, but never to think or fail. I'm not sure that can be called a relationship. Not really."

She shook her head, an understanding smile on her face. "No, I suppose it can't."

"I love Silas. He sees me as I am and loves me with all my faults. I don't want to wait when I already know."

She patted my leg, looking quite pleased. "Sounds a lot like me when I found Dashiell. There were people who warned me about rushing, of course . . . but I couldn't help it. He swept me off my feet."

That was a feeling I knew all too well. When it was real, there was nothing to be done.

We pulled up on the main road to Varinger Hall, and as we rounded to a stop, I saw my parents waiting for me on the front steps. Mother had her gloves on, which meant she didn't plan to be there for long.

"Oh dear," I muttered.

"That doesn't look good. Should I stay?"

"No. They'll want to talk to me alone. I'll send a letter once things calm down."

I stepped out of the carriage, turning to wave to Lady Eastoffe before facing my parents.

Father pointed, and I saw that, just in front of the carriage I'd gotten out of, another one was waiting.

"Get in," he insisted.

"Where are we going?"

My mother crossed her arms. "To the castle. You are going to beg King Jameson for forgiveness and smooth this over before another girl catches his eye."

"I would be delighted if that happened! Jameson deserves someone who understands his position, who's suited to be royalty."

"You are suited to be royalty," Mother insisted, coming down the steps. "*We* are suited to be royalty! Do you have any idea what you've done?"

"Claudia," Father said warningly.

"I haven't forgotten," she shot back. I realized then they were keeping secrets from me, and I didn't have the slightest idea what they were. "Hollis, I hate to disappoint you, but you cannot marry this boy. He's common. He's *Isolten*."

"Mother," I urged her under my breath. Lady Eastoffe was still right behind us.

"She *knows* she's a foreigner! That her son is! How could it be missed? Hollis, your departure has made us the laughing-stock of court. Now, you will get in that carriage and make this right before anyone realizes why you left. The king has been so generous with you! He adores you! And if you give him the opportunity, I'm sure he would do everything he could to make you happy."

"Perhaps he would, Mother," I replied, my quiet voice almost startling next to her barks. "But try as he may, he would fail. I don't love him."

She stared at me, refusing to budge. "Hollis, so help me, you will get in that carriage."

"Or?"

"Or you will be on your own," my father finished.

I watched him, trying to understand. Behind him, the front doors were shut tight, and my parents were in their traveling clothes. I only just then saw the trunk that I'd taken to the castle was sitting on the steps.

I was never going into my house, not if I didn't agree to go back to Jameson.

"I'm your only child," I whispered. "I know I wasn't a boy, and I was never as smart or talented as you would have hoped, but I have done my best. Don't lock me out of my own home."

"Get. In. The carriage," my mother insisted again.

I looked over at it, black and shiny and deadly. And then I looked back at my mother and father. And I shook my head.

That was my last chance.

With a nod of my father's head, the doorman picked up my trunk and threw it down the steps to my feet. I heard something smash inside it. I was hoping a broken bottle of perfume wasn't ruining what little I had left to my name.

"Oh my goodness," Lady Eastoffe said, hurrying out of the coach. "Help me with this," she said to her driver, who quickly came over to pick up the trunk. Lady Eastoffe looked up at my mother, not bothering to disguise the rage in her eyes.

"Do you have something to say?" my mother shot at her.

Lady Eastoffe shook her head, holding her arms around me as I stood in stunned silence. "I've gone through so much to keep my family in one piece. I don't understand how you can tear yours apart without so much as a second thought. She's your daughter."

"I will not take lessons from *you*. If you're so concerned, you can be responsible for her now. Wait until you see how she repays you."

"I *will* be responsible for her! I'm proud to have her as my own. And I wouldn't be surprised if she accomplishes more than all of us one day."

Mother dropped her voice. "Not if she's married to your pig of a son."

"Come," I whispered. "There's no point talking to them. Let's go."

Having the class to hold her tongue, Lady Eastoffe guided me back into the coach. I climbed back in on unsteady feet, taking the seat that looked out at Varinger Hall. I had plucked apples from those trees as a girl. Danced in the tall grass. I could still see the swing I'd climbed in the distance. I think, once, we were all happy here. Before they realized I was their only hope, before I let them down.

I watched as my parents went back inside, closing the doors behind them. It was the cold sound of them screeching shut that finalized what I had already suspected: I had no one but Silas now.

There were no friends waiting for me back at the castle, no apartments to comfort me. My family no longer wanted me for their own, and I wasn't welcome in my childhood home. And so I left, thankful only for the arm wrapped tightly around my shoulder.

TWENTY-NINE

In an effort to make sure Silas and I could get married within two short weeks, all repairs to Abicrest Manor were focused on the main floor. The Eastoffes intended to invite all the nearby families, both as a gesture of goodwill and as a chance to show them they weren't heathens. The floors were scrubbed, bringing new life to the stone. Furniture and tapestries the Eastoffes had brought from Isolte were aired out and placed where they were highly visible. Staff was acquired quickly, and the Eastoffes bought their loyalty with kindness and extra food.

In short time, I was grafted into the family, and much pain was taken to make sure that when it was official, it would be done through the best celebration they could afford.

"Is this the one?" Lady Eastoffe asked, looking at the fabrics brought in for me to choose for my wedding dress. She was lingering over my signature gold. "I have heard more brides are swinging toward white. It's meant to symbolize purity."

I tried to be discreet about rolling my eyes. "After leaving the castle the way I did, I worry white would only invite criticism."

Scarlet gasped at me. "Hollis! If you want white, you should wear it! Can you please pull this one out more, sir?" she asked, grabbing at a bolt of ivory fabric.

"No, no," I insisted. "Besides, Silas says I'm his shining sun. I think he'd like the gold."

"That's so sweet," Scarlet commented. "Then I think you're right. It should be gold."

My happiness was ever so slightly tainted by the knowledge that my parents were just on the other side of the plain, past the forest, and on lands that we'd held for generations, but that they refused to come see me. Too ashamed to return to the castle, they were staying in the country; they might as well have been on the other side of the continent for how close they felt. Without their approval, this was dangerously close to eloping. I was certain the reason Jameson had a hard time convincing the lords to approve of me was because of how much of the law circled around marriage. In most families, there were written contracts where the parties would make agreements upon goods exchanged to prove the match was being done for the mutual benefit of both groups. If an engagement was officially made, it took another contract to undo it, and if a parent made an agreement on behalf of their child, sometimes that took the work of a holy man to undo, if not the king himself. Eloping and marrying quickly without the express approval of one's family told the world those laws were insignificant, and it brought on unending judgment.

One look at Delia Grace's life was enough to prove that.

But where the family I was leaving had nothing to say, the one I was entering did nothing but fawn over me. The proof was in the preparation for my wedding, the fuss they made over gaining another daughter.

"Gold it is," Lady Eastoffe confirmed. "What do you want for the style? I know the sleeves of Isolten gowns can be heavy, but I thought maybe we could round the neckline. Try to pull the two together?"

I smiled. She had said this about dozens of things. The dress, my hair, the dinner, the music . . . All she wanted to do was build a new life for all of us.

"I think that will look quite lovely."

The tailor nodded in agreement and took his goods to begin his work. He said his shop could produce a gown in five days, so that would keep us right on schedule. As the tailor left, a maid walked in and whispered in Lady Eastoffe's ear.

"Absolutely. Show her in at once."

My heart leaped up into my chest. My mother was here, I just knew it. She was going to give me her blessing and let me wear a family heirloom and everything was going to be all right.

But my mother did not walk through the door. It was an older lady who looked to be a servant. She came over and curtsied before me.

"My Lady Hollis. I'm sure after so many years away, you won't remember me, but I work in your home, in Varinger Hall."

I studied the woman's face, but she was right, I didn't recognize her. "I'm sorry, I don't remember you. Is everything well with my parents? Is something wrong with the manor?"

"They are in good health, miss. They do seem quite sad. I think they regret sending you away, but that's not my place to say. But yesterday, you got a letter. I felt after everything you'd been through, it might do you good to have some comforting words, so I planned to come today. Just before I left, a second letter arrived, so I brought it, too."

She held out the neat little letters, and I recognized Delia Grace's handwriting immediately. The other was a mystery.

"Thank you very much . . . I'm sorry, what was your name?"

"Hester, my lady."

"Hester, I'm indebted to you."

"It's no trouble. It's the simple kindnesses in life, isn't it?"

I smiled. "Yes, it is. Do you need an escort home? Or a horse?"

Lady Eastoffe turned to summon someone to help, but Hester lifted her hand. "Oh, no. It's such a pretty day for a walk. But I best be on my way. Many happy wishes for your wedding, my lady."

She moved slowly, and I wondered how long it had taken her to get here on foot.

"We'll give you some privacy," Scarlet offered, pulling her mother from the room. I smiled at her in gratitude and started with perhaps the more frightening update, the one from Delia Grace.

Dear Hollis,

I didn't miss that she didn't bother calling me Lady.

You were right. The night you left, His Majesty was in need of a companion, and when I went to him mourning the departure of my closest friend, we related in a way we never had before. This morning I was gifted with a new gown. I think, at last, I am where I always wanted to be.

There is other news. A section of the South Wing caught fire the other day, and it was fortunate it didn't spread. No one is confessing to setting it, and though the rooms in question were supposedly empty at the time, my guess is it belonged to one of the Isoltens. They're all kept in that same area. There was a rumor that Jameson started it himself, which is a vicious lie. Keresken Castle is his home.

While His Majesty was out of sorts immediately after you left, he seems to be almost himself again these past few days. He's yelling less, and I talked him into throwing a tournament for the solstice, and the planning has lifted his spirits. I don't have the talent for making him laugh as you did, but he smiles for me sometimes. I'm the only person who can manage to get him to do that, so I'd say my place is relatively secure. My guess is, if he does care for me, he will be very cautious before offering his hand again. Honestly, there's a part of me that thinks he's waiting for you. Though I'm not sure why, after how you left.

This reminds me, there is a rumor circulating that you are a witch. With the way the king was acting, someone said you must have cast a spell on him to drive him to such madness. Don't worry, I quashed that one. Well, I tried. Then there was one about you being pregnant, which, with your carefree spirit, was much easier for people to believe. There's only so much one can do to quell rumors at court, as you well know.

Speaking of rumors, there is one that has been of particular interest to me. Someone told me that you didn't just leave the palace, but you left with the Eastoffe boy. The oldest one, the one who made the sword. They said that you were to be married to him any day now, and that you had been plotting to leave the castle with him for some time.

Naturally, Jameson needs me so much right now that I cannot possibly leave to come and investigate this myself, but if there is any truth to this, I am most anxious to know of it. I think, if this is true, it would do for Jameson what the eve of your engagement did for me: allow him to settle into the inevitable. I think he will be much happier himself once he knows your heart belongs to another.

For what it's worth, I am sorry things didn't work out. Just

because I'd hoped for Jameson for myself doesn't mean I wished
ruin upon you. Perhaps you won't believe that—I know I
wasn't the best friend I could have been in recent weeks. But it
is true. I'm sorry.

I must be off. I find myself in the center of so much attention
these days, and I don't want to disappoint anyone.

Hope you are well, old friend. Send my best to your family.

Delia Grace

I shook my head and folded up the letter. She might have been sorry, but she didn't say a word about wishing I was back, about missing me. I still missed her.

"But I bet she does," I whispered to myself. Delia Grace had a hard enough time mentioning her feelings out loud, so it was no surprise she'd be hesitant to put them in writing. But I knew her as no one else did. My guess was court life was a little lonely these days, even with all of Jameson's attention. I wouldn't be shocked to learn she missed me so much, it hurt to write it down.

Someday, I would mend all this.

I picked up the other letter, studying the delicate handwriting, and, flipping it over, I found the Isolten royal seal pressed into the wax.

"Valentina!" I whispered hopefully.

Dear Hollis,

I am both surprised and not surprised by your news. I think, if I had reconsidered before supporting the current rider at the tournament, I would have been much more satisfied with another.

I squinted at the words. Tournament? Pausing, I flipped the letter over and studied the seal again. If I looked closely, I could see where some wax had been melted away and the note resealed before being sent to me.

She warned she might write in code, so my guess was that she was speaking of King Quinten. Yes, I, too, would have gone with a different knight.

I wish so dearly that I could see you again. I could use another game of dice.

. . . talk to me? Be comforted by someone?

I have been working so hard on my garden, but I'm afraid the very rare flower that I planted has wilted. It's been difficult to stay bright without it.

I paused over that one, thinking it could only have one meaning and hating it.

She'd lost the baby.

I had to sit for a moment and swallow my tears. She'd been so nervous before, and then so happy once she was positive her baby was on the way. That was three now. . . . I couldn't imagine her suffering.

I do love that I have your letters to look forward to, so once you're married and settled, do take some time to write me all the details of your special day. I want to feel as if I were in Coroa again, standing beside you, eating honey cakes.

I'm sorry this letter is so brief, but since my garden has waned, I find myself easily tired. I will send you more news soon, telling you all the gossip about the gentry in Isolte, even though you won't know any of these people at all. The stories themselves are amusing, and I think it might keep you entertained out in the country.

Do take care of yourself, Lady Hollis. Stay well and write soon.

Your dear friend,
Valentina

I sighed. I wished she could be standing by my side, too. Tucking my letters into my skirts, I went to the only person I could talk to about this.

THIRTY

IF HE WASN'T HELPING WITH the renovations to the manor, Silas was always in the outbuildings with Sullivan, working on new pieces. It seemed, despite the rumors of our leaving together, he was still receiving commissions. The people of court had seen Eastoffe work firsthand at least twice now, and there was no denying their skill.

I could see him through the large, glassless window, hammering away on metal as Sullivan appeared to be polishing a piece toward the back.

"Good afternoon, sir," I said, setting myself down on the window ledge.

"My lady!" Silas called, wiping sweat from his face before coming over and kissing me. In the corner, Sullivan stashed his work under some straw. "To what do I owe the honor of your company?"

"I had a question for you."

Quietly, Sullivan crept out the door. If anyone took the time to watch, it was impossible to miss how sweet he was. He tended to live in his own world in his head, but he wanted to offer others privacy, too. Just in case.

"What do you want to know?"

"Do you remember how I was in charge of entertaining Valentina?"

He laughed. "Yes. And I remember you doing a smashing job because no one—I mean, *no one*—in the Isolten court could get her to smile, let alone talk."

"It felt like quite an accomplishment at the time. I wasn't sure, after we spoke, if you realized just how close Valentina and I were."

Silas raised his eyebrows, looking over at me. "I realized. As much as I was wishing you'd come just to speak to me, I could tell how worried you were for her. I was hoping it would be a very short-lived friendship."

I grimaced. "I know you and the Isolten royal family aren't exactly on good terms."

"You don't know the half of it."

"But all the same, I care about Valentina. She's entrusted me with some very important secrets."

He squinted, crossing his arms. "Such as?"

I sighed. "She just had a miscarriage. It's the third one she's lost."

Silas stood there, gaping at me. "Are you certain?"

"Yes. She told me under strict confidence about the first

two when she visited, and she just wrote me about the third. I'm worried for her."

He ran his fingers through his hair. "Three . . . I have to tell Father."

"No!" I insisted, putting my hands up. "I promised I'd keep her secret, and she trusts me. I'm only telling you so I can explain my following, very unreasonable request."

"Which is?"

"Do you . . . could we go to Isolte sometime soon?"

"Hollis." His face was aghast and his tone flat.

"Not for long!" I promised. "I know that Valentina is all alone, and I'm sure she's afraid the king may divorce her—or worse—now that she's lost a third child. I want her to know she has a friend."

"Then write her a letter."

"It's not the same!" I protested.

He shook his head, staring back at the fire. "I resigned myself to the fact that I wouldn't be able to give you the life you were going to have at the palace—"

"I don't want that life," I interjected.

"And I promised myself that, so long as it was in my power, I'd give you everything you ever asked for." He came closer, lowering his voice. "But Isolte is a dangerous place for my family. The king doesn't trust us, and we're not sure if the Darkest Knights would tolerate us, even for a visit. For goodness' sake, I was the one who convinced my family to finally leave." He clasped my hands tightly. "I can't go back there. Not now . . . maybe not ever."

I dropped my head but tried to not look too disappointed. Running off had caused much more of a mess than I'd bargained for, and I kept worrying I was taking things away from Silas instead of adding to his life. I didn't want this to be something else he worried about for my sake.

"You're right. I'm sorry. I'll write Valentina and try to be a comfort that way."

He kissed my forehead. "I hate to say no. For now, we need to take time for ourselves, start our lives." He smiled. "I feel like I've been waiting for you for ages."

"Well, not much longer, sir."

"Not much longer at all." He smiled, and the world felt right. I couldn't wait to become an Eastoffe.

"By the way," I said, walking back to the manor, "Delia Grace, who has been gifted a dress by the king, has heard rumors I'm to be married, and is *very concerned* about their validity."

He laughed heartily. "I'll bet she is. Tell her you actually ran off with some gypsies. Oh! No, no! Tell her you joined the monks of Catal and are now living out of a cave. I've got tools! We could carve your letter into a rock!"

"If we find any big enough."

I walked back, thinking I did need to tell Valentina something to encourage her, and I knew Delia Grace was probably pacing her room at this very moment wondering if I was a married woman or not.

Still, with all of that, there was only one letter I could think about writing today.

Blessed Mother and Father,

I'm sorry. I know I have disappointed you, not only with refusing to marry the king, but with the several years of squandered attention that led up to today. I rarely behaved the way you wished I would. Some of that is simply my nature, but the rest, I cannot explain. I didn't aim to be unruly. I simply wanted to find the joy in everything, and it's difficult to do that while sitting still and saying nothing. I apologize for letting you down.

I can't undo what's been done, but I do believe, in my heart of hearts, that His Majesty will find someone far better to wed, someone who will be a superior leader for Coroa. Even with my best intentions, my leadership would have proven disastrous, and I hope that my absence from my king's life will ultimately benefit the people of Coroa far more than my presence in it would have.

I believe I've found my equal in Silas Eastoffe. I know you're unhappy because he doesn't exactly live like a gentleman, even though his family is an old one in Isolte. And I know you're not pleased because he isn't Coroan, but I think this snubbing of Isoltens has gotten our people nowhere. The handful I truly know, I really care for. And I can't pretend I don't know better anymore.

I love Silas, and I'm marrying him in two days. I'm sending this to you as a last hope that you will find a way to forgive me and be present on the most important day of my life.

No, I wasn't the boy you hoped for. No, I didn't become queen. And yes, I shamed our family publicly. But why does *any of this matter? The games of court will put you into an early grave if you let yourself be swept up in them. You are still members of one of the strongest family lines in Coroa. You still have land and assets that put you above the majority of the country. And you still have a daughter who desperately wants to be in your lives. Please consider coming to my wedding. If not, I will wait until you are ready to see me again, trusting that this day will come. I may be poor in many other skills, but I've become exceedingly talented at hoping.*

   Two days from now, five in the evening at Abicrest Manor.
   With all my love,
   Your Daughter Hollis

THIRTY-ONE

"WITH THIS RING, I TAKE thee, Hollis Brite, as my wife. With my body, I swear to you my loyal service. With my heart, I swear to you my unending faithfulness. And with my life, I swear to you my devoted provision, for as long as our God should deem."

The ring that Silas made himself slid down my finger. After all the jewels I'd worn over the last few months, I asked for something simple, and though he disagreed, he delivered. Once the thin golden band was in place, I turned to face him, ready to recite the vows myself.

"With this ring, I take thee, Silas Eastoffe, as my husband. With my body, I swear to you my loyal service. With my heart, I swear to you my unending faithfulness. And with my life, I swear to you my devoted provision, for as long as the gods should deem."

The slightly larger ring settled into perfect place on his hand, and finally, I was married.

"You may kiss your bride," the holy man said.

As Silas bent down to kiss me, the ceremony was over, and applause went up around the room. The main hall in Abicrest Manor was surprisingly full. Neighbors from several estates had come to meet the Eastoffes for the first time. Many knew me from my youth or shared time at the castle, and they seemed very curious to see the person I'd chosen over a king.

The Eastoffes even allowed their staff, who had worked so tirelessly to make the manor presentable, to stand in the back for the ceremony, and I noticed happily that when some of them moved to pass out goblets of ale, their peers were the first ones to receive them. And there, in the middle of my guests, were my parents.

They weren't smiling. In fact, as the room was applauding and receiving drinks for the toast, they appeared to be arguing under their breath. I let it go. For better or worse, at least they'd come.

"A toast," Lord Eastoffe began. "To such wonderful neighbors and friends for supporting us as we settle in Coroa. To an absolutely perfect day for the happiest of celebrations. And to Silas and Hollis. Hollis, we have loved you from the start, and we are thrilled to have you join what has become the most scandalous family in Coroa, you poor, swindled girl."

The room laughed at this, myself included. I knew exactly what I was getting into.

"To Silas and Hollis," he finished.

The room chorused the words back, lifting their glasses. In an elegantly rehearsed move, the strings started up as the drinks came down, and everyone moved around the room to mingle.

"I have a sister, I have a sister!" Scarlet sang, crashing into me for a hug.

"Me, too! My whole life, I've wanted siblings. Now I get three in one day!" Saul wrapped his arms around my waist, looking to fill whatever space Scarlet left open. And when they were finally done, Sullivan crept over, blushing wildly, and hugged me, too. To my surprise, it wasn't just a quick embrace. He held on to me, palms flat across my back, breathing steadily, and I held him back, wondering if he needed to be hugged like this from time to time but was too shy to say so.

He pulled back, smiling. "Welcome to the family."

"Thank you. And thank you for my headpiece; I love it!" Sullivan's little project in the outbuilding that he'd rushed to hide was his wedding gift to me. The golden headpiece was quite brilliant, sitting smartly on my head with two tiny hooks to hold a veil down my back. Furthermore, he'd placed tiny loops in the front so I could string flowers into it, too, and the result was stunning. This would be what I wore every Crowning Day for the rest of my life.

He gave a little nod before stepping back. Silas nudged his brother's arm, their own way of communicating, and everything—*everything*—was perfect.

"Come here, wife," Silas, said, pulling me away. "I want to greet your parents before they find an excuse to leave."

Bypassing every rule of etiquette I knew, Silas walked right up to my mother and embraced her. "Mother!" he announced, and I stood back, trying not to laugh at the horrified expression on her face. "And Father," he said, reaching out for a handshake. "We're both so happy you could be here today."

"We may not be able to stay for long," my father said quickly. "We're planning to head back to Keresken tomorrow, and we need to oversee the packing."

"So soon?" I asked.

"We prefer our lodgings at the palace," Mother said plainly. "Varinger just echoes."

I supposed a house that big with so few people in it would leave one feeling rather small.

"Promise me you won't go before the dessert. Lady Eastoffe has ordered apple cakes, and apparently it's Isolten tradition for one to be crumbled over my head for luck."

Mother laughed, and I counted that rare event as a wedding gift. "You're going to be covered in crumbs?"

"Yes. But I figure I get to eat some of the dessert before anyone else, so I can't complain."

She shook her head. "Always looking on the bright side." Closing her eyes, she took a deep breath before speaking again. "I wish I'd been able to appreciate that more."

"There's still time," I whispered.

She nodded, tears in her eyes. I could see she was still

broken from everything that had happened, but it also looked like she wanted to move forward. I hoped there was still room for me in her heart.

"We'll stay for the apple cakes," Father promised. "But after that, we really do have to go. There are . . . things we have to tend to at the castle."

I nodded. "I understand. Will you tell the king how happy I looked? And that I wish him the same happiness?"

Father let out a long breath. "I . . . I'll say what feels appropriate in the moment."

That wasn't the answer I'd wanted. I'd hoped for a better future for the king, for his blessing on mine. Apparently, my parents didn't think this was a possibility.

I curtsied and let Silas lead me away. "I wanted them here, but that was hard."

"Everyone's adjusting," he assured me. "Trust me, this will smooth itself out."

"I hope so."

"You can't frown like that, Hollis. Not on your wedding day. If you don't cheer up, you're going to force me to ruin the surprise."

I pulled him to a stop, watching that satisfied smirk on his face. "Surprise?"

He started humming.

"Silas Eastoffe, you tell me right now!" I demanded, pulling on his arm. He laughed until he decided to end the suspense.

Turning to me, he took my face in his hands. "I'm sorry I

can't take you to Isolte. But . . . I can take you to Eradore."

I sucked in a breath. "We're going? Do you mean it?"

He nodded. "I have to turn in two hunting knives by the end of next week, and once they're done, we're setting off for the coast."

I flew at him, draping my arms around him. "Thank you!"

"I told you, I want to give you everything I can. This is only the beginning."

"Hollis, might I borrow you for a moment?" Lady East-offe asked, coming up behind me.

"I can go greet more guests," Silas offered.

"You're going to have a very spoiled wife," I warned him.

"Good!" he called, walking cheerfully to greet the closest couple.

"My Lady Eastoffe," his mother greeted me, and I giggled with delight.

"It's true! I'm finally an Eastoffe."

"Just as you should be." She wrapped an arm around me. "Before things get too hectic in here, I wanted to talk a moment. Would you join me outside?"

"Of course."

She nodded her head toward the door, and we made our way into the garden. The sections toward the back were still a little overgrown, but anything a guest might see looked pristine. The tall, thick walls of shrubs made a perfect place to wander and think, and I had spent much of my time out here in the sun over the last two weeks. Now that very sun was setting over the horizon, leaving the sky a beautiful shade of purple.

"It does my heart good to see you and Silas settled. Now no one can argue over your place, and I think it helps us, too. We're tied to Coroa forever," she said with a smile.

"It felt like such a tangled mess to get here, like it was going to be impossible. But look! It's done. And people came to witness it, to be friendly. My parents are here. . . . It's unbelievably perfect."

"It is," she agreed. "And I hope you remember this moment for the rest of your life. Marriage can be challenging, but if you can always come back to this place, to the love, to the vows, then everything will work itself out."

"I'll remember that. Thank you."

She smiled, stopping. "Anytime. Now, the wedding makes things official, but there are other traditions that need to be honored as well. And it's good luck to have something old, so I'm passing this on to you."

Lady Eastoffe reached down to her right hand and slid a large sapphire ring off her finger, holding it up in the fading daylight. "This ring was once worn by a great man in Isolte. It was given to his fifth-born child—his third son—and it has been passed down through the Eastoffe family for generations. I know our past means little here, but it is deep and rich. One day, I will sit and tell you all the old stories. For now, you must wear this, and you must wear it with pride."

She had stories for me. And I suspected Silas had tales of his own. Soon, they would be woven into my life as our histories became intertwined.

My fingers trembled as I reached out for this ring, one more thread in the tapestry. "It's beautiful. But are you sure? Shouldn't Scarlet have this?"

"I have other things to pass to her. But you are the wife of my eldest son, as I am the wife of an eldest son. It's a tradition. And we Isoltens are nothing if not traditional."

"So I've seen." As I spent more time in the Eastoffes' home, I saw how they did everything they could to preserve their way of life. There were dozens of little details in how they executed day-to-day tasks, and each one was accompanied by an explanation of its importance, delivered with great care. "If this is the custom, then I will take it. As long as you're positive Scarlet won't be upset."

Lady Eastoffe embraced me. "Putting this on your hand establishes you as part of our line; she will be overjoyed."

"You make it sound so—"

We were pulled away from our moment by a high-pitched wave of screams.

"What's that?" I asked.

We had wandered farther out into the tall bushes of the garden than I'd realized, and we couldn't see the house. As the screaming continued, we raced through the bushes, trying to understand. We crept up to the edge of a high wall of shrubbery, peeking around the side. There were at least a dozen horses by the entryway.

"They came for us," Lady Eastoffe breathed in horror. "They finally came."

THIRTY-TWO

THEY. THANKS TO VALENTINA, I knew exactly who *they* were.

"The Darkest Knights," I breathed so quietly I didn't think Lady Eastoffe heard me.

There were more screams, and I impulsively started running again. Silas was in there. Before I could get too far I was thrown to the ground. I heard my veil rip as I fell.

"What are you doing?" I asked, beginning to cry. "We have to help them!"

"Shhh!" she insisted, covering my mouth until I settled long enough to hear her. "What do you think you could do? We have no horses, no swords, no nothing. My husband and yours would command us to stay in place if they could, and so we shall."

"That's our family in there!" I insisted. "That's our *family*!"

She dragged me back behind the cover of some topiaries, and I kicked the whole way. I would not be kept from Silas.

"Look at me, Hollis!" I stopped fighting long enough to meet her eyes, and what I saw shook me to my core. How quickly she had gone from proud to broken, from lovely to disheveled. "If you think this isn't breaking me, you're wrong. But Dashiell and I, we made a deal. We made plans. And if one of us could ever make it out alive, that was what we had to do. . . ."

She pulled back skinny branches to see what she could. It was a shocking contrast, the beautiful sky, the scent of the flowers . . . and the violent shouts filling the air.

"Why won't you run? Why would you even make such a plan?"

When she didn't answer, I moved to stand, but she was on top of me again in an instant.

"I made promises to Silas, too. Now stay down!"

At the sound of his name, I stilled. Why in the world would Silas have a plan for me? Why didn't I know about it? Why was I cowering in the grass when he might be dying?

I covered my ears. I could hear the grunts of fighting still, and I wished I could yell out, to tell everyone to stop. But it seemed I'd already risked too much, and I couldn't bring danger to someone who had made vows to protect me.

"I don't understand," I insisted, over and over, whimpering out the words. "Why aren't we helping?"

She said nothing, only carefully looking beyond the bushes when she thought it was safe and then quickly darting back. Her hands were safely locked on to me, ready to hold me down again if I threatened to run.

I remembered what Silas had said. He'd told me the Darkest Knights' destruction was absolute. I wanted to vomit at the thought of Silas enduring absolute destruction.

The horror felt like it went on for an eternity. I tried to will Silas into living, into surviving whatever had just happened. Then I felt instantly guilty that my thoughts were of him and not anyone else. Saul still had so much living to do, and Sullivan was such a gentle soul that being in the room alone was probably enough to ruin him. And maybe my parents weren't perfectly content, but that didn't mean they didn't deserve more time to try.

After both too much and too little time, the cries and shouts died down and gave way to sick laughter. That's how I knew they were leaving. These men had finished their task and were now joking about their success. It was disgustingly satisfied, the sound of a job well done, the sound of many congratulations.

Then I heard another sound: crackling. We watched them ride off, making sure we could no longer hear the horses before daring to even stand.

"Please," I whispered. "Please." Then I risked opening my eyes.

The sound had made it clear, but I still couldn't believe they'd set fire to the house. We hurried from the garden, rushing though I worried our opportunity to help had passed. I pushed down my fear with each step, desperate to get closer, to see if anyone had lived. Only one corner of the house was in flames. There was a chance we could save anyone who was still breathing.

I stopped in front of the main door, afraid to step inside, terrified of what I was going to see.

"Mother?" A whimper came from the shadowy corner by the front door.

"Scarlet? Is that you? Oh, thank goodness!" She ran over, clutching her child as she wept violently. "My girl! I still have my girl!"

I looked at the house. Nothing stirred. Was she the only one left?

"Were those the Darkest Knights?" I asked, though I was already quite sure.

Lady Eastoffe whipped her head over to me. "How do you even know about them?" she asked, turning back to touch every inch of Scarlet's face, unable to believe she was still there.

"Valentina. Silas."

She shook her head, turning back to her daughter. "I thought they'd let us live in peace if we left, but I was wrong."

This made no sense. "Why would they do this to you?"

"Oh, Mother, they came in with masks down and swords drawn, stabbing at anyone in their way, even the maids. I don't know what happened to me. . . . I froze. I couldn't fight."

"You aren't supposed to fight. You *know* that," her mother urged. "You're supposed to run!"

"A man took me by my shoulders, he held me for a moment, and I thought he was just going to kill me slowly. But then he grabbed me by the wrist and threw me outside. I tried to run, but I still couldn't move. I crawled into the bushes and hid. I wanted to fight, Mother. I wanted to hurt them."

Lady Eastoffe held her tighter.

"They spared me, and I don't know why! And I watched . . . I saw . . ." She broke into sobs, unable to speak of it anymore.

I shook my head. I didn't understand any of this. Hitching up my skirt, I moved to go inside.

"What are you doing?" Lady Eastoffe asked.

"Checking for survivors."

Her blue eyes were hollow. "Hollis, listen to me. There won't be any."

I swallowed. "I have . . . I have to . . ."

She shook her head. "Hollis, please," Lady Eastoffe said, her voice alone a clear warning. "That will do you more harm than good."

The air of certainty around her words, as if this was nothing new, chilled me, despite the heat from the flames beginning to engulf the entire east wing of the manor. Maybe it was only in my head that we waited so we could live and go back to find survivors. Maybe it was already in hers that she knew we wouldn't.

"I have to . . ."

She lowered her head as I pressed forward.

I walked into the house and was almost immediately run

over by a servant carrying golden plates, running as if his life depended upon it. I sucked in a breath of hope, believing someone must have made it, but I instantly regretted the move as I coughed over the smoke.

Turning toward the great hall, where only moments ago we'd been toasting the future, I saw great tongues of fire devouring the tables and the tapestries and someone who looked to be Saul. He'd been brought down just by the door.

I dropped my eyes to the floor, covering my mouth to hold in the screams.

She was right. Simply seeing that had made the entire thing that much worse. Now, instead of the collective group dying, I had a face, an image. I was never going to forget the blood, the smell.

I wanted to keep going. I could try to find Silas. But the fire was set in more places than we could see from outside . . . and there were no cries for help. If Silas had made a plan for me, one in which I survived, I would have to walk away now. Because seeing him in pieces or being consumed by flames would not be something I lived through. And if I walked much farther in, I might not make it back out.

I coughed, struggling to breathe, and ran back outside.

Lady Eastoffe took in the horror on my face and nodded once. I looked over at Scarlet and had to guess my expression was a hollow echo of hers. She was lost in what she'd just seen, and I could see all the ghosts in her eyes. I walked down and embraced her, and she held on to me tight for just a minute.

Taking Scarlet's hand and mine, Lady Eastoffe turned toward the path they'd freshly laid out for my wedding and stared.

"Where will we go?" Scarlet asked.

"Varinger Hall, of course," I suggested dully.

Lady Eastoffe pulled her chin up and started walking. "Come, my girls. It won't do to look back."

But I did look back. I watched as the curtains carried the fire up, up, up. She was right; we had to keep walking.

It was obvious to me now that this family must have seen at least one moment like this before. How else could they step away from it so calmly, as if it was only a matter of time before another moment landed in their laps? Why else would they map out how at least one of them should try to live if they could?

Silas had told me about the Darkest Knights in a way that put some distance between them and him. But there was no doubt they'd come face-to-face before. It was just that this time, he didn't walk away from the meeting.

If we had been thinking, we might have gone by the stables for a horse. Instead, we walked in silence, trudging toward my childhood home. It ought to have given me a sense of security, knowing I was finally going to pass through the doors of Varinger Hall again. All I could think of was why I had to . . . I'd have rather stayed locked out forever. My ears were on high alert, listening for the sound of horses or screams or anything that might have told me to start running.

There were no horses, though. Or screams. Just us.

When we finally approached the front gate, a steward was waiting for us on the steps. He held out a lantern, seeing there were three shapes instead of two, that there were only female silhouettes, and that the fine carriage was nowhere to be seen.

"Wake up! Wake up!" he called into the house. By the time we were at the front steps, there was a small army of staff to attend our needs, including the sweet lady who'd brought me letters when I lived at Abicrest Manor.

"Lady Hollis! What has happened to you?" she asked. "Where are your parents?"

Instead of answering, I collapsed in a heap and screamed.

THIRTY-THREE

IT HIT ME THEN, THOUGH I'd been aware of it for hours. My parents were dead. My husband was dead. I was alone.

"They won't be coming home," Lady Eastoffe whispered to her on my behalf. Her face was steady but hollow, with two clear tracks down her cheeks where tears had washed through the soot and dirt. Even like that, she looked noble. She went to move up the steps and was cut off by one of the staff.

"We won't shelter you," he said, his chest puffed up. "Our masters hated your kind, and they—"

"Do you think any of that matters now?" Hester spat back. "They're dead. And Lady Hollis is the mistress of this house now, so you'd better get used to taking your orders from her. These are her people, and they will be fed and taken care of."

"She's right," someone else muttered. "Lady Hollis is the mistress of the house now."

"I'll see you to the drawing room," Hester said.

"Thank you. Come on, my girl. Up we go." Lady Eastoffe pulled me to my feet, and we dragged ourselves into the main drawing room, thankful for the fireplace. I crashed onto the ground closest to it, warming my aching hands. Scarlet was crying so quietly, only occasionally making a sound, and I didn't blame her. There was so much to feel. Sorrow for what we'd lost, guilt for being spared, fear of what might come next.

"It will be all right," Mother whispered to Scarlet, stroking her hair. "We will make a new home, I promise."

Scarlet leaned her head into her mother, and I could sense that this promise was not enough to undo what had just happened. My eyes flicked up to Lady Eastoffe, and I could see her gaze was unfixed, staring into nothing. She had the sense to make me stay put, she had the perseverance to make us get up and walk, and I had no doubt she would carry us both through the next few days . . . but I could see she was shaken, changed. This thing they said they'd been preparing for had come, and now she was left with the heartbreaking aftermath.

"Why would they do this?" I asked again, not really expecting any more of an answer. "They killed everyone save Scarlet, lit a fire, and took nothing. I don't understand."

Lady Eastoffe closed her eyes and drew in a labored breath.

"Unfortunately, dear Hollis, we do."

I looked up at Lady Eastoffe. "This has happened to you before, hasn't it?"

"Not like *this*," she said, shaking her head and finally settling herself into a chair. "But we've lost people before. And goods. Been scared out of our home. . . . I just didn't think the threat would follow us here."

I shook my head. "You're going to have to explain better than that."

She sighed, trying to steady herself, when the staff came scurrying in carrying trays and towels and large bowls of water. A maid placed a plate with bread and pears beside me, though I didn't think I could stomach anything at the moment. Lady Eastoffe thanked the maids as she dipped her hands in the water, washing dirt and ash from her face.

As soon as they were gone, she turned back to me.

"Do you remember our first day at the castle?"

It brought a weak smile to my lips, even as silent tears slid down my face. "I'll never forget it."

"When King Jameson recognized our name, I was sure one of two things was going to happen. Either he was going to unceremoniously punish us . . . perhaps put us in a tower or kick us out altogether. Or he was going to collect us, have us be one of his most visible families at court, constantly in service. I was shocked when he was willing to let us eventually settle wherever we wanted, that he let us settle at all."

"But why would he do either of those things?"

She rested her head on the high-backed chair, staring at the ceiling. "Because things like that tend to happen to those on the fringes of royalty."

I stared at her, trying to make sense of the words. "Royalty?"

"This is a bit of an untidy history," she started, leaning forward. "I'll try to keep it simple. King Quinten is the direct descendant of Jedreck the Great. The crown was passed to Jedreck's firstborn *son*, and Quinten is of that line, so the crown has been his. But Jedreck the Great had three sons and four daughters.

"Some married into other royal lines, some chose a quiet life of service to the crown, and others have died off, complete dead ends. The Eastoffe family is one of the branches of that family tree that still lives. The direct descendants of the fifth-born child, Auberon. The ring on your finger was his, given to him by his father, the king."

I looked down at the sapphire, completely well matched to Isolten blue, and I considered this. I couldn't find a single memory of our time together to support such a story.

"Besides Quinten and Hadrian, obviously, and us, there is only one other family that belongs to the Pardus line: the Northcotts. Do you remember them?"

I nodded. Etan had made an unfortunately unforgettable impression on me. There was no way that boy had a drop of regal blood in him.

"Between our three families lie the remnants of the royal line, of anyone else living who could have a claim to the throne. But . . . seeing as male heirs are usually the most viable, and my husband and sons . . . my sons . . ." She burst into tears, weeping uncontrollably. I bet she had wells and wells of tears. I certainly did.

Scarlet balled herself up into a tighter knot on her chair, feeling her own deep and dark grief; she'd seen too much today. So I was the one who jumped up and wrapped my arms around her mother.

"I'm so sorry."

"I know," she sobbed, holding me back. "And so am I. For your sake. To be orphaned so young. I'm so sorry, Hollis. I never would have agreed to any of this if I thought you were in danger. I thought they'd leave us be."

"But who are these Darkest Knights?" I asked, remembering that even Silas didn't have a definite answer for that. "Who would do this to you?"

"Who would be the only person wanting to eliminate any disputes for a throne?" she asked.

The answer came to my mind instantly, though I couldn't entertain it as a possibility. "Certainly not your king."

Then again, it didn't seem so impossible once I considered it. The very memory of King Quinten gave me a chill. He was the one who kept Valentina isolated, who forced his ailing son to be front and center at everything though it clearly pained the boy. If he treated people he supposedly cared about so poorly, then what would stop him from treating everyone else worse?

"A few weeks before we left Isolte, we went to the castle

to visit the king and celebrate his twenty-fifth year on the throne. You saw firsthand how old and vain he is. You saw how he torments those closest to him. But you certainly don't want to risk crossing him. So, even though we'd much rather have stayed home, we went. I don't think we concealed our exhaustion at these expositions well enough.

"When we came back home, all of our animals were slaughtered. It wasn't done by a wolf or bear, we could tell by the wounds. And our servants . . ." She paused to swallow down another wave of tears. "The ones who were left said that men in black capes came and took the others, forcing them into chains. There were a few who fought back, and we found their bodies piled under a tree.

"It was deliberate timing and a very strong message. He can't stand a threat to his line, which looks like it will die off very soon indeed. The Northcotts have the highest claim now. Some could have argued they've had the highest claim all along. I suspect he will go for them next. . . .

"But the Northcotts have been smart. You saw they were present when Quinten and Valentina came to visit. They never miss an event, making a point to stay on his good side, if such a thing exists. And though they have lost things themselves, they refused to be scared off by it. They might be harder for Quinten to move than he would guess."

I squinted. "The Northcotts have been attacked by the Darkest Knights, too? So this . . . army of sorts is not so anonymous as some people think? They're definitely the king's men?"

"I don't see how they could be otherwise," she replied with a tired shrug.

I sat there, perched on the arm of the chair, arms still stretched out to Lady Eastoffe. "Then your king is not only vain but foolish. If he has no heirs and he murders those who might lay claim to the crown, won't it fall into the hands of some unknown? Or worse, your country could be annexed if it is without a leader to defend it."

She patted my hand. "You have more wisdom than he does. Alas, you do not have as much power. So now, Scarlet and I are without a country, without a home, and without a family." She pressed her lips together, fighting more tears.

The events of a single evening had torn so many lives to shreds. Would I ever recover from it? Would she?

I looked down at my tiny hands. Too small to save anything, too weak to push back a horrific assault. But on my finger was a ring. I looked at the shining blue stone, remembering now that Lady Eastoffe had told me it was worn by a great man. And I looked at the plainer one on my left hand, the one that somehow seemed infinitely more valuable.

"You are not without family," I said. She raised her eyes to me. "I married into it today, so you have me. It's as binding as any law could be. And, despite my parents' qualms, I am their only heir. This house and property are mine. So they also belong to my family." She smiled, and even Scarlet perked up for a moment. "You are not lost."

THIRTY-FOUR

FOR ONE BEAUTIFUL SECOND AS I woke, I didn't remember what had happened. It was only after rubbing my eyes and realizing that the sun was hovering around midday that I recalled how I had walked into my house sometime near sunrise. I also realized I was on the floor. Looking up, I saw Lady Eastoffe and Scarlet were on my bed. After pushing my dresser up against the door, we'd all settled down for a moment to think, but thinking turned into sleep within moments.

My parents were gone. Sullivan was gone. Lord Eastoffe. Little Saul.

And Silas.

What was the last thing Silas had said to me? He'd said, "Good." I'd told him he was going to have a spoiled wife, and he was quite pleased by the prospect. I tried to hold on to that moment. In that image, a hint of my veil was in the corner because I'd looked back over my shoulder. His smile was impish, as if he were planning things I didn't have the imagination to build up on my own. "Good," he'd said. "Good."

"I've had a thought." Lady Eastoffe had stirred and was moving quietly from the bed, leaving Scarlet to rest.

"Oh, thank goodness," I sighed.

"I can't guarantee it's a good one, mind you, but it might be all we can do." She settled next to me on the floor, and I couldn't help but think that, even in her rumpled, mourning state, she looked so poised. "I think Scarlet and I need to go. And I think you need to stay here and start your life."

"What?" My heart started pounding. "You'd abandon me?"

"No," she insisted, cradling my face. "I'd protect you. The only way I can ensure that your life will not be in jeopardy is to distance myself from you as quickly and widely as I can. I cannot be sure that King Quinten will not come again once he finds me alive, even though I am old, and neither Scarlet nor I could hope to hold the throne. He will always be a shadow over my shoulder. The only way you will be safe is if I'm anywhere that you aren't."

I looked away, trying to find holes in her logic.

"You've inherited quite an estate, darling girl. Take your time to mourn and then, when you find someone new—"

"I will never find someone new."

"Oh, Hollis, you are so young. There's so much ahead of

you. Have a life, have children. It's the most any of us can hope for in such dark days. If my leaving means keeping you away from what happened last night, then I do it happily.

"But please know," she pleaded as she ran her hand down my dirty hair, "that being parted from you will be as difficult to bear as being parted from my sons."

I tried to find the good in this, in being left behind. The only thing I could see in it was that she loved me as much as I loved her, as much as I suspected we both had for a while. And that was something, in the middle of so much sorrow: to know that I was loved.

"Where will you settle?"

She looked at me as if I'd missed something. "Back in Isolte," she said matter-of-factly.

Oh. When she said she was going, she really meant it.

"Are you mad?" I shot back a little too loudly. Scarlet stirred and rolled over, still asleep. "If you are so certain your king is trying to kill you, won't going back make it all too easy for him to finish the job?"

She shook her head. "I think not. It may not be written into law, but Isolte *tradition* states that it's males who count when it comes to royal succession. That is why our line is so much more threatening than that of the Northcotts: they are descended from one of Jedreck's daughters. But"—she paused, thinking of all the little details—"she *was* the first-born, and that sometimes holds weight in Isolte. In the past, there were pockets of people who favored her son, Swithun, and her line has been so strong and upstanding, which couldn't be said for many of the other lines before they died off. . . . ."

Her eyes suddenly went somewhere else, as if looking at a picture in the ground I could not see. "I think the king hasn't bothered with the Northcotts as they've managed to nearly cut off the line without much help. . . ." She blinked a few times, coming back to her point.

"Dashiell and I raised our children to know who they were, whose blood they carried, and how that made them enemies of the king. They understood why we set guards outside their doors some nights, why we visited the castle to pay homage for even the smallest event in King Quinten's life. If Scarlet and I die, it will be with honor. If you die? It's because of our association. That would be too much for me to carry."

I stood, moving to the window. Mother always said that when you absolutely must make a decision, do it in sunlight. As a child I thought it was her way of making me wait for answers that she never wanted to give, ones I always seemed to ask before bed. But sometimes I still did it. I hoped it would clear any clouds in my mind.

"Do you intend to just march up to King Quinten? Tell him you're his faithful servant after he just murdered your family?"

"Indeed, I do." She closed her eyes for a moment, taking her own words in. "I will confirm his hopes that the male line has ended, and then I will swear my loyalty. Even if it wouldn't save you, I think we'd have to go back. For better or for worse, Isolte is our home, and I want to protect it, try to save what good there is while there's still time. Because one day, that wicked old man will die. He will die and leave a fractured kingdom, and I would be shocked if anyone could muster the will to mourn him.

"It's risky. He could kill you on sight and truly end your line. Have you considered that?"

"He could," she allowed, resigned to a truth that I supposed had been a part of her since the day she married, "but my life has been a long one. I have used it to love, and I have used it to mother. I have used it in worry and in fleeing. Now I will use it to guard. I will guard Isolte by going back to it and you by leaving. So, you see, we have to go."

The sun was giving me nothing. I could see it, I could even feel its warmth . . . but it didn't change a thing. I turned, burying myself in her arms.

"I don't know if I can do this alone."

"Nonsense," she insisted in a tone that was unmistakably motherly. "Think of all you managed to accomplish in the last few months. If anyone could manage this, it's you. You're a very smart young lady."

"Then will you listen to me when I say it's foolish to go back?"

She chuckled. "You may be right. But I can't spend my final years in hiding. I must face my monster."

"A monster," I echoed. That was exactly what Quinten was. "Quite frankly, I'd rather face a dragon than be alone here."

"I will write you so often that you will be drowning in letters. I will write even when there's nothing worth writing about, to the point you may start to wish we were never related at all."

"Now you're the one talking nonsense. I love you the way I loved the rest of your family: from the first day, wholly, and without reason."

"Stop. You'll make me cry again, and I already hurt from doing it too much." She kissed my head. "Now, I need to make arrangements for burials. You do as well. . . . I hope it won't offend anyone if we don't make a ceremony of this. I just want to put my dead to rest."

She looked down and cleared her throat. Except for the quick outburst the night before, she'd been working hard to keep her emotions at bay. I suspected it was for my sake.

"And then," she began again, her voice less steady than before, "we'll see if there's anything salvageable from the manor, and, assuming the weather is fair, we'll leave as soon as we're able. I need to write the Northcotts. It would probably be safest if they sent Etan to escort us. . . ."

She spoke continually throughout the day, placing all her energy into her planning, and I was awed. My pain took up too much space for me to think of anything else.

THIRTY-FIVE

THE NORTHCOTTS RESPONDED QUICKLY, OFFERING to house Lady Eastoffe and Scarlet for as long as they should need. A date was arranged, and Etan would bring a carriage to make the journey as comfortable as possible. They seemed thankful to have a way to help at such an awful time, but the whole thing made me uneasy. If the Northcotts were in a similar position, why in the world would they collect themselves all in one place?

"They've made it this far by the grace of Quinten's own arrogance and his seeming disregard for the female line. I dare say it will carry us all a little farther at least," Lady Eastoffe speculated, though it did nothing to comfort me.

"I still think this is risky," I huffed, crossing my arms. "Would you please consider—"

"Forgive me, mistress, but there's a parcel for you," Hester said, hobbling in with her sweetly slow gait. "It's rather heavy, so it's near the door."

"Heavy?"

She nodded, and Lady Eastoffe and I exchanged a look. "Thank you, Hester. By the front door?"

"Yes, mistress."

Lady Eastoffe followed me as I made my way downstairs. I was still adjusting to being called the mistress of Varinger Hall. It felt like one more weight I had to bear, and I didn't think I could hold much more.

"Huh," Lady Eastoffe said. "It's not that large. I wonder why it's so heavy."

On the circular table my parents usually covered with flowers sat a small chest with a letter atop it. I reached out to take the note.

"Oh," I gasped, looking at my hands, which quickly started trembling.

"What is it?"

"The seal. It's the royal seal." I swallowed. "This is from King Jameson."

"Do you need me to read it?" she offered.

"No." I hesitated. "No, I can do this." I broke the seal and turned the letter around, seeing the familiar handwriting. How many times had I received letters written in this hand?

My dearest Hollis,

Though you may think it unlikely after all that has passed between us, I was most heartbroken to hear about the recent

death of your fiancé and parents. Anything that grieves you
will always grieve me, and I write to send you my deepest
condolences.

    As a member of the gentry, you are, of course, entitled to an
annuity. Based off the hope and assumption that you will live
another fifty years, I have decided to give you the entire sum
up front, as a sign of my forgiveness for any past indiscretions
and my current shared sorrow.

"Oh my goodness." I dragged the chest over and flipped
it open, gasping with Lady Eastoffe at the sight of so much
money.

"What is this?"

"The king offers me compensation, which is customary
when a member of the gentry is widowed."

"Even though you were only married for a few hours?"
she asked incredulously.

"I told you, there are a lot of laws surrounding marriage. I
think so people wouldn't enter it lightly. But I'm a widow . . .
even though Jameson only calls Silas my fiancé here."

"I would comment on how peculiar it is, but when I think
of the lists and lists of customs in Isolte, I have no room to
speak." She picked up a handful of the golden coins. "Goodness, you are rich indeed, Hollis."

I returned to the letter.

    I hope this will keep you living in a station that you are both
accustomed to and deserve as a highborn lady and one of the

sweetest women Coroa has ever known.

In another matter that I hope will bring you more joy and no grief, I have become very close with our friend Delia Grace. She is to be my official escort for the solstice, which is not too far off. Perhaps the festivities would draw you out of any sorrow you might be feeling as well. Come to Keresken and let us take care of you. With the loss of your parents, it must be particularly isolating out in the country, and you will be most comfortable here.

You will always have a special place in my heart, Hollis. I beg you to let me look upon you with my own eyes and see you happy once more. It would make my joy complete. I hope to see you soon.

Your humble servant,

Jameson

"He also invites me to court. Soon," I said, passing her the letter. "And it sounds as if he's finally paired up with Delia Grace."

"Ah! Well, that's good news, isn't it?"

"Yes," I replied, though I wasn't sure my tone was convincing. I was still sorting out my feelings when it came to Delia Grace. Sad because I missed her so much, hopeful that she might miss me. Guilty over the way things had played out in the end, and happy for her success. At least one of us could have what we wanted. "Maybe it would be good to see her again. It might be good for all of us to tie up loose ends."

"Then I think you should go. It might do you good to

have a distraction, something to look forward to, and we'll be leaving soon ourselves. This house is beautiful, but it's awfully big for one person."

I threw myself into a chair in a manner my mother would have described as petulant. And in that moment, I wished she were here to tell me so. What sum of money might I have paid to have my mother scold me one more time? I pushed the thought away and looked over at Lady Eastoffe. "I suppose you're right. You usually are."

She chuckled and left to go finish her letter.

"If you'll excuse me, there's something I need to take care of."

"You needn't ask me," she said, looking up from the table. "You're the lady of the house."

Oh. That's right. I raised my chin. "Well, in that case, I have something to do, and I'm going no matter what you say."

"That's more like it."

I moved down the entryway stairs and out to the stables, where the horses were in the middle of being groomed.

"Good day, mistress," the groomer said. "I'm sorry, I didn't know you were coming."

"Nothing to be sorry for," I insisted, touching his shoulder. "I need to borrow Madge for a short ride."

He looked me over. "But you're not in riding clothes, my lady," he noted. "Perhaps I could get the carriage?"

"No. I'm not worried about my clothes. I just . . . I need to think."

An understanding passed over his eyes, and he brought out my beautiful, dark horse.

"If anyone asks, you haven't seen me."

He gave me a wink, and I pulled on the reins as Madge went into a gallop. We rode fast, but I had no fear that she would bolt or buck me off. She, like I, was singularly focused.

Like I had over the last few days, I took Madge through the deep woods, heading west. She knew the terrain and handled it expertly, protecting us both from trees and roots as we made our way to my home away from home. Abicrest Manor.

The mounds of dirt beneath the large willow tree were a strikingly bright shade of brown, and they remained several inches higher than the ground surrounding them, though years would erode that to nothing.

I didn't know if it was custom or just a measure of kindness the Eastoffes chose to extend, but the servants were buried alongside their masters, making nearly two dozen graves lined up in neat rows on the outskirts of the property. This didn't include others, like my parents, who had a tomb in the mausoleum beside the great temple, or those unfortunate neighbors who had resting places of their own.

We had very little to bury in the end. We found two of those sacred silver rings among the ashes. I guessed at which one was my father's, not sure if I was right, and buried them both with their owners.

I felt guilty as often as I felt sad. It was all a matter of timing. If we'd walked back a few minutes sooner, I'd be gone as well. If Lady Eastoffe had chosen to involve her son with the giving of this ring, he'd still be here. If, if, if. If was a question that gave no answers.

I tied up Madge on a low-hanging branch, scratching behind her ear before I walked down to the temporary stone that marked where what little remained of Silas was laid.

"I've tried to talk her out of leaving. I've tried twenty different times with as many excuses as I can think of. . . . I don't think it's going to work."

The wind blew through the leaves.

"Well, no, I haven't tried begging, but it wouldn't become me. I'm meant to be the mistress of Varinger Hall now. She keeps saying things that remind me of my place. But the thing is . . ." I bit back the tears. "All I wanted to be was the mistress of *your* home. And now you're gone, and the house is hardly standing, and I have so much, but it feels like I have nothing."

The branches rustled.

"I *am* grateful. I know that living through a situation where I surely ought to have died is a gift, but I cannot think of why in the world the gods would spare me. What use could they possibly have for me?"

There was no sound.

"Jameson has invited me to court. I can't believe he found the will to forgive me. My guess is it must be rooted in pity." I shook my head, staring at the horizon. "I will offend the king if I do not go, and I have already given him enough reason to hate me. My only fear is, I think . . . I think I will be forced to let you go."

I started crying, wiping the tears with the sleeve of my gown. "I used to feel like there was something pulling me to you. I didn't know what it was, but ever since I first saw you, it felt like there was a string around my heart, tugging me to wherever you were." I shook my head. "I don't feel it anymore. But I long to."

I wished so badly he could answer, that he could just give me one of those quick whispers of truth that he always seemed to have on hand. But he couldn't. He never would.

I couldn't feel him.

"I just needed you to know that, even though I don't feel you, I'm going to remember you. And if I one day find the will to love again, I will only *know* if it's love . . . because you taught me what that was. Before you, every glimpse I'd seen of it was a lie. And I didn't know that until you came into that room, holding a golden sword, silent and proud.

"You took me without a single word. I don't know if I ever told you. I was yours from the very start. From the second our eyes met, I was lost for you. And you promised to love me without condition, and you did. Thank you so much, Silas. Thank you."

I looked around. I would have to lock this season into a corner of my heart, and it would have to keep beating.

"I love you. Thank you." I kissed the tips of my fingers and touched them to the stone. Madge lifted her head as I climbed up into the saddle, and this time when I rode away, I didn't look back.

THIRTY-SIX

I WAS STRUGGLING TO FIND enthusiasm for most things these days, including things I enjoyed. Eating was hard; dressing was hard. Everything was hard. So it was impossible to will myself to be cheery for the likes of Etan Northcott to visit my house, especially considering he was only coming to take away what remained of my family

Still, willing or not, he rode up the drive on a horse alongside a stately carriage that was a shade or two darker than the blue I typically associated with Isolte. I stood at the front steps, waiting to greet him as propriety dictated. His face was as somber as it was when I first met him, which left me wondering how anyone ever knew his true mood. He dismounted and walked up to me, and I extended my right hand in greeting.

"Sir Northcott. Welcome to Varinger Hall."

He reached out to take my hand in greeting, but froze in his movements.

"What's the matter?"

He kept his eyes on my hand. "You're wearing the ring. That doesn't belong to you."

I showed him my left hand. "According to this ring, it does. Please come in. Your aunt and cousin are expecting you."

I moved into the house, the click of his boots echoing behind me. This house needed people in it to dampen the noise. I kept my voice low, hating that I needed to tell him anything, but knowing I must.

"I feel I should warn you. Lady Eastoffe is holding up well, all things considered. She's thrown herself into planning and caregiving. I don't know if her grief will come to the surface soon, but be on the watch for that."

"I will."

"And Scarlet . . . she's not herself at all. I don't know if you were told, but she was in the room. She saw everything and was thrown outside. We're not sure why."

His mask slipped a little, and he looked genuinely pained for her sake. "Has she told you about it?"

"No. She's hardly said anything. I hope she comes back to us, because I love her so much. But you might have to brace yourself for her to stay this way. I haven't known what to do for her, and I don't think Lady Eastoffe does, either. I think the best we can hope for is that time will erase her pain."

He nodded. "And how—" He stopped quickly and cleared his throat. "How are you?"

I was sure I failed at hiding my shock that he would care. Or, if not care, ask.

"The only person I felt comfortable sharing my true heart with is gone. All of my family and most of his have left with him. . . . It's too much to feel at once, so I'm taking it in pieces. And I think that's all I could tell you about it."

I didn't trust Etan with the fact that I covered my face with my pillow at night so no one could hear me cry. I couldn't tell him how much guilt I carried for living when so many didn't. Though I didn't consider Isoltens my enemies anymore—well, maybe just their king—I also didn't consider Etan anything close to a friend.

"I am sorry," he said.

And I wished so badly that I could have believed him.

"They're in here," I answered, showing him into the parlor where Lady Eastoffe and Scarlet waited.

Lady Eastoffe's face perked up, and she stood to greet her nephew. "Oh, Etan, you darling boy. Thank you so much for coming. I'll feel much better on the road now."

Scarlet looked up at him, but then let her eyes fall away.

Etan turned to meet my gaze, and I gave him a shrug that said, "See what I mean?"

"I am always prepared to serve you, Aunt Whitley. We can leave as soon as you're ready," he offered.

"Let's spare no time," she replied. "The sooner we're back in Isolte, the better."

And my crushed heart found new ways to break.

Etan helped Scarlet down the front steps. Her silence seemed to frighten Etan, who kept looking back to me for assurance. I didn't know what else to say; she was who she was for now.

The three of us were a study in how grief changed people. Lady Eastoffe moved on with impressive perseverance, Scarlet folded in on herself, and I . . . well, I was taking each day as it came, afraid to make any plans that took me any farther down the road than that.

I waited outside the door of the carriage, and she gave me one last embrace.

"Goodbye, Hollis," she eked out. "I'll miss you."

"I'll miss you, too. When you're feeling up to it, write me."

"Should I send letters here or to the castle?"

I shook my head. "I have no idea."

She sighed. "Let me know when you do."

Etan offered her a hand, and she took it as she climbed up into the coach that would take her away from me.

"You don't look convinced," Etan noted quietly.

"I'm not. I wish they would stay."

"It's better for them to be with their family."

"I am their family; I'm an Eastoffe."

He smiled. "It would take a little more than that."

I wanted to contradict him, but Lady Eastoffe came down the front steps, the pair of gloves on her hands passed down from my mother's belongings. I was not going to ruin our last moments with an argument. Etan walked away, mounting his horse, presumably preferring to be on the lookout instead of cooped up in the coach.

"I checked our rooms," she assured me, "but there wasn't much we brought in the first place. We should have everything."

I couldn't help but smile at her thoroughness. "There is one thing," I said, turning to face her. I may have disagreed with everything he was as a person, but Etan had been right about how Jameson viewed me. Maybe he was right about this, too.

I started to slip her ring off my finger.

"Oh, Hollis, no! No, I insist."

"It belongs in your family. Scarlet should have it," I urged.

"No, thank you," she muttered from the coach.

Lady Eastoffe dropped her voice. "I don't think she wants to have anything to do with our legacy anymore. Can you blame her?" I shook my head. "You said you were an Eastoffe," she reminded me. "This is your ring."

"I don't know."

"Well, then, wear it for a while, and if you still think it should be mine, you can come deliver it to me in Isolte. Deal?"

I smiled at the thought of seeing her again. "Deal."

"When do you leave for the castle?" she asked.

"In a few hours. I'm hoping to arrive early evening, when everyone will be at dinner. The less attention I can draw to myself, the better." I couldn't begin to imagine the reception I was in for at Kereshen.

"I want you to know . . . if, for some reason, the king sees you and your feelings are rekindled, there's no shame in that. I thought, as Silas's mother, you would trust it if those words came from me."

I sighed. "I appreciate the thought, but I've known for a long time that I don't want to be near a crown ever again. And . . . Jameson . . . I don't know if he ever really loved me. Or if I ever really loved him. My goal is to reinforce how well-suited Delia Grace is for the throne, and then . . . honestly, I don't have much of a plan after that."

"You will adjust."

"How will I know?" I whispered. "If something happens to you, how will I know?"

"I've already told the Northcotts to send word. But you needn't worry. I'm an old woman. King Quinten might have been threatened by my sons, but it's unlikely he cares about me one way or the other. And Etan will keep us safe on the road."

I looked over at him skeptically. "If you insist."

We stood there for a moment. There was nothing left but goodbyes, and I wasn't ready for them.

She bent down and kissed both of my cheeks. "I love you, Hollis. I miss you already."

I nodded, stepping back. "I love you, too."

I so badly didn't want to cry in front of them. I couldn't bear to be the cause of any more pain.

"I will write you as soon as I'm able," she promised.

I nodded again, knowing I couldn't trust my voice

anymore. She ran her hand down my cheek one last time and climbed into the coach.

Etan, looking rather impressive upon his horse, came over to me. "I will keep them safe, you know. Whatever your opinions of me or my king or Isolte, you have to believe I would give my life for my family."

I nodded. "So would I. But my family gave their lives for me instead." I inhaled deeply. "I'm sorry. It's still painful."

"It will be. For a long time. But it gets easier."

I must have looked rather pathetic indeed for the likes of Etan to show me some level of mercy.

"Thank you. And I do believe you'll look after them. I pity anyone who would come up against you," I vowed.

He gave me a quick nod of his head. And then they were off, slowly riding out of my world. I briefly wondered what kind of life I would have at all if they weren't with me.

I watched them until they were at the end of our drive, and once they turned, I stayed outside until the coach disappeared over the crest of the low hill. And then I stood a little bit longer because I could not walk into that huge house all by myself.

It must have been quite a while, because when the steward came up beside me, I noticed my cheeks felt a little burned from the sun.

"Mistress Brite?"

"It's Eastoffe," I corrected him.

"Yes, very sorry, mistress. Old habits, you see. We need to

know which trunks to load?" I took a deep breath and went inside. But I couldn't make it past the foyer.

There may as well have been a wall between me and the rest of the manor for how hard it felt to walk inside. My breathing was a little shallow, and I could tell that if I didn't get ahold of it, I might faint. I clutched the big circular table and inhaled deeply.

"I . . . There are two trunks by my bed. Anything I've forgotten I'm sure will be provided at the castle," I instructed, and that was enough to buy me more time.

He bowed and went upstairs to fetch my bags. I took a seat on the bench near the window, intending to watch the world outside Varinger Hall until it was time to leave. A funny sensation tickled at my chest, and I scratched at it, trying to get it to leave me alone. Then a cascade of feelings washed over me. I was frightened to move forward but knew I couldn't stay still. I was uncertain of the company I was about to keep but knew I couldn't stay alone. I never quite got to the end of one thought before a new one rushed over it, sending me down another stream of questions I wasn't prepared to ask myself.

The slant of the sun in the sky shifted as time passed, and I felt that funny tickle in my chest again. But no. It wasn't an itch or a tickle or anything of the sort. It was like . . . like a string tugging on my heart.

My breath sped up as I focused on the sensation, wanting to make absolutely sure. Yes. Yes, it was the same. And, whatever might befall me, I had to follow it.

I looked out at the sun just as it began to rest on the tips of the distant trees. I didn't have much time.

I ran up to my room, grabbing leather bags from my armoire; Madge wouldn't be able to carry any trunks. I folded up three of my simpler dresses and fit them in a bag with a brush and some perfume. In another, I went over to the trunk Jameson had sent me and started shoveling in coins.

"Hester!" I called. "Hester, I need paper!"

I switched out my shoes for riding boots, shoving the little ones in my other bag. It wasn't much, but it would have to do.

Hester hobbled in, hands holding out paper and ink.

"Thank you." I snatched it. "Listen, Hester. I know everyone is already planning to tend the house, but I'm not sure how long I'll be gone now. I'll write as soon as I'm able."

"Yes, mistress."

"And this box?" I said, pushing it over to her. "Hide it. I need it safe."

"Yes, mistress."

I wrote frantically.

> *King Jameson,*
> *By the time you read this, I will be in Isolte. I pray you will forgive me for once again not being there for you when I said I would. I'm hoping from the depths of my heart to be able to come and bless your marriage to any woman you choose one day. But I cannot come to the castle yet. Like many things in my life, it's harder than I was prepared for.*

I wish you to be the happiest of any king on all of the continent, and I hope my path will bring me to you again sometime. Until then, I remain your most humble servant.

Hollis

I folded it up hastily and placed it in Hester's waiting hand. "To the castle. As quickly as you can, please."

"Yes, mistress. And please," she added kindly, "please stay safe."

I nodded, grabbing my cloak and heading for the stables.

I checked stall after stall until I found Madge. "There you are, girl!"

I strapped on a saddle as quickly as I could, realizing just how fast the daylight was burning. Once I'd finished, I flung the bags across her back and hoisted myself atop her.

She was my girl through and through, sensing my urgency and moving at top speed. I had an idea of the general direction they were heading, but I didn't know the roads that led to Isolte. I blew a kiss when I passed near Silas's grave and prayed that if I stayed on this course, I'd find them.

The roads were very empty today, and painfully dry. I could feel the dirt coating my skin as I barreled down the countryside, hunting for a carriage.

"Come on, girl!" I encouraged her, coaxing Madge into chasing the sun toward the west.

I was starting to think I'd gotten myself in too deep this time. I didn't know my way, night was coming, and I was all alone. Eyes squinting, I searched the horizon at every turn, hoping I'd find . . . a blue coach and a tall, thin rider moving beside it!

"Wait!" I yelled, riding maniacally toward the coach in the distance. "Wait, I'm coming, too!"

They didn't hear, so I kept calling out. It was Etan who noticed me first, motioning to the driver to stop. Scarlet popped her tired head out of the window to see what the fuss was about, and her mother followed shortly after.

"What in the world are you doing here?" Lady Eastoffe demanded. "You look a state. Are you all right?"

"No. I am not." I exhaustedly dismounted and walked over to them, my muscles screaming in pain. "I am not all right with any of this. I cannot go back to that life, and I cannot let you leave without me."

Lady Eastoffe tilted her head. "We've been over this."

"No. *You've* been over it, but I will not be left without a hand in making the choices of my own life. I am now the mistress of Varinger Hall, and I am your daughter. . . . You must let me speak my piece."

She opened the door, climbing down to stand beside me. "Very well."

I took deep gulps of air, dirty and exhausted and not really sure how to say what I wanted to.

"I'm an Eastoffe. And I still wear his ring, and yours. You are my family," I said simply. "As such, I refuse to leave you. If you are heading into danger, then . . . then I can't let you go without me."

"This is nonsense," Etan protested.

"Oh, go back to ignoring me!"

"Can't you go back to hating us?" he shot back.

"I don't hate you," I said, staring into Lady Eastoffe's eyes. "Well, maybe you," I offered to Etan. "But not all that much."

"Oh. Thank you *so* much for that."

"Etan," Lady Eastoffe said firmly, rolling her eyes. It was enough to silence him, and she turned her attentions to me. "Do you really want to leave your people? Your home?" she asked quietly. "We've done it ourselves, and I assure you, it's much harder than you think."

"I want to honor you. To honor Silas. To live a life, long or short, that is more than the pettiness of court or the isolation of my home." I wrung my hands, pleading, trying not to cry. "I don't want to harm King Quinten, if you can believe that. Too much blood has been spilled, and I don't want to cause any more. But I want answers. I want to find a way to make it undeniable. I want that man to look into my eyes and own that he killed my husband, to tell me why."

"Hollis . . ." she began gently, her conviction seeming to waver.

"I cannot go back," I vowed. "And if you won't let me in your carriage, then I'll be forced to follow you on this rather impressive horse. I'm afraid you'll find me quite persistent."

She looked over at Scarlet, who, for the first time in weeks, smiled.

"It seems you are decided."

"I am."

"Then into the carriage with you. Sir, could you tie this horse to the back? I'm sure Lady Hollis will want her with us."

"You cannot let her in that carriage!" Etan insisted. "She can't come with us."

"I don't take orders from you, sir. I'm following my family. And as we know, nothing is more honorable than to give your life to your family." I gave him a determined stare, and he sighed, trotting to the front of the carriage while Madge was tied up to the back. I removed her bags to pull inside with me, and only calmed once we were moving.

"That's not very much," Scarlet pointed out.

"Only half of it's clothes," I informed her, pulling out a handful of gold.

"Is that your money from the king?" Lady Eastoffe asked quietly, as if anyone would hear over the wheels.

"Not all of it. But I figured we might need some. For basic needs. Or bribes. Or to renovate Varinger Hall if I'm forced to go back."

She laughed. "Silas always liked that about you. Your determination. But let me remind you, this won't be easy. I have no certainty of what's waiting for us in Isolte."

I took in the solemn looks on her and Scarlet's faces, and I watched the rigid figure of Etan outside the window. I knew I was walking into the unknown, possibly even death. But the tugging feeling in my heart was calmed, so I knew it was better to walk into that than back into everything I already knew.

"Don't worry, Mother," I assured her. "I'm not afraid."

ACKNOWLEDGMENTS

Hey there, gorgeous. Thanks for reading my book. I like you.

Fun fact: I didn't put this all together on my own. So if you enjoyed it (and, quite honestly, even if you didn't), please take a moment with me to thank the people who put their time and energy into this project:

My wonderful agent, Elana Parker, who has always had my back. Which is impressive considering how much hand holding I need. Also, the whole team at Laura Dail Lit, including the lovely Samantha Fabien, my international agent, who makes it possible to share my stories across the globe.

My supertalented editor, Erica Sussman, who shines my words until they sparkle, and Elizabeth Lynch, who's worked beside her to make this book so pretty.

Speaking of how pretty it is, there's Gus Marx who shot the cover photo, and Alison Donalty and Erin Fitzsimmons, who designed it.

The gang at HarperTeen: Aubrey Churchward, Sabrina Abballe, Shannon Cox, Tyler Breitfeller, Sabrina Abballe,

Ebony LaDelle, Jane Lee and countless others who perfect and promote my ideas. Seriously, this little section could go on for days.

It takes armies to make books, and I'm so thankful to everyone who has put their hands on it.

Northstar Church, who has given me constant support and prayer. Specifically, my small group: Erica, Jennie, Rachel, and Karen, who listen to everything on a weekly basis (without getting bored!) and keep me encouraged.

My parents, Bettie and Gerry, and my mom-and dad-in law, Jennie and Jim. They genuinely think I can do anything, which is what parents do, I know, but it seems like they just do it really, really well.

My hubby, Callaway. He's the best. You're all jealous of me, and you have no idea.

My Guyden, who has inherited my gift of giving good hugs and offers them to me often. Which is great, because I need them.

My Zuzu, who is the world's best cheerleader and makes it impossible for me to doubt anything for more than, like, fifteen minutes.

Finally, but most important, I want to give my unending thanks to God. Writing was handed to me as a rope when I was drowning. To this day, the amazing generosity of Christ my savior has continued to floor me. The opportunity to tell stories for a living is still absolutely astonishing to me . . . and that's only a fraction of the goodness I've received.

And I already thanked you, but thanks again. You're keen.

Hollis will
follow her heart in

The Betrayed

ONE

As the carriage rolled on, I looked over my shoulder out the tiny rear window, as if someone might be coming after me. I reminded myself the notion was ridiculous; there wasn't anyone left in Coroa to follow me. Not anymore.

Silas—my husband—was dead, as were my parents. I still had a few friends at court, but they were far more loyal to King Jameson, and that would be especially true in the wake of me jilting him the very night he planned to propose. As for Jameson himself . . . at least it seemed I had his forgiveness for running away with a commoner—a foreign commoner, no less. Even so, Delia Grace had taken my place by the king's side, and I didn't want it back.

That was everyone. The only other people I cared about were in the carriage beside me. Still, I looked.

"I spent the majority of my adult life doing the exact same thing," my mother-in-law, Lady Eastoffe, commented, placing a hand on my lap. Across from us, my sister-in-law, Scarlet, slept on the other bench. Even in sleep, there was something about her posture that said she was ready to wake in a split second, a demeanor she'd adopted since the attack.

Just out the side window, Etan, proud and irritating on his horse, kept watch. He surveyed the thin mist, and I could tell by the way he kept tilting his head that he was listening for signs of danger.

"Hopefully after this trip, we can all stop looking behind us," I commented.

Lady Eastoffe—no, she was my mother now—nodded, looking solemnly at Scarlet. "Hopefully, once we reach the Northcotts, we'll find a way to confront King Quinten. After that, everything will be settled . . . one way or another."

I swallowed, reflecting on the finality of those words. One day, we would either walk out of King Quinten's palace victorious, or we'd never walk out.

Studying my new mother, it was still shocking to know she'd willingly walked into a marriage that tied her so closely to such a wicked king. But, then again, I'd unwittingly done the same.

The Eastoffes were descendants of Jedreck the Great, the first in the long-running line of kings on the Isolten throne. Isolte's current ruler, King Quinten, was descended from the first *son* of Jedreck, but not his first *child*. The Eastoffes were descendants of Jedreck's third son. Only dear old

Etan—a Northcott—could boast a lineage dating back to Jedreck's firstborn child, a daughter who had been passed over in favor of a boy.

Whatever the history, Quinten saw all Eastoffes and Northcotts as threats to his reign, which was coming to a swift close unless his son suddenly took a turn to better health.

I didn't understand it.

I didn't understand why he seemed intent on driving away—no, *murdering*—men who held royal blood. Prince Hadrian was not exactly the stoutest of souls, and when King Quinten himself died, as all mortals do, *someone* would have to take the throne. It made no sense to me that he was killing off everyone with a legitimate claim to it.

Silas included.

So, here we were, determined to ensure that the ones we lost didn't die in vain and painfully aware of how likely we were to fail in the process.

"Who goes there?" We heard the barking call over the squeaking of the wheels. Instantly, the carriage pulled to a stop. Scarlet was immediately upright, her hand pulling out of her skirts a small knife I didn't know she'd been hiding.

"Soldiers," Etan murmured. "Isolten." Then louder, he called: "Good afternoon. I am Etan Northcott, a soldier in His Majesty's—"

"Northcott? That you?"

I watched as Etan's face softened, his eyes squinting. He was suddenly much more at ease.

"Colvin?" he called back. There was no answer, so I took it to the affirmative. "I'm escorting my family back home from Coroa. By now you will have heard about my uncle. I'm bringing his widow and daughters home."

There was a pause, hinting at the confusion this created, when the soldier started speaking again.

"Widow? Surely you don't mean Lord Eastoffe is dead?"

Etan's horse bucked beneath him, but he steadied him quickly. "Indeed. And his sons. I was charged by my father to bring the rest of the family back to safety."

There was an uncomfortable silence.

"Our condolences to your family. We will let you through, but we must do a security check. Protocol."

"Yes, of course," Etan agreed. "I understand."

The soldier approached to examine our carriage while another walked around the outside, looking beneath the frame. By his voice, I recognized that the one looking in on us was the one Etan had been speaking with. "My Lady Eastoffe," he said, tipping his head toward Mother. "I'm so sorry for your loss."

"We thank you for your concern. And for your service," she replied.

"You ladies are lucky to have been met by the best regiment in Isolte," he said, puffing his chest. "This road is usually crawling with Coroans. They set fire to a border village not two weeks ago. If they'd come upon you, I don't know what would have happened."

I swallowed, looking down, then turned my eyes back

to the soldier. The connection of an additional lady in the Eastoffe family and the direction we were coming from all came together for him in an instant. He squinted at me and then looked back to Etan for confirmation.

"My cousin Silas's widow," he explained.

The soldier shook his head. "Can't believe Silas is gone . . . or that he married," he added, looking back at me. In his head, he seemed to be amending his thoughts, tacking on that what he really couldn't believe was that he'd married a Coroan.

Not many people could.

His eyes shifted from slightly judgmental to entertained. "Can't blame you for wanting to get out of there," he said to me, lifting his chin to the road behind us. "I don't keep up with much going on in Coroa, but it's impossible not to hear how your king has all but gone mad."

"Really?" Etan asked. "It's not as if he was that sane in the first place."

The soldier laughed. "Agreed. But apparently some girl rejected him, and he's been erratic ever since. Rumors are he's taken an axe to one of his best boats, right there on the river where anyone could see. We've heard that he's got someone new but isn't faithful to her in any sense of the word. Heard he set his castle on fire a few weeks ago, too."

"I've been to Keresken," Etan said flatly. "A fire could only improve it."

It took everything in me to bite my tongue. Not even at his worst would Jameson want to destroy the pinnacle of

Coroan craftsmanship that was Keresken Castle.

The only rumor that might pain me if true was the thought of Jameson seeing other girls behind Delia Grace's back. I hated the idea of her thinking she'd finally gotten what she wanted and being so very wrong.

The soldier barked a laugh at Etan's quick wit, then became serious. "With how unpredictable he's been, there's talk of a possible invasion. That's why we have to check the carriages, even with those we trust. Seems Crazy King Jameson could do anything at this point."

I could feel myself blushing and hated it. None of this was true, of course. Jameson wasn't crazy or planning an invasion or anything of the sort . . . but the look of suspicion on that man's face told me to keep my thoughts to myself.

Mother placed a comforting hand on my knee and spoke out the window to the guard. "Well, we certainly under-stand and thank you again for your thoroughness. And I will make sure to say special prayers for all of you once we're safely home."

"It's clear," the other soldier called from the opposite side of the carriage.

"Of course it is," he replied loudly. "It's the Eastoffes, you nit." He shook his head, then backed away from the carriage. "Move the barricades!" he called to the others. "Let them through. Stay safe out there, Northcott."

Etan nodded to him, keeping his thoughts to himself for once.

As we came upon the border, I could see dozens of men

outside the window. Some saluted, showing their respect, while others simply gawked. I feared that maybe one of them would connect me to the girl who had allegedly driven her king to madness, that they'd demand that I get out of the carriage and go back to him.

No one did.

I'd walked into this journey willingly. More than that, I'd chased it down. But that one incident made me aware that I wasn't just crossing a border; I was stepping into a different world.

"It should be smooth sailing to the manor," Etan said when we were clear of the crowd.

Scarlet placed the knife that she'd kept tucked under her demure little hands beneath the folds of her skirts again. I shook my head; what exactly had she planned to do with that anyway? Mother reached over and wrapped an arm around me. "One obstacle down, countless more to go," she joked.

And, for what it was worth, I laughed.

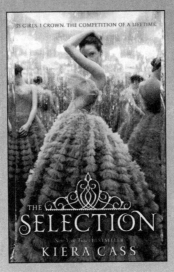

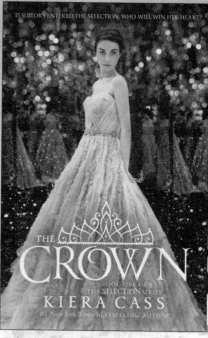

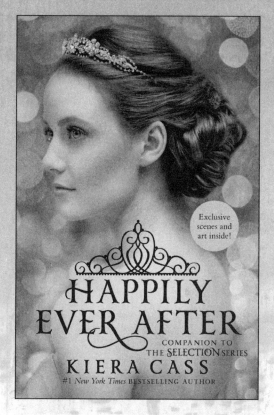

SHE'S CAPTURED THE KING'S HEART.
BUT WHO'S CAPTURED HERS?

A royal romance for the ages from #1 *New York Times*
bestselling author KIERA CASS